BLOOD,
WHITE
AND
BLUE

First published in Great Britain in 2018
by Urbane Publications Ltd
Suite 3, Brown Europe House, 33/34 Gleaming Wood Drive,
Chatham, Kent ME5 8RZ
Copyright © James Silvester, 2018

A CIP catalogue record for this book is available
from the British Library.

ISBN 978-1-911583-90-5
MOBI 978-1-911583-91-2

Design and Typeset by Michelle Morgan

Cover by Michelle Morgan

Printed and bound by 4edge Limited, UK

URBANE

urbanepublications.com

BOOK 1 IN THE **LUCIE MUSILOVA** SERIES

BLOOD, WHITE AND BLUE

JAMES SILVESTER

Urbane
PUBLICATIONS

urbanepublications.com

"For Dad."

PROLOGUE

The grounds of the British Embassy, *Prague, 1968.*

A ferocious and unwelcome sweat brought on by the August heat, erupted on the brow of the young Civil Servant as he raised the gun in an awkward and wholly unfamiliar movement, his aim distorted by the shaking in his arm and his nervous clenching of the revolver's grip.

"I could stop you," he intoned, straining against the agony he felt in his arm to keep the weapon levelled on his foe. "I *should* stop you."

"Be my guest," replied the second man, pushing his black trilby back above his brow and defiantly staring beyond the wavering gun barrel into the eyes of his accoster. "You might as well finish the job; it's the least you can do after this."

The second figure was as young as the first, but stood straighter than his counterpart, his features were more cruelly arranged, and he wore an altogether fiercer expression on them, no doubt borne from the furious rage he felt towards the gunman before him. But while his face was etched with anger, his opponent's radiated only anguish.

"Oh, I think I've finished the job well enough, don't you? The whole Embassy knows by now, that you are a traitor, nothing more than a Communist Patsy."

"Bastard!"

"Language, Old Boy," the first man smirked through his obvious pain, as though trying to enjoy his moment to the full but his heart denying him the pleasure. "You can't pretend you don't deserve this, or that you didn't know the moment was coming. It was always coming, ever since you decided upon betrayal."

"Then put a bullet in my brain and get it over with, will you? Spare me your gloating."

From across the courtyard, the gunman slowly lowered his arm, a twinge of sadness further diluting the loathing which he had yearned to surrender to.

"No," he answered, simply, eliciting a frown of reluctant curiosity in response. "There's only one place you can go, old boy. In seconds, security will descend upon you and drag you back to Britain in chains. You'll be paraded across the front page of every paper in the land, your face jeered at nightly on every television unless you run."

"Run where?"

"To your suitors, of course; to the Reds. The Dubček regime is doomed and the Hardliners are waiting in the wings. I'm sure they'd welcome you with open arms, after all, you're the man who killed the Prague Spring."

"You're not serious…" the desperate man half-whispered, almost incredulous at what he was hearing. "You really can't be serious."

"What's the matter? You always wanted to make your mark on history, and now you have. Whether you run or not, you'll be remembered forever for this," came the response. "You can either spend your life reeling from your castigation in a prison cell, or else you can embrace it here as a hero; a hero of sorts anyway."

There was no choice that he could see, the other man's logic was sound, and he had always considered himself a logical man; that was what had gotten him into this mess to start with. But a lifetime here, with *them*?

"We were right about you," he said after a moment. "All this time, we were right about you. This is a death sentence just the same as if you put a bullet between my eyes, you know that. But then, you never did have the courage to fire a gun, did you, Geoff? And that arm of yours doesn't look strong enough to take the shot anyway, does it?"

"No," Geoff quietly conceded. "But it isn't just my gun you need to be wary of, and you never did have the courage to take a bullet, to be the one to take the pain, did you Alex? That's why you'll run."

The sun was getting hotter and Alex could hear the sound of boots getting closer. He turned his back to Geoff, to the Embassy and to his country, the country he had pledged to serve, and stepped closer to the gate, through which lay whatever he could turn into his destiny. As he stepped through, he turned back, just one more question on his lips.

"Why did you do this?" he asked solemnly. "Just so you can say you stopped the man who betrayed Britain?"

"Screw Britain," the slighter man replied with equal solemnity from across the courtyard. "You betrayed me."

He nodded, his acceptance of the answer as reluctant as that of his situation and drew his first breath as a man on the run from his country.

"Goodbye, Geoffrey," he shouted through the gate. "Don't get too comfortable, don't ever let your guard down. Hell is a lonely place and that's where you're sending me. Don't be surprised when I come back looking for company." He doffed his trilby in faux salute to the Embassy, then turned and set off at a jog into a life in the chaos and fear of a Russian invasion.

"Goodbye, Alexander," Geoffrey whispered back, before the heat and his emotion overpowered him and he fell to the ground, his knees, and his gun dropping uselessly to the cobbles.

ONE

Present Day – *The Ocean.*

She'd been ready for them this time. This time, it was going down very, very differently. The previous night they had caught her unawares, the bastards in there with her; one of them grabbing her legs, another yanking back her long, dark hair and still another twisting her arms up her back; a filthy hand covering her mouth while another moved quickly and lecherously over her body, tugging at her white uniformed trousers, stained with that evening's menu, until they gave way and the trio gorged themselves on her vulnerability.

"Just having a laugh," they'd jeered as they left her, humiliated on the floor outside her quarters. "Every newbie gets a debagging on their first trip," they'd snorted as she tucked her legs up to her chest and wept tears of rage and anger, "We're just the ship's Equal Ops team, making sure everyone gets their fair share!"

They'd laughed and crowed as they disappeared, and she'd laid there for an age, shaking and quiet, hating them for their actions and herself for her failure to prevent them. She had crawled into her bed, intending to weep herself to sleep but refusing, the moment her head touched the pillow to succumb to self-pity, instead calling upon the resolve that had pulled her from the mouth of the cave years earlier. God forgive and help them, she sincerely prayed as she finally closed her eyes, because they knew not who they dealt with.

The smirks had still been on their faces as she'd entered the galley the next morning, tempered only by their obvious surprise that she had shown up at all. She bore no outward sign of the attack, her fresh uniform was pristine and the long, dark hair they had pulled the night before tied up beneath her chef's cap. She had looked each of them squarely in the eye, not a word passing her lips as she took her place on the line and busied herself with breakfast prep, adamant in her mind that nothing they could do would prevent her from doing her job.

Already alert to the likelihood of a repeated episode of their 'banter', it was the sudden silence as the chop of fruit and the clunk and splash of pot washing abruptly ceased that told her it was time for the next assault.

This time she was ready. She stamped down hard onto the hand reaching for her legs, a loud crack accompanying the scream of its owner, and she twisted quickly around, bringing the kitchen knife in her right hand slashing down across the cheek of her nearest abuser, who dropped to his knees clutching his face. The third of the unholy trinity lurched forward, a blade of his own clumsily slashing the air until it was knocked from his hand by a panful of boiling water.

"Fucking foreign bitch!"

The would-be knife man thrust his scalded hand into the dishwater as she dragged the first of her felled attackers across the cramped galley floor towards the open hatch on the wall known to the crew as the gun-port door, in reality little more than a square hole through which the food waste and rubbish was deposited. Picking up the tub of peelings and leftovers from the side with one

BLOOD, WHITE AND BLUE

hand, Lucie tipped it to the edge of the hatch, spewing its contents into the ocean below.

As if on cue, a succession of dorsal fins began to ominously rise from the depths, following hungrily in the ship's wake, the trail of leftovers almost magnetically drawing them in.

"Just banter mate," Lucie Musilova spat with every ounce of her fury, as she dragged the struggling oaf to the hatch's edge, her resentment and rage granting her the strength to lift him and force his torso through it, where she held him by his belt, the ocean – and the fins – only feet below, "I'm sure you understand."

His arms flailing, searching desperately for a non-existent hand hold, the hunter turned prey twisted his body to escape the woman with his life quite literally in her hands in sheer desperation, the anger in her voice enough to convey the unlikelihood that this was a bluff.

"Fucking hell, you crazy bitch, you wouldn't!"

The two other cowed abusers stood nervously across the galley table, one still clutching his face and the other his hand, but both wearing expressions of shock and fear.

"Come near me, and he drops," she shouted defiantly at them, the frothing emotion within her rendering her unsure as to exactly how hollow a threat it really was. They deserved this, damn them. Each one of them deserved it, for what they had done to her and for all she knew every other woman who had ever sailed with them. But she couldn't go through with it, could she? She'd been a Woman of God, someone who helped and forgave, not condemned to execution... It was only when her screaming quarry emphatically increased the strength of his squirming in response to the squat snout breaking water beneath him that reality clawed its way back into her mind; the potential of her role changing instantly from killer to saviour as the panicking man began to wriggle himself free of her grasp in terror, and she squeezed harder with her arms around his legs to try and keep him safe.

The door to the galley slammed open and in poured a handful of wide-eyed crew, led by a middle aged, bearded Officer, a Commander's rank on his epaulettes.

"Lucie!" The Commander shouted, his own eyes as wide as his men's and shock clinging to his voice as tightly as Lucie clung to her abuser's legs.

Her senses returned, and once more in control of her raging emotions, Lucie railed against the squirming of a body consumed by blind panic, his contortions loosening him once more from her grip.

With a final effort brim full of resentment and stress, Lucie hauled the weeping man back, his fingers scrambling to the metal floor as she pulled him back through the hatch to safety, and she stood there, her body aching and her mind exhausted, staring in contempt at the figure on the floor, while the newcomers quickly swarmed around, though none immediately found the courage to apprehend her.

The danger averted, the Commander crossed over to her, stopping only to stare in disgust at the two other injured attackers, curtly ordering them both to seek medical attention then consider themselves confined to quarters pending investigation.

He stepped over the third member of the self-appointed 'Equal Opps Team', who still clung to the floor as though fearful it would give way, whimpering softly.

"Get that man to sick bay," he barked; two men instantly picking him up and half walking, half carrying him out of the galley.

Standing in front of Lucie, his expression turned to one of sympathy and worry and he shook his head gently.

"Well, Lucie," he sighed, his tiredness evident, "I'm afraid you've really fucked things up this time."

TWO

"A little clichéd, wouldn't you say?"

It had been hours since Lucie was hauled from the boat and frog-marched through Southampton docks, past the gawping inquisitives for whom the parade of a tall, slim, striking woman with dark hair reaching down her back, was a distraction from the boredom of queuing for the ferry to Cowes, and deposited in a dull, grey secure room at the end of the pier.

"It's another one of that Polish lot," she'd heard one hiss in response to the profanity she'd aimed at the guard and his wandering hand. "The sooner we're out of bloody Europe, the better."

It was far from the first time such comments had been aimed at her, but each one served as another reminder as to why she'd signed up for the Merchants in the first place, another reminder that she wasn't welcome here anymore, in what was supposedly her own country.

Dressed at least in her own civilian clothes – flared, worn jeans and a blue paisley shirt, enveloped in a long, black overcoat – she stubbornly resisted giving in to the situation by blowing expertly on the harmonica she kept in her coat pocket, amongst the discarded tissues and forgotten sweet wrappers. It was either that or re-read the crinkled tabloid rag thrown in the room for her for the third time and hoping that this time it somehow magically contained articles with a bias other than foreigner-bashing, or attacks on Kasper Algers and Co. – a small band of MPs who still dared to put their heads above the parapet and defy the alleged 'Will of the People', and so the harmonica won easily.

A fair few years had gone by since she had frequented the pub circuit in Bury with her small group of friends, blasting out rock covers and blues standards to audiences of varying levels of intoxication, but the skill had never left her and neither had her love for the music and its unique ability to at once soothe, caress and admonish. Lucie was quite content to lose herself in her playing before the door banged unceremoniously open, breaking her from her self-induced trance.

"They wouldn't let me bring my cello," she replied to the odd man now stood in the doorway, her voice full of sarcasm.

Returning the harp to her pocket she took in the new arrival through her enchanting brown eyes, as he closed the door and sat across from her at the small table in the centre of the cramped room. Rapidly balding and not especially tall, the bags under his eyes betrayed a tiredness which was obstinately refuted by the sharpness of his stare, which remained fixed on Lucie as he sat. His dress was unremarkable; a simple, if well-cut suit and a reasonably expensive looking shirt, worn tieless and open-collared. Over one arm he carried a beige raincoat, which he now hung on the back of his chair, and in his hand was a black file which he snapped open, finally dropping his eyes from her to the papers it contained.

"Lucie Musilova," he began in a crisp, clear voice. "Thirty-five years old, born to a Czech mother and a British father who remained unmarried. Parents deceased, the father from testicular cancer, the mother in suspicious circumstances which remain unresolved. Childhood spent between both countries, leaving you fluent in both languages as well as Slovak, Polish and a smattering of Hungarian. Prior to your tour of duty with the Merchant Navy and the current… unpleasantness…"

"They assaulted me," Lucie interrupted, her anger clear but understated, "they deserved every bit of 'unpleasantness' that came their way."

The stranger's eyes once more fixed on her; fierce but not completely devoid of sympathy.

"I'm sure," he concurred simply, in a tone which discouraged further discussion of the point.

Dropping his gaze once more to the papers, he picked up his thread.

"Prior to your tour with the Merchants, you trained as a Military Chaplain with the RAF and served in Afghanistan for a time."

"That's none of your business…"

"During which time, you were injured in action – your right knee, I believe - were awarded the George Cross for heroism and immediately afterwards resigned both your Commission and your Holy Orders…"

"I said, that's none of your fucking business."

Lucie fixed the stranger with a fierce stare of her own, not allowing the surprise at how much he knew of her to show on her face when he sat back, smiled and slapped the file closed. She was unsettled, anxious and she didn't like it; her mind looking for a way to take back as much control of the situation as she could.

"Look, can't we just get on with the arrest? I'm not in the mood for a round of 'This is Your Life.'"

"Nor I in hosting one, and I'm not here to arrest you, although if that remains your preferred option it can of course be arranged."

The realisation that no identification had accompanied the stranger's arrival piqued Lucie's anxiety further and she sat bolt upright, catlike, ready to pounce as soon as the situation demanded, although the oddly calming smile of the stranger was enough to convince her that such an effort was not immediately necessary.

"No."

"Good. The truth is, I want you."

The resentment and anger of the last few days bubbled once more in Lucie's gut and she raised an eyebrow in warning at the statement.

"Excuse me?"

"Oh, not in the Biblical sense, or anything like that," the stranger scoffed. "There's a job I need completing, one which I think you might be particularly well suited to."

Realisation began to dawn on Lucie, one she met with a pinch of amusement and a healthy dose of scepticism.

"So, you're supposed to be a spy, are you?" She grinned.

"I really prefer to think of myself as a Civil Servant."

"Brexit Britain's own Bond, James Bond?"

"Actually, my name's Lake."

"Not even James Lake?"

"Mr. Lake."

Lake's tone had lost its avuncular inflection and Lucie knew that the conversation was now serious, even if she doubted the veracity of his claim.

"You don't look much like a spy."

"That's largely the point, Ms. Musilova."

"Yeah, but come on. I mean, no offence but you hardly fit the image, do you?"

"And it's a damn good job not," Lake icily replied, "It's fair to say I wouldn't have risen to the glories of the Office I presently hold if all eyes in the room turned to me the moment I strode to the bar, dressed in black tie. Believe me, many a state secret is hidden beneath a well-worn toupee, or 'twixt a cardigan clad bosom."

A smirk played at Lucie's lips, despite her reluctant acknowledgement of the odd man's logic.

"Perhaps so, but there has to be a balance somewhere."

"How so?"

"Well, as you've just read, I've been on military missions, I've just been thrown off my ship for nearly feeding a guy to the sharks. No disrespect but you're no spring chicken; what's to stop me just getting up and walking out?"

A raised eyebrow and the slightest hint of a smile, fuelled with just a hint of subtle arrogance, met Lucie's words and she inwardly questioned her own blitheness.

"You wouldn't make it up from your seat."

"Oh, really? It strikes me it would be a rather unmatched contest."

"Then let's even the balance, shall we?"

Lake reached into his inner suit pocket and pulled out a small, short barrelled gun, placing it on the table and sliding it over towards Lucie, who looked at it, frowning; her nerves at the weapon's appearance mixing sharply with the uncertainty which once more niggled her.

"As I see it," Lake began, "you have three options: Prison for attempted murder, and given the current political climate, I'm not sure your ethnic status would garner much sympathy for you in the courts. You take the job I am offering you, and your debt to society will be considered paid in full, or…"

"Or?"

"You can pick up the gun and threaten to shoot me if I don't let you walk out to your freedom. In which case, I give you my word I will not pursue you."

BLOOD, WHITE AND BLUE

Lucie's brow furrowed at the simplicity of the offer.

"The gun isn't loaded," she cautiously ventured, in response to which Lake retrieved it from the table, pointed it to the ceiling and fired; the noise echoing around the small room, causing Lucie to clasp her hands to her ears and duck as ceiling dust and plaster coated the table in a brief shower.

Lake returned the gun to the table and offered a half smile.

"It seems to be working just fine to me."

Cautiously raising herself, Lucie looked into the eyes of this strange, surely insane man, reasoning that with such apparent instability on display, spy or not it was unquestionably better that if there was a gun in the room, she be the one to hold it.

Lake looked calmly back, unmoving and seemingly unmoved by his actions of a moment before. The gun, its authenticity proven, lay once more on the table between them, smoke continuing to rise from its barrel and its handle achingly close to Lucie's fingertips.

She would have been lying to herself if she said she was not intrigued by the game, for a game this now undoubtedly was. The gun was close, much closer to her than to Lake, who sat back in his chair, between her and freedom, making no effort to inch forward.

Her mind was made up. Erratic or not, she would take the gun and warn him not to follow her. She would have to quickly find some alternative clothes and hide her hair under something, but after that she could surely take advantage of one of the many ferries steaming away from Southampton docks. Keeping her eyes firmly on Lake, Lucie chose the precise instant to lurch forward, fingers outstretched for the object of her escape.

Instead of the reassuring grip of cold metal, Lucie felt only the impact of the table hitting her square on the chin, knocking her head – and her- backwards into her chair which almost toppled over with the sudden movement.

Stunned, she shook her head clear of stars and stood to launch herself at Lake, stopping dead when she saw the gun had slid down the table, which he had raised sharply with an extended leg, and was now pointing nonchalantly in her direction.

"Let's call that Lesson One," Lake suggested as she rubbed her chin and stared angrily back at him. "When your enemy focusses your attention on one thing, always be aware of what else is going on behind their back; or in this case, under the table."

"Nice," Lucie begrudgingly admitted, her ego more bruised than her chin would be but her interest also aroused by this curious and well-prepared man; enough certainly to play along for now. "But if you think this means I'll work for you, you're madder than you look. The second you let me out of your sight I'll be gone."

"Yes, well I had a feeling that might be your attitude," Lake answered dispassionately, opening his folder once more and pulling from it a tattered and dusty A4 envelope, its carelessly stuffed contents bursting through rips and tears at the corners. He tossed it over to Lucie, who caught it, her curiosity awakened.

"What's this supposed to be?" she quizzed as she opened the envelope, only for her stomach to sink as though an invisible fist had pummelled into her gut, as she pulled the contents free. Crowning the papers was an ageing, dull photograph, though the eyes of the woman it contained were quite the opposite, their beauty still powerfully evident despite the absence of life behind their stare.

Lucie's emotions instantly drove home their advantage, claiming her in a tumultuous avalanche which brought a crack to her voice and tears to her eyes.

"Bastard," she croaked through the lump in her throat, her face red with rage as she stuffed the papers, photograph and all, back into the envelope. "You complete bastard."

BLOOD, WHITE AND BLUE

Lake was unmoved, both by her words and the emotional trauma he'd inflicted. Instead he simply picked up the envelope from the table and returned it to his folder.

"Perhaps I am," he mused, almost to himself, "but if so it's at least for the right reasons."

He shifted forward, his expression breaking into something approaching earnest, and his voice mirroring the change as he met Lucie's still wet and resentful eyes.

"I need you, Ms. Musilova," he entreated, "and I can't have you running off on some voyage of self-loathing while there's work to be done."

The sudden sincerity intrigued Lucie, despite her revulsion at his tactics and she returned the look without comment.

"Complete the task I have for you and not only will your record be expunged, but the case of your mother's death will be re-opened. I know the desire to know what happened still burns inside, just as it would for anyone. I can't promise that knowing will make any difference but work for me and I'll at least help you put the flame of ignorance out."

Lucie stayed silent for a moment as she fought back the assault of her emotions. Beneath all of Lake's charm, his eccentricity, his bluster, here was another man seeking to control her, to manipulate her actions. No better than the scum on the boat, this was at heart just someone else trying to bend her to their will, but this time with a carrot instead of a stick.

"Ask me."

"What?"

"All this bollocks with the gun, the file, trying to twist me whichever way you want me to twist, fuck all that. If you want my help, ask me for my help."

Lake's posture relaxed as the half-smile returned to his face.

"I have a problem," he said simply, "will you help me?"

"You forgot to say please."

"Don't push it."

Lucie returned the half smile, glad to see the balance of power tip at least a little back towards her.

"So, what's this job you have for me?"

Lake's mouth spread into a full grin for the briefest of moments, before being instantly replaced by a serious frown.

"A threat has been received, Ms. Musilova," he began. "A threat against a leading figure on the Government benches."

"So why does that affect me? Surely stuff like that's par for the course?"

"Well yes and no, this case is a bit different."

"How so?"

Lake narrowed his eyes and looked back at her with an expression of utter seriousness.

"Because this time the threat has come from a ghoul."

"A ghoul?" Lucie laughed out loud in incredulity. "You mean like a ghost?"

"I do indeed," came the mirthless response. "A Ghost from Prague."

THREE

A short time later, the unlikely duo had been ushered into Lake's car by the waiting chauffeur and were heading out of Southampton in the direction of London, while the eccentric man expanded the briefing, punctuated by the occasional curse articulated at the less aware of the morning's rush hour drivers.

The car itself was nothing special, in fact quite the reverse. An ageing Rover 214 SEi, in British Racing Green with grey trim was their carrier; a car which the bland suited driver described as a 'classic' but which to Lucie's mind served better to emphasise Lake's point about the value of the unexpectedly unspectacular in his field. As the car merged onto the A27, Lake, reclining in the back seat next to Lucie, was ready to explain the reasons for his supernatural warnings of earlier.

"You've heard of Alexander Huxley, I presume?"

Lucie nodded, turning her head from the window towards him.

"The defector? He was the British operative in Prague during the sixties who fled the embassy and joined the Hard-Line Communists against Dubček when the Russians invaded."

"Top of the class," Lake acknowledged. "What isn't so well-known is that there was another operative in Prague at that time who was captured and tortured by the Communists before eventually being released, apparently alongside Huxley. After a long career in the intelligence services, that operative entered politics and is tipped by the Press to shortly become a significant figure within the government."

"Who?"

"Sir Geoffrey Hartnell," Lake answered immediately, the fierceness of his gaze at once assuring Lucie of the severity of the consequences which a lack of secrecy on her part would bring.

"Oh yeah… he's quite pro Europe isn't he?" she quizzed.

"Quite so. He's in his seventies now," Lake explained, "but he's as energetic as ever and he's hugely respected on the international scene; he's one of the few politicians we have left we can say that about. With Brexit turning out to be the catastrophe it is, he's widely seen as a steadying influence on the Ship of State. He currently Chairs the European Affairs oversight committee and has been extremely critical of the government's vacuous approach to everything European since that damn referendum was called, but despite that, the PM is under pressure to hand him the Foreign Office Brief at the impending reshuffle. God knows we need someone competent in there handling things."

Lucie soaked up the information as a thousand questions began to form in her mind.

"Everyone knows that MPs and Public Figures on every side of the Brexshit argument have been getting death threats from all manner of numpties and keyboard warriors ever since the referendum was called. What's different about this one that's got your knickers in a twist?"

"Primarily who it came from, and how it was delivered," Lake responded, frowning a little at the coarseness of his companion.

"Not just an anonymous e-mail or letters cut from newspapers, then?"

"I'm rather afraid not." Lake's frown deepened, accompanying the deeper seriousness in his tone. "This one arrived in the Diplomatic Bag from Prague, written under the government's own headed notepaper and signed by none other than…"

"Alexander Huxley," Lucie finished. "I suppose it's reasonable in a way; resentment at the elevation of a colleague while you find yourself in exile. Shit like that could really eat at someone I'd imagine."

"Quite," Lake agreed. "But arriving in the Bag suggests that the writer has an accomplice within our own walls who shares his resentment, if indeed the threat is genuine."

"Can't the Embassy look into that?"

"They are," Lake assured her, "in as much as they can. They aren't really equipped to conduct an investigation of that sort, and of course no-one is likely to put their hands up and admit to posting the threat."

"Or to working with Huxley…" Lucie mused.

"Well that's the other problem," Lake explained, a note of worry accompanying his words, "Alexander Huxley is dead."

The revelation startled Lucie into a seated attention.

"Dead?"

"As the proverbial Dodo," Lake confirmed. "Hartnell was sent to retrieve him during the Velvet Revolution in '89, but by then he'd already been killed by his KGB handlers, presumably to prevent any chance of re-capture at a time when the Communists were at their most vulnerable."

Lucie continued her assimilation of the data, her mind rushing through variables and possibilities as the ageing car bumped uncomfortably on.

"So, either the whole thing is a hoax," she pondered aloud, "which given how the threat was received is unlikely, or else someone with more knowledge of the case than is publicly known is wearing 'Alexander Huxley' as a mask to revenge him from beyond the grave..."

"Those are both workable hypotheses," Lake agreed as they drew ever closer to London, "ones which you'll be considering with your new team shortly."

"Team? I thought this was a job for me?" The thought of working with others was anathema to Lucie, her sudden enthusiasm for the case dipping at the news.

"Your unique experiences and skills will prove essential to us, I'm sure," Lake answered, ignoring the irritation in her words, "but so will those of the others."

Lucie sighed in frustration. "So, I'll just be another suited and booted drone with an MI6 name tag?" she spat contemptuously.

"We're not 'Six'," Lake corrected.

"MI5 then."

"No."

Puzzlement added itself to Lucie's frustration and she pressed on. "Then what the hell are we?"

Lake turned to her and twisted his mouth into the annoying 'not-quite-a-smile' of his, clearly relishing his new subordinate's current frustration.

"We are the Security and Intelligence Service for Cross-Boundary Affairs," Lake smirked.

"The what?"

"The 'Overlappers', Ms. Musilova." Lake returned his stare to the window as the car continued on its way. "The 'Overlappers'."

Lake said little else during the journey and for the moment Lucie was content for that to be so, as the silence was at least preferable to another smugly delivered drip of information and Lucie's own thoughts contained much to occupy her for the rest of the trip.

The whir of unbalanced wheel bearings began to plague Lucie's ears just as the ancient vehicle pulled into the kerb outside a graffiti coated row of takeaways in a part of Camden Lucie didn't recognise. Lake and the chauffeur immediately stepped out from the car, somewhat to Lucie's surprise, who nonetheless followed suit.

"Don't tell me this is your office?" she frowned at Lake, who stood outside what was evidently once a fish and chip shop but was now hauntingly empty, save for the remnants of kitchen equipment visible behind the street art adorned windows.

"Oh no, no, no," Lake answered, shaking his head. "This is your new home."

As if on cue, the chauffeur dropped Lucie's bag on the pavement next to her and she looked from it to Lake to the building with an almost murderous incredulity on her features.

"You have got to be fucking kidding me," she exhaled, "a bloody chippy?"

"Don't be ridiculous," Lake retorted, I wouldn't ask you to live in a fish bar! There's a vacant flat above it you can get to around the back."

The assurance offered little comfort to Lucie, whose resentment continued to grow.

"I already have a flat," she protested, reliving her anger at the difficulties of securing tenancies in the hostile environment of a Britain still wrapped up in its distrust of anything foreign that wasn't served in pint glasses. "It's in Manchester. That's where I live."

"You've moved," Lake replied, mirthlessly. "Your belongings up north can follow you, but for now this will suffice. There are basic furnishings and supplies inside, a small pot of cash and an adequately stocked fridge, and if you feel like something more exotic to eat then you shouldn't have far to look for it, this is Camden after all. Here."

He held out a dull, plain Yale key and dropped it into Lucie's hand before turning back to the car.

"Going so soon?" Lucie sarcastically queried, "not popping in for a battered sausage?"

Lake squirmed just a little at the vulgarity and shook his head.

"Best I'm not seen with you too much around here," he insisted, "we don't want to give anyone the impression that we're friends. Get some rest, settle in and I'll be in touch tomorrow."

With that, the strange little man who had plucked Lucie from a certain police cell barely hours before resumed his seat in the rear of the Rover as the chauffeur began to rev the tired and resistant engine.

"Wait!" Lucie bellowed as the car's engine began to gain a second wind. "You haven't told me!"

"Told you what?" Lake quizzed through the car window.

"How did you know about me? About my arrest, all the shit on the boat, any of it?"

Lake was silent for a moment then offered an answer.

"Your Commander and I were at school together," he revealed with his usual nonchalance. "He didn't want to see you sent down and thought I might be able to use you."

"Let me guess," Lucie began, falling back on the sarcasm ingrained in her defences to mask her surprise at her former superior's concern, "Eton?"

"No," Lake answered as the car began to inch from the kerb, "East Bartonfield Comprehensive, we had detention there together most afternoons."

The car sped away, and Lucie stood, watching after it for a moment, assimilating the events of the past few hours as best she could, until her self-consciousness compelled her to move rather than become an object of attention for the passers-by on the street.

Heaving her bag to her shoulder, Lucie ducked down the alley beside the dilapidated fish bar and located a wooden door in faded red towards the building's rear which opened with the Yale key to an unlit and poorly carpeted staircase. At the top, Lucie took in what was, for now at least, to be her new abode. Three doorways greeted her from the small landing; one leading to a bathroom only just big enough to fit the compulsory toilet, sink and corner shower, and decorated in a dull lime green that she couldn't imagine ever having been popular. The next door led to a modest bedroom, replete with double bed, dressed in the type of eiderdown that could have adorned a spinster in a Dickens' novel, small bedside cabinet and, curiously, a hat stand, while the third led to a conjoined living room and kitchen.

Stepping into the living room, Lucie flicked on the light switch, inviting the unshaded glow of a high wattage bulb to attempt to improve the room's appearance. She stood on a carpet threadbare to the point of baldness and untacked from seemingly every part of the skirting board. A two-seat sofa, probably as old as the building, took up residence in the middle of the floor, a small TV set in front of it and a coffee table stained with the spillages of decades pushed to the side. The kitchen was home to a fridge-freezer with what sounded like a straining motor, only marginally quieter than the car she had just stepped from, a hob oven and a microwave. The walls were yellow with nicotine and age and the possessive stench of chip fat clung intransigently to all that she could survey. Lucie had always valued solitude, but here in this place, it served only to deepen the depression she had felt herself sinking back into in the weeks before her assault.

Feeling the tell-tale build-up of emotion inside her, Lucie gulped it back and pulled her phone from the bag, swiping her music onto shuffle. Pulling back the curtains, she flung open the window, hoping as much to let some freshness and positivity in as to let the chip smell out. Crossing into the bedroom, she flung her bag down and knelt beside the bed, her bad knee aching on the hard, carpet-less floor. Clenching her hands together she inhaled deeply, fighting to retain control of herself and her emotions. This was all becoming too much; the attack, the journey back to Britain confined to quarters, waking up this morning expecting arrest and charge and instead being dragged into the bizarre world of this strange little man with his folder and his ancient car who had deposited her here in this stinking, filthy flat, barely fit for habitation. Was he really a spy? He certainly knew a hell of a lot about her and that file of her mother's death was enough to stop Lucie running straight down the stairs and out into whatever the world held for her next. Plus, she'd be lying if she told herself she wasn't curious about this whole notion of Czech spies and old scores to be settled. And while the flat smelled bad, it was still better and roomier than the prison cell she had expected to be spending the night in. Most of all though, she was tired, so very, very tired. There was still fight in her, she would always be sure of that, but Lucie knew she needed time and rest to consolidate it, and for tonight, it was spent.

The sound of traffic, louder through the open widows, served as a melodious accompaniment to the cold which joined it, enveloping Lucie in a blanket of melancholy she did little to try and dispel. Instead, as though ossified into her prayerful posture, she clamped her eyes shut and allowed the bleakness to gnaw at

BLOOD, WHITE AND BLUE

her once more, as it did every night, each time leaving her with less and less of herself to hold onto. And as it ate at her and she allowed her mind to fall into a painful and uncomfortable sleep, her dreams fell back as they always did to the fear and horror of Helmand.

FOUR

She stayed silently, unmoving in that position for some hours before stiffness and cold plucked her from the distress of her slumber just long enough to shed her clothes, switch off her phone, slam the window closed and crawl under the itchy bed sheets where she remained until the noise from the living room woke her with a jolt.

Sitting upright in the bed Lucie blinked the tiredness from her eyes and turned her ear to the door, relying on the heightened sensitivity such situations bestowed to confirm the noise. It came again – the scrape and thump of wood across the floor – and she slipped deftly from the sheets, taking a t-shirt and jogging pants from her bag and pulling them on within seconds. With no obvious weapon to hand, she moved on her toes to the edge of the living room door, reasoning that if they – whoever 'they' were – were in the living room, she could make it to the kitchen and retrieve one of the chopping knives from the block on the counter before they could properly react. Indeed, she guessed, that would likely be her only chance.

Inching out onto the landing, she carried her weight on the balls of her feet and prayed that creaking floorboards were not a feature of her new home. The living room door was open and peeking in, Lucie could see two figures. One of them, a woman dressed in jeans and a bright red jumper was sat on the small sofa, which had been dragged some way across the room, stretched out so as to take up both seats, while the second, a grey suited and grey-haired man with a thin face and uncompromising eyebrows, was leaning against the window sill, his hands in his pockets. Neither looked especially inclined to move and the thought that this was perhaps the most nonchalant burglary of her experience crossed Lucie's mind. Whatever their motives though, they were here, inside her flat, and while it was not an abode she yet felt a particular warmth for, she was damned if she was going to allow herself to be a victim again.

Tip-toeing to the edge of the door, Lucie filled her lungs and dived into the room, vaulting the kitchen counter and grabbing the knife as planned in one movement. Holding it expertly towards the two strangers, she flung the unbrushed, untidy hair from her face and demanded the identities and purpose of the intruders, peppering her question with a liberal dose of profanity.

Neither of the pair answered or even made a move of surprise; the man barely raising one of his impressive eyebrows at her, while the woman simply offered a sympathetic smile.

"I said, who the fuck are you and what are you doing in my flat?"

Lucie's words were answered not by the protestations of the pair, but the new sound of footsteps behind her. Spinning around once more, the knife pointing resolutely in the direction of the doorway, Lucie exhaled in tedious frustration as Lake stepped into the room, casually adjusting his cuffs as he walked.

"Ah, good morning Ms. Musilova," he opened, stepping past her and picking up his customary folder from the coffee table, "awake at last I see. I did warn you not to only pay attention to what's in front of you…"

"You…" she caught herself before saying the word that had popped into her mind. "So, this is the deal is it? I get to live knee deep in chip fat in the arse-end of nowhere, in a flat you have full access to and there's nothing I can do about it? Well not to frighten you or anything pal but just to give you fair warning, I keep an untidy home and I shit with the door open, so bear that in mind before you pay any little visits, ok?"

"I'll certainly keep that in mind," Lake responded, grimacing, which only served to further incense Lucie.

"Who the hell do you think you are, waltzing in here uninvited? And who the hell are Tweedle-Dee and Tweedle-Dum here, and what are they doing apart from making the place look even more untidy?"

Lake looked at her with his typical calmness.

"Who I am, Ms. Musilova, is the man who helped you avoid custody yesterday and as for the identity of my two colleagues, well let's deal with that now, shall we?"

He crossed over to the far wall, straightening his cuffs and brushing himself down.

Lucie meanwhile took a deep breath and replaced the knife, standing by the kitchen, her arms folded and her expression somewhat less than welcoming.

"So, this is the big briefing, then?"

"Well unless anyone fancies a 'chip butty' for breakfast."

The comment and the condescending manner in which Lake affected a Northern accent was sufficient to halt any further remarks from Lucie, at least for the time being.

Lake stood by the far wall, facing the room and its collection of occupants.

BLOOD, WHITE AND BLUE

"Lucie Musilova, meet Della Quince and you may recognise Kasper Algers MP."

Lucie was shocked to have his name confirmed. He had seemed familiar to her, but his seemingly perpetual position of head down, staring at the carpet had made it difficult to be sure. At the mention of his name though, Algers raised his head just enough to nod the hint of a greeting in Lucie's direction, the man clearly uncomfortable at his presence in her flat. Lucie though wanted more from the man who had built a nationwide following through his progressive opposition to Brexit and the problems it had created.

"You?" Lucie quizzed, somewhat incredulous. "You're a spy?"

"I'm the Member of Parliament for Camden West," came the slightly indignant response, "and that's all I am."

"So how do you fit in with all this?"

Algers' severe expression relaxed into one resembling a teacher struggling for patience as he thought about his answer.

"I've a duty to my constituents, Lucie," he quietly answered, "and to the country. It's just that not everyone is privy to all the ways I carry out that duty."

Lucie was about to press further but the woman on the sofa now stepped up, her arm outstretched, ready to take Lucie's hand.

"But rest assured, most Saturdays he holds constituency surgeries and chats to old ladies about traffic lights, pot holes and the rowdy teenagers down the street. I know because I'm sat with him handling the diary."

Lucie gripped her offered hand and smiled as the woman continued.

"Good to meet you, I'm Della Quince."

"Lucie Musilova," Lucie answered. "It's a pleasure."

The handshake lasted just a moment longer than Lucie had

expected, and was accompanied, she was sure, with a soft and supremely subtle thumb stroke across the bridge of her hand.

Della was older then Lucie, perhaps by as many as ten years or more, but the maturity took nothing away from her beauty. Her hair was a lighter brown than Lucie's and greying only in parts and only very slightly, while it matched hers for length. Her face, though hinting at lines in the usual places was alive with an unusual vivacity and a sparkle in her eyes which Lucie struggled to find any other word for than 'naughty'.

The brief contact with Della warmed Lucie's mood and as the older woman returned to the couch, the younger sounded a question to the room.

"So, what? I'll be licking envelopes in Kasper's office by day and stalking defectors of yesteryear by night?"

"Not quite," Algers smiled, sympathetically.

"At least, not yet," Lake clarified. "As far as the world is concerned, you, Mr. Algers and Ms Quince have yet to officially meet, and that is how it will stay for the moment."

"Then why bring me here now?"

"Because you need to know *how* you are going to meet."

Algers returned to his statuesque pose and Lake began thumbing through the damn folder of his.

"I hope you have a list in there of any other MPs secretly on the payroll," Lucie said. "What is it, one in each Party and an Independent for good luck?"

"It's not exactly like that," Lake answered, "there are no other Parliamentarians 'on the payroll' as you say, and outside of this room, nobody is aware of Mr Algers' other interests."

Lucie was confused. "So, why…?"

"We took advantage of an opportune vacancy," Lake said absent-mindedly, still thumbing through his copious folder. "Mr. Algers'

BLOOD, WHITE AND BLUE

predecessor in the Seat proved something of a disappointment; the sexual harassment allegations were bad enough, but he would so insist on hiding away his ill-gotten gains from the various seedy sources and Russian backed think tanks that funded him all over the Cayman Islands. In the end, we thought we'd have to sit through a whole new round of 'tax leaks' to get him de-selected, so it was a real turn up for the books when his boat capsized on the Thames last year..."

Lucie grimaced at the words, remembering the headlines at the time and the stampede of politicians to the press rooms to declare the event a 'tragic loss' for his constituents and the country, only to hastily backtrack on their sorrow when details of the allegations against Jack Malcolm, an otherwise unextraordinary career back-bencher, found their way into the tabloids some weeks later. It was those headlines, and the women who came forward afterwards that spawned a hashtag and turned the voters against the Party they had flocked to since the Seat was created, instead putting their faith in Kasper Algers – a man whose military career ended with him refusing promotion and resigning his commission to spend the next couple of decades elbow deep in Community work in London's poorest areas, before standing as a Pro-European Independent candidate at the subsequent by-election, and winning by a landslide. The distaste rose in Lucie's stomach as she churned over the events in her memory.

"Are you saying that you killed Jack Malcolm?" she demanded of Lake, hoping the disapproval on her face at least matched what she was feeling inside. Lake though frowned in obvious irritation that she was asking at all.

"What I'm saying, is that every cloud has a silver lining and the people of the late Mr Malcolm's constituency are far better served by our friend, Mr Algers, here."

"And the women who came forward, they were fakes?"

"Not at all, the allegations were all true, Malcolm was a nasty piece of work. I'll admit though that the resultant social media outcry was rather useful for us."

Lucie looked over to Della, whose face, Lucie noticed, was missing the mischievous smile it had thus far held, and whose eyes flashed with regret at Lake's comment, but who also gave a slight, almost imperceptible shake of her head, as if to tell Lucie not to give in to the anger brewing inside her. Algers, for his part, remained silent and rigid, his lined face unreadable.

Inhaling deeply, Lucie opted not to press further and stayed silent, while Lake finally found the relevant pages in his folder and pulled them out, resuming his position in the centre of the small room and contenting himself that all eyes were upon him.

"Right then," he began, authority in his tone. "You're all aware of the threat against Sir Geoffrey Hartnell and the unusual circumstances surrounding it, so there's no point in going over old ground. For the sake of focus however, here's a reminder of the problem to hand."

Lake slipped a sheet of paper from his folder and passed it to Lucie who took it.

"Pass that around would you, Ms. Musilova?"

Lucie took in the contents swiftly and received confirmation straight away that Lake had not been overreacting in his response to its receipt. The threat itself was simple enough; a couple of lines typed in Ariel Twelve, the hallmark of a Civil Service document, which read, 'Looking forward to catching up Old Boy. If you don't recognise me after all this time, I'll be the one firing the trigger. Love, Alex'. More disturbing though was that it sat on letter headed paper from the desk of the Ambassador from the Court of St. James to the Czech Republic, the Ambassador's stylised signature a couple of inches below.

BLOOD, WHITE AND BLUE

Lucie committed the contents to memory and passed the sheet to Della to examine.

"So," Lake began again, "What matters now is getting to the bottom of all this. By fortuitous circumstance we have the opportunity to search the stable for a 'horse's mouth' to speak to, as it were Hartnell is due to fly to Czechia on Thursday on the latest of his 'good will' visits to European allies as he tries to undo some of the diplomatic damage done recently by the Foreign Secretary, among others. It's an unofficial trip, personally financed and not sanctioned by the government, but nonetheless there will be a number of people accompanying him, including several journalists of note and a handful of cross-Party like-minded MPs, including Mr. Algers, here."

He nodded over to the window ledge where Algers leant, staring at the floor, his clenched hand tapping rhythmically against his chin in either ignorance or deep contemplation of Lake's exposition.

"Mr Algers, you will be spending your time liaising with our contact at the embassy and trying to find out how the message was sent."

Algers barely grunted a response and Lucie looked curiously at the obvious resentment on his face.

"Once there, we're also engineering a suitable opportunity for you, Ms. Musilova, to be 'noticed' by Hartnell," Lake continued, unperturbed by the silence of his audience.

"And how do 'we' do that?" Lucie quizzed when nobody else did.

"Hartnell will make a tour of the city," Lake answered, his voice at its authoritative best. "As one of his stops, he's agreed to meet with representatives from a local campaign group resentful of the British media's attitude towards EU migrants since the referendum. He'll meet them outside their premises at 11:30am, pose for photographs and assure them that a cross Party group of MPs will be working tirelessly to ensure that the rights of 'the three million' will not be eroded and that stories of racist attacks against EU nationals are exaggerated and broadly untrue."

"Which is a lie," interjected Lucie, Lake ignoring her and continuing.

"Also waiting for him will be this man…"

He reached into the collection of papers pulled from his cavernous folder and took from within them a photograph of a young, shaven-headed man with a goatee beard, thin mouth and cruel, piercing blue eyes. Beneath his chin was fastened a casual sports jacket of the kind worn by millions of young men across the continent.

"This is Nathan Fostrow," Lake announced, sticking the picture to the wall behind him with a hard ball of ancient blue-tack. "He holds the dubious honour of being one of the internet's most persistent Trolls; he's been blocked on social media by almost every member of the Cabinet and a sizeable amount of backbenchers from all Parties, not to mention journalists and presenters. He doesn't tend to stop with famous faces either."

"What's his particular beef?"

"He's a Brexiteer," Lake answered, "and a pretty extreme one at that, even by the standards of the government's more divisive figures. Mr Fostrow is of the opinion that anything short of the compulsory repatriation of the three million EU Nationals living in Britain would represent a betrayal of the 52% who voted to Leave."

Lucie felt her gut churn as Lake spoke; the opinions of this 'Fostrow' every bit as vicious and cruel as the expression he wore in his photograph.

"Charming man," she muttered quietly as Lake continued.

"During Hartnell's short speech, Fostrow will be watching him from an apartment window, from which he intends to douse our elected representative with the contents of three tins of paint."

"No prizes for guessing the colours."

Lucie looked to Della, who had made the remark and returned the wink the older woman offered her.

"Any specific motivation for expressing himself in this way?" Lucie queried.

"Well Mr Fostrow, it's fair to say, is rather dismissive of Sir Geoffrey's moderate stance on European affairs and would welcome nothing more than to publicly humiliate him in front of the TV cameras and on a foreign stage, no less. He can publicise his Brexiteering credentials and let the EU communities in Britain know exactly what he thinks of them in a single protest."

"Never mind the bollocks!"

All heads in the room turned to Algers, still leaning against the faded paint of the window sill, unmoving save for the deepening of his scowl, "How do you plan to use this 'Fostrow' to get Lucie in with Hartnell?"

"I was coming to that," Lake answered quietly, his eyes narrow and focussed on the surly MP, his voice and expression suggesting any further interruption to be unwise.

"As it happens, Mr Fostrow's apartment block will also be temporary home to Ms. Musilova, who will have travelled to Prague to express her support for the policies of Sir Geoffrey and her personal admiration for you, Mr Algers."

Lucie and Algers exchanged a silent glance as Lake continued.

"As Mr Fostrow sits ready with his tins of paint, you, Ms. Musilova will be in the room next door, and will, at 11:27am precisely, after becoming suspicious of the sounds coming from your new neighbour's apartment, accost him and deprive him of his tools. Fostrow will be 'arrested' by our contacts in the Czech police and Hartnell will be made aware of an attempt to humiliate him, vanquished by none other than your good self."

Della leaned forward, her hand touching Lucie's shoulder.

"You could always take a bow at this point," the older woman chuckled, with what Lucie reckoned was a customary cheekiness in her voice.

"Piss off," she laughed back before Lake 'ahem'd' his way back in charge of the discussion.

"Hartnell is nothing if not 'old school' and his personal code of honour will ensure he attempts to repay your favour with some sort of reciprocation, be it a drink, or dinner, or whatever. Then it will be up to you to use that opportunity to ingratiate yourself with him."

"I can't wait," Lucie responded, her voice dripping with a sarcasm which left Lake distinctly unimpressed.

"I would remind you that Hartnell is our best and may well be our only lead in uncovering the truth behind the threat. It would be unwise for you not to take advantage of the opportunities presented to you."

The almost sinister stare which moments before had been locked on Algers, was now firmly directed at Lucie, along with the quietly threatening tone of voice. Though she had met him only the day before, Lucie had formed an opinion of Lake as an unpredictable, if generally harmless eccentric, but the sudden change and edge of seriousness in him, whether implied or otherwise, unsettled her and convinced her not to make light of his words.

"Ok," she answered, "I get it."

Lake's tone switched again, almost instantaneously as he brought his presentation to a close.

BLOOD, WHITE AND BLUE

"This will provide us with a suitable cover story. No need for false names and laboriously manufactured biographies; the best cover is always normality, you are who you are."

"And what might that be?"

"The child of a British father and a Czech mother ostracised because of Brexit, and with an unfortunate history of getting into trouble."

Lucie could only nod in reluctant agreement.

"You have travelled back to Prague, partly because you see Hartnell as the British politician most capable of ending the xenophobic madness engulfing the country, and partly because your other political idol happens to be Mr. Algers, who now also happens, thanks to your recent change of address, to be your MP."

Lucie smiled to herself in ironic acknowledgement that the cover was only partly fictitious. Algers, while not quite her idol, was indeed a man for whom she had a long-held admiration, thanks to his unapologetic anti-Brexit stance and his unswerving support for the EU Nationals. He had in fact become something of a hero to many and his maiden speech to Parliament had passed into legend, after he had used it to describe Brexit and the campaign behind it as 'the last vainglorious wank of a dying man', earning himself an army of followers and an immediate suspension from the Chamber in the process. Lucie shared not only that sentiment but the disdain for pomp and ceremony that Algers had displayed. She had followed his career, ever since, and she couldn't help but feel a modicum of disappointment at his less than enthusiastic response to meeting her.

Lake, for his part now seemed as eager to conclude the conversation as he had earlier been to begin it, returning his papers to his ever-present folder and snapping it shut.

"Well, I think that's everything for now," he muttered, almost under his breath as he pulled an envelope from his inside pocket and handed it to Lucie. "Your flight ticket to Prague and room reservation, I trust I can rely on you to find your own way there?"

"Hang on, hang on," Lucie protested, "that can't be it? I don't know anything about this Fostrow bloke, he could be dangerous, how am I supposed to overpower him?"

"Don't be modest, Ms. Musilova," Lake responded tensely, the pair now stood inches from each other and neither apparently inclined to make their discussion any less taut. "Your record makes clear your abilities; if anything, I'd say Mr Fostrow is fortunate his room doesn't look out over the ocean, wouldn't you?"

Lucie could feel her response brewing inside her ready for delivery but felt Della's hand on her shoulder; a quiet warning not to proceed, and though she had met this woman only minutes before, she felt an undeniable confidence that she could trust her and chose, for now, to withhold her intended riposte.

Lake continued to look into her eyes, as though wishing to ensure she had every opportunity to articulate her resentment, before his face once more reverted in an instant to the casually deadpan expression it typically wore.

"Well, then, if there's nothing else, I suggest we all leave separately, and I look forward to hearing of your endeavours in Prague. My apologies for the necessity of commandeering your living room, Ms. Musilova, good morning all."

He crossed to the living room door without another word, only for Lucie to pipe up while looking at her travel documents.

"Wait, is that really it? I mean, what happens after Hartnell 'notices' me, what am I supposed to be looking for in the first place? This is all a bit new to me, you know?"

"One thing at a time, Ms. Musilova," Lake answered over his shoulder having reached the top of the stairs. "Just be sure to be in your apartment listening for Fostrow at precisely 11:27am. Everything else can wait for now."

With that, he was gone, his footsteps descending rapidly towards the front door.

"I am so getting a new lock," Lucie mused as the door closed behind him.

Algers now approached her, his arm outstretched in greeting, but his face still displaying nothing but frustration, an emotion that Lucie most emphatically shared.

"Look, I'm sorry about all this," he said sincerely, clasping her hand in a strong grip. "Nobody needs a front room full of spies first thing in the morning, especially the bloody B-Team you've ended up stuck with." He was smiling at last, if only slightly, and the delicate Scottish hint to his accent had a calming effect on her as he spoke.

"It's fine," she smiled back, "it's just been a lot to take in this past couple of days."

"Aye, I remember. I've got to go, I can't be seen with you until we officially meet in a couple of days. I'm sorry but I won't be able to be in touch or help you until then, but from what Lake's said about you I'm sure you'll be fine."

"Thanks," Lucie responded, grateful at least for some genuine words of confidence. "And it really is good to meet you by the way, you've done a lot for people being screwed by Brexit and it's appreciated."

"Ah, I've not done enough," Algers replied, an obvious discomfort with praise rising on his face. "Now have today to yourself, get to grips with everything, then head to Prague tomorrow and I'll see you after you sort this Fostrow bloke. Della, I'll be in the car."

Algers too quickly descended the steps and Lucie welcomed the sense she got that Algers was a man she could genuinely count on, although it worried her a little that she wouldn't be able to call on him until after this Fostrow business, the details of which were still sketchy at best in Lucie's mind.

"I'll have to go too," Della said as she stepped forward and embraced Lucie warmly. "Here's my number, if you want to meet up later and have a drink, find out a bit more about us before getting on the plane, then give me a call."

Lucie took the scrap of paper with the number scrawled on it and looked up to smile at Della, but she had already gone, having descended the steps in double quick time, the slamming of the front door punctuating her departure.

Lucie stood alone in the suddenly empty apartment, a familiar melancholy descending on the room, akin to when the party is over, and the guests have all departed. Lucie looked again at the number and smiled, understanding growing within her that this particular party was very much yet to begin.

"Thanks," she said aloud to the empty room. "I will,"

FIVE

It was a few hours later that Lucie found herself negotiating her occasional nemesis, the London Underground. She was an intelligent and capable woman, she had crossed subway systems the world over with comfort, from Prague to New York to Japan. She had navigated wounded and leaderless troops through hostile terrain back to base while under fire, with nothing but the stars for reference, but neither that, nor any of her considerable life experiences so far could put her at ease with the intricacies of the Victoria and Circle Lines. The air was warm and stale, the commuters as impatient as they were ill-tempered, the maps unclear and the attendants, at least the ones she encountered, were surly at best.

Nonetheless, despite her reservations, Lucie found herself on the cramped and uncomfortable train that evening, breathing in a heady mix of fast food, e-cigarettes and other people's body odour and listening to the unwelcome sounds of someone's beatbox, punctuated by some of the more extreme political views of her experience being openly opined within earshot. In the days of her youth, Lucie could remember tube rides with her mum when they would both happily speak Czech, while maybe five other languages could be heard up and down the carriage, spoken without any fear of offense being taken or violent reaction being provoked. Sadly, it seemed to Lucie, that sense of ease, or perhaps more that lack of fear seemed to now to be gone, dying along with so much of what she knew to be Britain, in the early hours of 24th June 2016. In its place hung an ever-present wariness which Lucie saw holding passers-by in its grip, possessing people with an almost subconscious terror of appearing to say or do anything that could be perceived as 'unconventional' or 'non-conformist', for fear of falling foul of the current standards of 'Britishness' now demanded of residents.

The train stopped at her station, the doors opening to their consistent warning to mind the gap, and she followed the horde through tunnels and up steps into the night air, walking the short distance to the bar Della had recommended on the phone. A handwritten paper sign had been taped to the inside of a glass panel on the door which instantly soured Lucie's mood and rammed back down her throat the uncertainty and worry that had afflicted so many, since the referendum, people and businesses alike: 'STAFF WANTED', it read, 'NO EUs'.

Stepping through the doors, she saw her new friend waiting at a table, dressed in a black turtle neck, jeans and knee length boots, her hair bunched up atop her head and the mischievous smile firmly in place emphasised by the red lipstick which now adorned it.

Della stood to welcome her, kissing the air next to Lucie's cheeks and gesturing her to sit down.

"Rum and coke, wasn't it?" Della asked, passing a glass full of the mixture, replete with ice, lime and superfluous umbrella to Lucie, who thanked her and clinked it against Della's own glass, the two women taking a sip and returning them to the table.

"It's really kind of you to take the time to meet me like this," Lucie said, "I must admit this has all been a bit of a whirl. And finding you all in the flat this morning was a shock to the system to say the least."

Della grinned in apology.

"Lake always likes to keep newbies on their toes, he's famous for it."

"He might have given me a bloody heart attack," Lucie spat, raising the glass to her lips and taking another, deeper sip. As she returned the glass to the table she felt Della's hand cover her own, and she turned to see a serious, but concerned look on the older woman's face.

"Look, I know you won't be too happy about it, but Lake gave Kasper and I a bit of background on you. I heard what happened to you on that boat, and before, in Afghanistan, so with everything over this last couple of days and what we have to do, I suppose I just wanted to make sure you were ok and welcome you to the team properly."

"I half-expected he had, and it's good of you to take the time," Lucie answered, sincerely, smiling back at her new friend.

The music in the bar began to thump louder, breaking her trail of thought. She took another drink to collect herself, leaning in to be better heard. Della offered her the widest smile she had seen in some time, instantly putting her at ease; a sensation that had been alien to her since at least the day she had walked up the gangplank of her ship.

"I'll bet you've had a few questions whiz through your head today," Della grinned.

"Just the odd one or two," Lucie smiled back, "first among them what the hell are the 'Overlappers'?"

Della laughed.

"Well," she began to muse, "we're exactly what it says on the tin really. Strictly speaking, Five deal with internal security while Six handle external affairs. Occasionally though there will be threats more indeterminate in source and cross boundary in nature that require a more independent eye, and that's where we come in."

"Can't Five and Six just run joint investigations when that happens?" Lucie asked, sensing as soon as she spoke the words that she was displaying a degree of naivety with her question, a feeling only intensified by Della's repeated laugh.

"Five and Six don't really play well together," she explained, "mainly because they're two cheeks of the same arse."

"So, what does that make us? The bit in the middle?"

More laughter emanated from Lucie's new friend who nodded in enthusiastic acceptance of the analogy.

"Absolutely," she concurred, "we are officially the arse crack of espionage."

She raised her glass in mock salute to the new label and Lucie clinked her own glass against hers.

"How long have you been doing this?

"Oh, longer than I'd like to admit," Della answered, clearly uncomfortable with the subject which she immediately sought to change. "Listen, it's a bit louder in here than I thought it would be, do you want to finish up and head somewhere else?"

"Absolutely," Lucie grinned, "and unless London's changed beyond all recognition then I know just the place."

*

A short tube ride and shorter walk later and the two friends were sat in the corner table of a half full bar, just across from a quartet playing their smooth, slow jazz to themselves as much as the punters.

BLOOD, WHITE AND BLUE

"That's more like it," Della grinned, raising her gin and tonic first to the band and then to Lucie.

"I could join in if you like?" Lucie smiled back, holding her Blues harp at the ready in a mock pose which brought a laugh from the older woman.

"Oh, brilliant," she chuckled, "is there a spot for me?"

"What do you play?"

"The fool mostly, but when I get out of bed in the morning, my bones click so much I sound like a maraca band…"

The women laughed heartily together and sat back to drink and take in the ambience, Della eventually leaning back in to pick up their conversation from earlier.

"Lucie," she began, "I know how this must all feel, believe me, but don't let it overwhelm you. You handled a lot worse than this in Afghanistan; you're smart, you can take care of yourself, you'll be absolutely fine."

"Maybe," Lucie concurred, "but let's just say I'd not planned to be involved in any more of this 'Queen and Country' bullshit, certainly not after the vote."

"You planned on a simple, quiet existence stacking shelves in Tesco for the rest of your life, did you?"

"Is that such a bad life?"

"Not at all," Della answered, "but it's hardly 'you' is it?"

"No, I suppose not," Lucie sighed in agreement. "I just hope this is all as simple as Lake says it is, that I'm just slapping a guy with a paint tin in his hands and asking a few questions of an old man. I'm not in any rush to get involved in the rough and tumble again, that's all."

"I'm sure you'll be fine," Della reassured.

"It's not me I'm worried about, Della… this is going to sound stupid, and I'm sure it's nothing like that in real life but I've seen spy movies, I've read the books; you might not have to abseil into hollowed out volcanoes but sooner or later in this game somebody gets killed, and that's fine, I don't mind being the one who dies if it means someone else doesn't. But if somebody gets killed that means somebody has to pull the trigger."

Della was quiet for a moment, and Lucie could feel her new friend's eyes on her, studying her, perhaps for weaknesses, perhaps out of concern, she didn't yet know her well enough to decide, and neither did she know herself well enough, it seemed, to decide which of those 'somebodies' she would rather be.

"Lucie," Della began after the pause had hung between them long enough, "as far as anyone can tell this is a simple job. Having some keyboard warrior arrested and finding out who's behind some elaborate prank with official stationary, that's all."

"As far as anyone can tell," Lucie repeated.

"You want a guarantee?" Della laughed, "Sorry darling, I can't offer you one. All I can say is that this should be straightforward, and it's not like the old days with the KGB around every corner. That said there are times, I suppose, when lethal force is necessary."

Lucie cringed, swallowing her own drink, the ice clinking loudly as she put down her glass with a little too much power.

"There's that damn expression again, 'necessary'. It's never 'necessary' to kill anyone, Della, never. I was a Chaplain, for God's sake; have you never heard that bit about 'Thou shalt not commit murder?"

"It's not murder if it's in self-defence," Della gently countered, gesturing to the barman for another round.

"That's just your interpretation," Lucie gloomily responded, "it doesn't make it true."

Her momentary silent introspection was broken by the waiter placing another two drinks down in front of them and collecting their empty glasses, which Della took as her cue to offer him a seductive wink.

"Keep them coming and I'll have a tip for you later," she grinned up at him, wickedly. "If you'll keep a tip ready for me too that is?"

The young man blushed noticeably and turned back to the bar, an embarrassed smile on his face, while Lucie shook her head and gave an exasperated smile at her companion's behaviour.

"It might not be true," Della said, picking up her previous thread in a heartbeat, as if her brief proposition to the waiter had never occurred, "but then again it might be. But what is true is that if you ever find yourself in that position then I hope you'll make the right decision and that you can come to terms with that. You have a talent for this sort of work Lucie, you really do, there's no point in fighting it, you may as well just lie back, enjoy the ride and…"

"Think of England?" Lucie interrupted, a sarcastic smile on her face.

"Anything that doesn't bring up your lunch, dear," Della winked back. "Oh, and while we're on the subject of unwavering National pride, don't let our mild-mannered benefactor Mr. Lake, fool you. I've never met a more ruthless bastard than him; he's so wrapped up in the Union Jack that he threw his own wife off a motorway bridge a few years back when she got mixed up in a case…"

Lucie spat her drink back into her glass at Della's nonchalant delivery of the bombshell, staring up at the older woman in incredulity.

"He did what?"

"No-one knows all the details," Della shrugged, her voice irritatingly casual. "It seems she was a double agent playing him for information. When he found out he chased her to the overpass at Knutsford Services and dropped her into rush hour traffic, just outside Burger King. No-one could accuse him of lacking commitment then; in fact, he's probably the only one of us left in the Service who does it all for Queen and Country, for the Blood, White and Blue…"

"The what?"

"Patriotism," Della said, a smile breaking onto her face, albeit in cynicism rather than joy. "Or at least Lake's version of it. That's what he used to call it; he'd say you'd never be at your most effective as an operative until you felt it in your blood, as though Britain itself was coursing through your veins… Not that he's a 'my country right or wrong' sort, he's too clever for that. But the good of the country – the Blood, White and Blue – that has to mean something to you."

A frown came to Lucie's brow and the bitter taste of bile to her mouth as she mulled over Della's words.

"Stupid expression," she hissed, her emotions taking a sudden and absolute grip on her. "I've had as much of that as anyone should ever have to."

Della raised her eyebrow in silent encouragement of her new friend to continue and Lucie drained her glass before responding.

"It was Afghanistan," she briskly explained. "When they bring the bodies of the fallen home, they always drape the coffin in a Union flag, as though it makes losing a loved one to some politician's flight of ego all the easier if you wrap the body in some final expression of jingoistic pointlessness."

She looked into her glass and tutted at its empty state as her rant continued.

"A damn disgrace is what it is Della. It turns a funeral into a pantomime and makes a mockery of everything the flag is supposed to stand for, at least what it was supposed to stand for, before it was hijacked by the wannabe Nazis… believe me Della, I've had my fill of the 'blood, white and blue."

Lucie felt Della's hand close over her own and she let it stay there just for a moment without looking up at her, the slow caress of her thumb oddly soothing.

"We're not all like that, Lucie," Della's voice had taken on a tone of calm maturity with an almost maternal inflection that wooed her back from the edge of her dark thoughts. "Some of us just want to do as good a job as we can and try and make this shithole a little bit brighter before we pop our clogs."

Lucie couldn't help but laugh and she straightened herself up in her chair finally, sliding her hand back across the table and pushing the hair from her face, tiredness adding to the stress in her mind by stinging her eyes.

"Sorry," she sighed through her smile, genuinely appreciative of the effort her new colleague and friend had made in meeting her, "I get a bit carried away with myself sometimes."

"Don't we all," Della reassured her, raising the new glass deposited by the nervous waiter. "Here's to getting carried away."

SIX

Though she had only intended to be out for an hour, several more had passed before she had put the key in her lock and begun the unfairly tortuous climb up the stairs to her flat. She had left Della still in top form, throwing back shots and chatting up waiters and waitresses alike, but while her new friend appeared able to weather the storms of excessive alcohol consumption, Lucie knew her body well enough to know she needed at least some sleep if she were to make it to the airport with the clear head she always needed to travel.

She awoke with the entirely expected but always unwelcome dry mouth and unsettled stomach, thanking The Lord in her morning prayers for at least sparing her the chore of packing, having not yet emptied her bag from her unexpected move. Eschewing her typical shower and barely rubbing her toothbrush against her teeth, lest it trigger another round of the pounding in her head which had failed to endear itself to her moments before, Lucie settled for a quick basin wash and a good dose of deodorant. Likewise, she reasoned that a change of underwear was not yet essential and certainly not worth the nausea inducing neuralgia it would provoke. Keeping her neck as immobile as possible she dressed herself in jeans and patterned shirt, texted for a cab and made her way slowly downstairs.

*

After directing the cabbie to the drive thru window of the nearest fast food venue, and having swiftly consumed something that vaguely represented food, Lucie began to re-join humanity. The cab driver was friendly enough and sufficiently worldly-wise to understand Lucie's delicate state and so kept his cheery banter to a minimum, rightly expecting that the size of his tip would correlate significantly with the brevity of his conversation.

The car eventually swept into Heathrow and after suitably rewarding the driver for his understanding, she made her way into the terminal and through to the departure lounge. Lucie took her time, still not wanting to aggravate the debilitating ache across her eyes with excessive movement, all too reluctant this morning to bear the punishment of a body whose warnings she had ignored the night before.

Walking too slowly to politely avoid the grim faced and despondent newspaper vendor, she took the proffered free copy and slipped it into her bag while she searched the terminal for the increased rarity of a coffee large and strong enough to satiate her, but which would not require a mortgage application and three forms of ID to procure. Finally locating something on the more modest side of overpriced, Lucie squeezed between the bickering couples and drunken groups to perch herself on a wooden stool beside the border rail, from where she could view the departure boards and observe the multitudes as they dashed from here to there, desperate to embark on what, depending what provision the far from secure 'Brexit Deal' made for airspace agreements, could be their last foreign trips for some time. Taking a sip from the scalding coffee, she pulled out the freebie paper and grimaced, immediately regretting her decision.

There they were, lined up between the pages, pontificating on the economic downturn that was beginning to bite and leaving readers in no doubt which people – or groups of people – were to blame. Quotes were fired like inflammatory bullets, as though those speaking them were engaged in some hateful competition, the winner of which would be crowned undisputed champion and defender of the 'Will of the People', whatever that was interpreted to be that month, with all who defied them forever condemned as traitors and enemies to be vilified and loathed.

Lucie scanned their comments, which variously within the same article condemned immigrants for laziness and benefit dependency, whilst taking jobs away from the indigenous population and pressurising emergency services, despite the NHS relying on them to function. One particularly fatuous remark sought to blame certain communities for wasting police time by insisting on reporting hate crimes against them. The ignorance did little to ease Lucie's hangover and she was about to toss the paper to one side when she turned the page and her eyes were drawn to a picture of the man she was flying to meet, Sir Geoffrey Hartnell MP.

The picture took up a good portion of the page's top half and was accompanied by a 'humorous' feature line reading 'A Grave Affair' and a few reams of text, short on minutiae but knowledgeable enough to sketch an outline of the bizarre scenario. The infamous Alexander Huxley – a man thought to be dead – had threatened Hartnell's life and with the popular MP about to fly to Prague on a personal mission of goodwill, was the government right to be treating this lightly?

However new to the world of espionage she may have been,

BLOOD, WHITE AND BLUE

Lucie was savvy enough to know that this was bad. She plunged her hand into the inner pocket of her overcoat and dialled the number that Lake had provided her during their car journey from Southampton docks, the unmistakeable tone of the man himself answering after barely one ring.

"Have you seen the papers?"

"Yes, but they're not the worst of it. The story was broken online by one of these 'Alt Right' lunatics, I'm sending you a link, watch it before you take off. It would seem not only that rumours of Mr. Huxley's passing have been somewhat exaggerated, but that his friend in the Embassy has chums of their own among the internet's shadier characters."

The line went dead, followed seconds later by the beep of a newly arrived text message. Opening it, Lucie pressed her thumb to the link it contained and watched as a browser opened up to reveal a skinny young man, stood before a wall covered with reports and clippings from Right Wing dailies from across the world. The youngster frowned into the camera with a ferocity that suggested it was his face's default position.

Lucie had encountered such people before. Usually they proved to be socially dysfunctional keyboard warriors with long retained virginities, raging at the unfairness of the world to similarly minded fantasists on YouTube. Occasionally though, one of them would ride a current of opinion to the promised land of higher hit counts, copious subscribers and the lucrative advertising revenue they brought. And once they had reached that point, more often than not in Lucie's experience, they had begun to genuinely believe the poisonous click-bait they spewed. She could tell in an instant that this was one such individual.

"Long serving Member of Parliament and Enemy of the People, Sir Geoffrey Hartnell, is to fly to Prague this week with his usual cross-party cabal of saboteurs and traitors in tow, on the latest of his vanity missions to countries in the EU."

The voice of the figure matched his expression, each syllable spoken as though Hartnell's actions were a personal insult and almost daring viewers to disagree with him. It was precisely the sort of performance that turned Lucie off from social media, but she forced herself to continue with the unsettling display.

"In reality, Hartnell and his team of Remoaners are doing everything they can to betray the Will of the People..." Lucie grimaced at hearing that damn expression again. "... and scupper the chances of a meaningful Brexit. But this time it won't be such an easy ride for Hartnell as he's flying into a warm welcome from his old friend Alexander Huxley. Now anyone who paid attention in school will remember that Huxley was also a traitor to Britain and defected to the Communists in Prague in 1968 ahead of the Russian invasion, and for reasons not yet clear, Huxley, who before today the world thought dead, is keen to say hello to his old friend with a bullet between the eyes."

The narrator lifted a sheet into view which wiped the grimace from Lucie's face and replaced it with a look of cold concern. It was a copy, poorly scanned but a copy nonetheless, of the very document she had studied in her living room only the previous morning – the death threat itself.

"How the hell do you have that?" Lucie mused aloud as she continued watching.

"Death threats to politicians are ten a penny," the angry young man continued, "but this one was sent from the British Embassy in Prague itself. And if I were Hartnell right now, I'd be bricking myself that my treachery against Brexit is so strong that even an infamous defector hates me for it, and I'd be looking over my shoulder when the plane lands, that's for sure."

BLOOD, WHITE AND BLUE

Lucie paused the recording and drained the last of her coffee from her cup, cursing. The tell-tale signs that this 'simple assignment' were about to become more complicated did little to quell her mood; instead she could only find herself agreeing with this young crusader, whose name according to his video channel was Stephen Nelson, that Hartnell should be on his guard.

"He might well do that, Mr Nelson," she pondered as her flight number was displayed on the board. "He might well indeed."

SEVEN

Shuffling through the Terminal gate, wedged between eager tourists and intoxicated stag groups, Lucie put the video and the inevitable storm it was doubtless already brewing from her mind and focussed on her imminent return to her mother's homeland. Though she had long adhered to George Bernard Shaw's famous belief that patriotism is at heart the conviction that one's country is superior because one was born in it, and the idea of being 'proud' of where one was born puzzled her, so too did she understand and share the desire to love one's country and one's heritage.

She did indeed love her Czech heritage, just as much as her British, but the resentment born of Brexit penetrated far and wide, causing her last stay in the country to be marred by inflammatory ill-feeling on the part of a presumed friend, directed at Lucie's British half. It had been that fall out as much as anything that had led her to sign up with the Merchants in the first place, after realising, perhaps belatedly, that neither country was yet prepared to reciprocate the love she had always held for them.

The trepidation chewed away at her, robbing her of the refreshing sleep she craved as the plane cut nonchalantly through the skies, until it finally dipped its wings over Prague and she reluctantly opened her eyes to the familiar sight below; a sight which had once filled her heart with joy, but today left her mouth dry with an after taste of bitter saccharine.

Clearing passport control, Lucie strode past the holiday makers haggling fares with intransigent cab drivers and climbed aboard a neglected bus which heaved itself through parts of the city rarely touched by tourists and sightseers, but which served as a magnate to those who had ever called this place home. Far from the bright lights of Wenceslas Square or the tourist traps of Old Town lay the blues bars and drinking dens that Lucie knew so well; seedy establishments yes, but brimming with character. They were places where the real musicians played, and the real people drank to forget the woes of their real and everyday lives.

Climbing from the bus, her bag over her shoulder, Lucie headed straight to just such a venue, a small but well populated bar with fading yellow paint on the stone walls and chipped and stained oak tables standing somewhat indiscriminately about. In the far corner on a high bar stool sat a balding man in late middle age, whose tightly closed eyes and furrowed brow wrinkled his black skin and whose fingers picked exquisitely at the strings of the acoustic guitar he held. The mournful, haunted, American tones which accompanied his playing, were the only English Lucie could hear uttered in the room, and with a bellyful of Brexit Britain lying undigested in her gut, that suited her just fine.

Dropping her bag to the floor, she climbed onto a vacant stool and ordered a large beer, slipping casually back into the Czech she hadn't spoken for months during her brief exchange with the barman. Finishing her drink almost immediately, she ordered another and closed her eyes. She hadn't expected to be overjoyed to be back in the city, but even she was surprised by how dispassionate she felt right now. This had been after all her home, at least for a few years, and it saddened her to realise how little warmth she felt for it after leaving the last time in the manner that she did. Deep down she still loved Prague, she always would, but right now it was a cold, reluctant love which she bore rather than relished, as though the city were an ex-lover with whom she no longer wished to speak, but whose embrace could never be matched by any other.

The beer was going down far too quickly, and Lucie could feel the edge of the blackness beginning to caress her emotions. It had been days since she had taken her medication and her decision to try to fight off her depressive episodes alone was starting to feel unwise. Too many more beers and she would be helpless against the enveloping cloud she could feel stalking her now, waiting for her to lose her grip. Though she yearned to lose herself in the music, she knew that right now, that too would be fatal, and with reluctance she passed a fresh, crisp note to the barman and pulled herself up to the floor, swinging her bag back to her shoulder and heading to the door. The night air, already cold, was made chillier still by an unexpected and entirely unseasonal smattering of snow that year, a thin but not insignificant layer of which now coated the streets Lucie trudged through in search of her apartment.

It wasn't long before she found the place, though its grim, soulless exterior offered no suggestion of home comforts awaiting her within. After being buzzed through the tall, wooden main doors, she collected her key from a surly and disinterested night manager who didn't seem to care too deeply about her proffered ID and the reservation Lake had provided in his bundle of travel documents. The building was long, thin and ancient, its stone walls and floor sparse and bare save for a faded copy of the building regulations and a lazy sketch of a fire alarm assembly point blue-tacked to the wall. Following the instructions Lake had provided in the envelope, Lucie dipped out of sight of the anyway bored night manager and peeled back the corner of the laminated building regulations, revealing a dull key, taped to the cracked wall behind them; the means, Lake's note had explained, by which she would gain entry to Fostrow's apartment the next day. Pocketing it silently and re-sticking the note, Lucie turned to the only other visible feature; the stone staircase which stretched up depressingly before her, twisting out of view on its way to a top floor she felt suddenly loathe to reach. Cheap digs indeed.

Heaving herself to the top, Lucie paused both to invite air into her burning lungs, and to stop, at least for a moment, the tell-tale spinning that was beginning to tease her head. As she refocussed on the door to her room, her eyes fell on its adjacent neighbour and she felt her stomach churn, as much in apprehension at her forthcoming 'mission' as of a consequence of her drinking. Almost without realising it she found herself at her neighbour's door, her hand raised ready to knock and a stream of resentful cynicism in her throat.

The continuing churn of her gut convinced her that she was in no shape or mood to swap barbs with a pound shop Nazi and she stopped her knuckles from rapping on the painted wood, instead turning the key to her own door and switching on the light. It was if anything even more sparse than the hallway downstairs, devoid of any furnishing save a single bed and small bedside table pressed against a cracked stone wall. To her left, Lucie noted a tiny, door-less alcove in which sat a toilet, sink and un-adorned towel rail. The room was cold, and the tired looking iron radiator clinging to the wall emitted more the impression of unwillingness to alter that fact than it did any heat.

Lucie didn't care, she had slept in worse. She threw her bag in the corner and peeled off the clothes she had travelled in, depositing them in a crumpled heap on the floor and pulling a voluminous faded t-shirt, retrieved from her bag, over her head. She went to the side of the bed to begin her prayers, but her knee was beginning to ache in the cold and she told herself that The Lord would not begrudge her missing one night. The black mood which had toyed with her in the bar was still hovering around, threatening to creep out from the back of her mind and bring with it a broken and nightmare fuelled slumber of hated memories and old fears. She tried her best to shut off the road to those thoughts and reached for her phone, twisting its headphones firmly into her ears and switching out the light. The temperature was rapidly dropping, and the ancient radiator spluttered and gurgled in protest at the job expected of it.

Still Lucie didn't care, pulling the blanket over her head and clamping her eyes shut tight. The music of her youth and her hatred of the present would keep her warm.

BLOOD, WHITE AND BLUE

EIGHT

Reality dragged her to cognisance in an instant early the next morning and she sat upright, blinking for a moment to help her mind catch up with her body. Her mobile and the headphones lay on the bedside table where she had unconsciously deposited them in the night, meaning that the wailing sound which had woken her had come from elsewhere.

Swinging her legs from the bed she smarted at the pain and stiffness in her bad knee, no doubt brought on by the coldness in the room, and she stretched her leg out a couple of times to loosen the joint. Opening the window, the wailing noise increased, and Lucie soon spotted its source; a young man, leaning out of an apartment window a few buildings down the street and howling his misery and his opinion of the woman who had left him to the world. The world, it was transpiring, was proving less than sympathetic in response, with other windows now opening to profane demands for silence. Glancing at her watch as the hands ticked over to just after six o'clock, Lucie could well understand the reaction, but was disinclined to join in the remonstrations. Who, after all, had not felt a similar despair in their lifetime?

The cold beginning to tease her bladder, Lucie crossed to the small bathroom and washed and refreshed herself as best she could, brushing the tangles from her long, dark hair and tying it back into a ponytail while she dressed in a cleaner variant of her regular attire. Plugging her dead phone in to charge, she pulled on her overcoat and headed out into the chilly morning to search for coffee.

A short tram ride into town led her to the back-street bakery she had once frequented daily, and she ordered herself a small pastry and large Americano, a little disappointed that she no longer recognised the face behind the counter. Pulling a free paper from the stand beside the till, she took a seat by the window and sipped her coffee as the city began to reluctantly heave itself to life and its occupants scurried here and there. Glancing down at her paper, she saw staring back at her, for the second day in succession, the face of the man she was to save from humiliation later, Sir Geoffrey Hartnell MP. Photographed at the head of his small band of cross-Party politicians, Algers among them, the shot had been captured as they greeted the Czech Premier the previous day.

"I bet your room wasn't so bloody cold," she heard herself mutter, before her eye was caught by the STOP PRESS box in the corner of the front page.

"Assassination threat from beyond the grave", the box proclaimed in Czech as Lucie quickly scanned the page. "Visiting British MP, Sir Geoffrey Hartnell, is the target of a terror plot, it emerged yesterday, orchestrated by none other than Alexander Huxley, the infamous defector thought to have died in Czechoslovakia before the Velvet Revolution. The UK government took the unusual step of commenting on the rumour, claiming it to be, "clearly ludicrous", while Hartnell himself joked that instead of extra security, he should make a call to the Ghostbusters."

Lucie cursed. However much Hartnell and the government may try to laugh it off, the fact that it had made the front page of a Czech Daily proved that the story had legs, and if she failed to stop Fostrow's little protest later it would only add to the problem and make her efforts to get to the bottom of the threat even more difficult than they seemed.

Resentment began to filter its way back into Lucie's thinking as she finished her breakfast and tossed the paper onto an empty table for someone else to read. For all her experience in the military and her recent struggles on the ship, she did not relish the prospect of confrontation, physical or otherwise. She had learned how to defend herself and if challenged would not shy away from a fight but the idea that she enjoyed violence or was in any way keen to get involved in scuffles was a myth Lake was choosing to believe. Lucie had been a Chaplain. A military Chaplain, yes, but nonetheless a woman of the cloth, and she still to this day chastised herself for her failure in that role; getting involved in a punch up with a hard right Brexiteer was no way to salve her conscience. Della had done her utmost to reassure her that it would not come to that, but Lucie couldn't imagine that a man with a history of online agitation who had gone to the trouble of arranging a stunt like this in the first place was likely to back down just because she knocked on the door and said 'boo'. It was only logical to expect she would have to restrain him in some way and hoped that Lake's police contacts arrived quickly to get the arrest taken care of.

Glancing at her watch she saw it was barely 7:30, so with the best part of four hours to play with she decided to make the short journey across the river to Letna Park, one of her favourite places in the city. The panorama from its top terrace was in Lucie's opinion unparalleled, but it was the tranquillity of solitude rather than the view that Lucie was interested in as she travelled. In these past few days her mind, never her most stable of assets, had been buffeted with all manner of realities, scenarios and the emotions that accompanied them, and the park offered the perfect venue for her to properly deal with them, rather than allow them to deal with her as had until now been the case. She had experienced on too many occasions the effects when she allowed circumstances and events to take root in her mind and trigger the dark feelings she was prone to. She knew that a few moments of personal reflection would help her to process things properly. Letna, early in the morning, was the perfect environment for her to do that, and as she sat on the bench overlooking the city from on high, she filled her lungs and emptied her mind, relinquishing all thoughts of spies, politics and protestors and wishing with all her heart that the moment could last forever.

NINE

The temptation of infinity unfortunately proved too great to resist, at least temporarily, Lucie having neglected to keep proper track of the time until disturbed by the staff setting up tables and tents in the beer garden for later in the day. Cursing her own self-indulgence, Lucie hurried back across the river and towards the dubious welcome of her apartment, the minute hand on her watch ticking a little too close to 11:10 as she boarded her final tram.

By the time she reached the building, several photographers and camera crews were already in place and Lucie slipped by them as casually as she was able, pausing finally for breath at the bottom of the winding stone staircase she had already grown to loathe. The clock above the reception window read 11:20 and she felt a gentle caress of relief at the knowledge she was still here to deal with the situation as planned, despite the error with her timings.

Taking a deep breath, she heaved her way to the top of the steps and paused, just as she had the previous night, outside the door of her target. It wasn't yet time and she was a little sweatier than she had imagined she'd be on her grand debut in the world of espionage, but with a few more deep breaths and a spare minute to compose herself, she could at least be sure she was ready for the inevitable scuffle.

11:25. Hartnell would be there now, the noise coming up the steps from the outside world confirmed it. Giving in to the vanity of her situation, Lucie found herself muttering through a selection of 'one-liners' that surely must come with the territory, starting at 'Hands up, Picasso' and running through to 'Bad luck, Salvador', before deciding this was a skill she really needed to work on and resolving to come back to it later.

Shaking her head free of glib remarks, she watched the second hand on her watch tick closer to twelve, its every movement tightening the knot in her gut. Reaching into her pocket she pulled out the key she had retrieved the previous night and held it ready to push into the lock as she counted down the longest fourteen seconds of her life. *Ten seconds…* she pressed the key against the lock, pushing as lightly as possible to mask any sound. *Six seconds…* the key fully slotted home, she turned it in the lock, praying for the absence of any metallic squeak or scrape. *Three… Two… One…*

Lucie slammed open the door and stood at her authoritative best in the entranceway, the bang echoing through the archaic corridor.

"Alright Fostrow, the paint job's been cancelled…"

She bellowed the words, hoping to maximise the shock factor and add to her target's surprise, only for that same element to stun her as she surveyed the room.

There as expected was Fostrow, just as Lake had described, but that was as far as Lucie's expectations matched reality. Not a paint pot was in sight, her target's hands instead cradling the unmistakeable stainless-steel barrel and grip of an Arctic Warfare bolt action sniper rifle.

BLOOD, WHITE AND BLUE

Crouching by the window, the skinny, sallow-faced figure swung the lethal beast around to the door, his face an explosive mixture of anger and surprise. Though shocked by the weapon's presence, the memories of Helmand that so routinely tortured her nights came to Lucie's instant rescue, sending her into an instinctive dive and roll the moment she saw the muzzle swing in her direction; two shots whooshing past her and into the paint and plaster of the open doorway she had stood in seconds earlier.

Lucie's roll took her closer to Fostrow, quicker than he could re-adjust his aim. The would-be shooter struggled to keep hold of the gun as she got to her knees and gripped the barrel, sending another shot upwards into the ceiling. They wrestled for possession of the weapon, the skinny Fostrow proving deceptively strong and wiry, but Lucie herself was no pushover and she began to gain the upper hand, the look in her eyes sufficient to tell him that if he were to defeat her, it would be only after the hardest battle of his life. Fostrow, likewise on his knees began to lose balance and tip backwards, before he swung his forehead backwards and brought it crashing onto Lucie's brow, stunning her for a moment, the man slipping the barrel from her fingers as she shook the stars from her eyes.

Taking advantage of her momentary weakness, Fostrow pushed Lucie onto her back, pressing the rifle against her throat and pushing down with all his strength. Lucie, her senses restored, pushed back as she struggled for breath. As her attacker leant forward to press home his advantage, Lucie wriggled herself enough room to bring her knee up hard into his groin, the release of pressure on her windpipe instant as he rolled from her, his hands clasping his injured crotch and pure anger burning out from behind his eyes. In an instant, Lucie had scooped up the fallen weapon and got to her feet, covering Fostrow as she went to the window and looked out to see Hartnell and his group give a final wave in front of the building opposite before returning to vehicles and heading off to the next destination on their whistle-stop tour of the city.

The immediate threat to Hartnell at least now passed, Lucie allowed herself a lungful of relieved breath and pushed the rapidly forming questions and resentments to the back of her mind, hoping that the promised custody officers would soon be present, and she could get on with finding out why the hell she had found herself with a gun pointed at her instead of a paintbrush.

"Ok, time for you to start talking…" She didn't finish the sentence she had begun as she turned away from the window, as Fostrow, hitherto silent, had used her distraction to slip a sizeable knife from the sheath on his belt and hurl it towards her head, her last second turn of gaze the only thing preventing it hitting home.

Shocked by the flashing metal, Lucie was unprepared for Fostrow launching himself at her, and knocking the rifle from her hands, sending it sliding across the floor. Gripping her throat and pushing her head against the wall with one hand, he raised a second knife in his hand, thrusting it towards her face before she caught it and held it at bay.

"Fucking bitch," Fostrow spat at her, his face so close she could see the stains on his teeth and smell the fetid breath behind them.

The strength in her arm beginning to fade, Lucie surrendered herself again to the instinct which had kept her alive in the desert. Letting go of the wrist squeezing her throat, she straightened her hand into a chop and swung it against her opponent's neck with all the fight she had in her, an instant daze coming into his eyes as the blow scrambled his senses. Her survival instinct still in control, Lucie rolled from the wall, pushing Fostrow back into the position she had occupied, and twisting his knife arm up towards his chest

BLOOD, WHITE AND BLUE

and with a low, jarring cry of rage, she pushed it hard and deep into his heart.

"Lucie!"

She woke from the brief intensity of her possession to stare at her handy work in as complete a sense of shock as she had ever felt, her expression mirrored by that of the dying Fostrow, whose lips fluttered uselessly as though fruitlessly attempting to articulate some final protest. In the doorway meanwhile stood Della, her attempted intercession having come just too late and her face etched in the same dismay that was hastily consuming Lucie, who looked up at the older woman and back to the man who thanks to her was struggling to draw his final breath.

His blood, spilling from the wound in his chest was coating Lucie's hands in painful resentment and she shook her head in mute apology, the only gesture she could now make, as the would-be assassin closed his eyes and slumped into a final and undignified heap at her feet.

TEN

Explanations were no good to Lucie now and she pushed away those that Della tried to give, running in to her own apartment and thrusting her hands under the tap, clearing the blood as best she could before throwing her bag over her shoulder and pulling her phone free from the charger she had plugged it to earlier that day.

"You see?" Della persisted, "I tried calling you, bloody hell, we all did! Why the hell didn't you have your phone on you?"

It was true, Lucie could see, her phone displaying multiple missed calls and unopened messages, but that did little to salve the wounds she had opened within herself through her actions and she turned on her friend with tearful fury.

"No!" Lucie stormed. "No, that does not make it alright, that does not let you off, not you, Algers or Mr fucking Lake, wherever he is! You told me, all of you that this would be simple, routine. Just stop some overzealous troll from chucking a bucket of paint over an MP! Well bullshit! The paint that guy's covered in in there isn't going to wash out so easily. For God's sake Della, there's a man lying dead in a room you sent me into, and I'm the one that killed him!"

"You had no choice," Della attempted to reassure, earning a contemptuous glance for her trouble. "Look, I only found out an hour ago that there was more to Fostrow than we realised; all the indicators were that he was largely harmless, gobby and a troublemaker but not someone who'd go in for something like this! We tried getting the message to you and I busted my arse trying to get here before you."

Lucie simply shook her head, trying her utmost to restrain the fury building within her.

"I spent so long, so long climbing out of that pit," she croaked, almost to herself, "and now you've pushed me right back down again… damn you all."

Della stepped closer, placing her hand on Lucie's shoulder who shuddered at the touch.

"Lucie, the police will be here soon, we've already paid them off but you'll need to answer a few questions, just to get the story straight."

"Yeah? Well you did such a good job of gathering the intelligence, why don't you take care of the police too?"

Lucie pushed past her, ignoring the pleas in her ear and set off at pace down the steps and out onto the snow dusted street, her eyes wide and frightened and her lungs burning as though each of the deep breaths she took contained not a trace of oxygen. Her body, stunned and bruised, kept moving forward, as though spurred on by the auto pilot of distant memory, until she could walk no more; her sapped energy leaving her propped against the side of ancient, gothic stonework, heaving air inside her and fixing her eyes tight against the wave of tears that threatened to engulf her.

"Bastard," she hissed in anger to no-one and everyone at once, "bastard!"

Sinking into a crouch against the aged building, Lucie sunk her head to her knees and gave into the still welling tears, the roar of anger that had been building since the moment the rifle had swung towards her finally forcing its way past her lips and into the open. She cursed herself as much for her reaction as anything else; she was no newcomer to the world of violence and death, she had snuffed out life before, but the last time had caused her to run away from the RAF she had dreamed of serving in, and the God who had called her to a service of His own. And in the midst of her rage and anger she hated herself still further that she couldn't tell if her tears were for the man she had killed, however vile he may have been, or for herself because there was nothing left for her to run away from.

She shouldn't have unloaded at Della, it wasn't her fault, Lucie should have known to keep her phone close and Shakespeare's centuries old warnings of the best laid plans at the forefront of her mind. Perhaps that was why she had left the phone and taken herself out of contact for the morning though; a subconscious defiance of being dragged back into a world of dog-eat-dog violence and danger, a deep-seated hope that the less attention she paid to this new reality, the easier the grip on her soul would be.

She slipped her hand into her pocket, intending to call Della and apologise for her outburst, to help her with the police matter, although it had sounded as though Lake's wallet was taking care of that, but her movement was interrupted by an all too familiar voice addressing her.

"Wondering where next to run to?"

Lucie gave a cynical laugh, refusing to turn her head towards the newcomer.

"Why bother?" she responded. "You'd only follow me there too.

It doesn't look like there's anywhere I can run to without somebody trying to find me, not even my own mind..."

"That's just as well, it strikes me that few places are as dangerous to be alone as the recesses of one's own mind, perhaps the likes of ours especially."

Lucie nodded in casual acceptance.

"Do you know what the worst part of depression is?" she quizzed her new companion. "It's those days when you have the urge to just give in to it. It's when you find yourself actually wanting to feel the pain, because then at least you feel something, and it's been a part of you for so long that if it went away, you're scared it'd take the rest of you with it and there'd be nothing left..."

"If you'd given in to it Ms. Musilova, it would be you in that apartment right now having your outline drawn on the floor in chalk. You stood and fought, as I had every confidence that you would."

"I should have known," Lucie opened as Lake sat down on the pavement alongside her, the ever-present dark rings under his eyes heavier even than usual. "You said you wanted an expert but what you really wanted was a gun-for-hire with a plausible motive. Since when was an expert welcome in Brexit Britain?"

"I didn't know Fostrow would be armed," Lake said in a straightforward tone, "but I did know that if the situation was more complicated than we anticipated you would be able to handle it."

"I could have been killed."

"But you weren't."

Lake carried with him two takeout coffee mugs wrapped in branded cardboard holders and he passed one to Lucie who accepted, neither of the pair yet making eye contact.

Lucie raised the cup to her lips, the hot coffee washing past the lump in her throat but failing to remove it, as she stared ahead down the street towards the main road where crowds were beginning to mill.

"You didn't say I'd have to kill."

Lake shrugged slightly and sipped from his own cup, joining her in her melancholic gaze.

"You've done it before."

"And I don't think I've ever come to terms with it."

"Well, that's your problem, we all have our crosses to bear. Like it or not Miss Musilova, you're good at this kind of work and as long as your debt to society remains unpaid, and as long as I hold the file on your Mother's death, I intend to see that you continue in it."

Lucie's cynical half-laugh sounded again, and she shrugged, realising the uselessness of arguing with him.

"Well it's done now, you can find someone else to ask Hartnell questions."

"I'm afraid not," Lake replied. "You're very much involved now. The Czech police, or at least those portions of it amenable to the monies I offer are aware of your role in the late Mr Fostrow's death and were you to try and leave Czechia without fulfilling the rest of your side of the agreement, you may find your journey a short one. Besides, our friend Mr Algers is presently informing Sir Geoffrey of your valiant effort to save his life."

"You bastard," Lucie spat, having fully expected such a retort but resentful of it nonetheless. "You utter and complete bastard. You really would have me arrested wouldn't you? Even after saving you the embarrassment of a dead MP on your watch?"

Lake drained his coffee and nodded in a simple confirmation.

"Yes. Intelligence work sometimes requires a degree of ruthlessness, you'd do well to remember that if you are to continue the impressive start you've made."

BLOOD, WHITE AND BLUE

"As ruthless as you were when you dropped your wife into traffic?"

Lucie regretted the barb as soon as it slipped from her lips, her face reddening under the immediate and intense stare of her superior. The age until he spoke was one of the longest and most uncomfortable of her life and for the slightest of moments she felt a genuine flutter of fear as to how he might react.

"My wife, Ms. Musilova," Lake eventually began, his voice harder and more threatening than she had until now experienced, "the manner of her demise and the circumstances in which it came to occur are categorically none of your concern."

Lucie nodded, contrite as Lake followed up with the expected threat.

"And unless you want the *Daily Mail's* next anti-foreigner headline to be aimed in your direction, I suggest you take your mind off idle gossip and return it to the job in hand."

"Ok," she answered quickly, "point taken."

"Good. Now I suggest that as your current apartment is likely to prove unavailable for some time, you take an hour or two to make alternative arrangements before you are introduced to the surely supremely grateful Sir Geoffrey Hartnell later this afternoon."

"I can't wait," Lucie snapped back. "Don't I even get the rest of the day off?"

"No," Lake instantly replied, rising to his feet and tutting at the damp posterior he now possessed from sitting alongside Lucie in the snow. "Find yourself somewhere to stay then text Mr Algers your new address, you'll find his number has been sent to you."

Lucie too rose to her feet and scrolled through her phone to find Algers' number there as promised.

"And then?"

"And then wait for instructions, Ms. Musilova," Lake clarified as though it should have been obvious, which, Lucie conceded to herself, perhaps it should.

The pair made eye contact for the first time since he had joined her, but instead of anything profound, he merely reached out his hand towards her.

"You've finished your coffee I see; may I take your cup?"

"Oh," Lucie replied, a little taken aback by the unexpected normality of the question. "Yeah, thanks."

He took the paper cup and turned to depart but stopped after only a yard and returned to look at Lucie.

"I know it's hard," he said, the faintest trace of sympathy infecting his hitherto cold and business-like voice. "And I know this isn't something you want to do. But Hartnell may well be the best hope this country has for anything other than a disastrous future right now, and if there's a genuine threat to him we need to neutralise it, by any means necessary."

"I made a promise," Lucie countered, "to someone even more important than you. And I've broken it today."

Lake nodded in seemingly genuine understanding.

"Then spend the next couple of hours making peace with that," he suggested. "Spend them in penitence, in prayer or in self-flagellation if you feel it necessary. But when the call comes this afternoon, be ready. Be ready to save lives if the situation demands it and to take others doing so if your cold rational judgement tells you to. However you come to terms with the reality of this, just be sure you are ready."

The pain and rage still bubbled within her, and the inherent logic of his words in no way stilled her heart's disquiet, but she nodded her silent acquiescence to Lake and watched him as he set off again towards the masses of civilisation.

"Oh, and Ms. Musilova?" he called over his shoulder.

"What?"

"Make bloody sure you keep your phone with you this time."

ELEVEN

Finding a new room was the easy part, far easier than the prayer Lucie had spent the next hour trying to say before putting repentance on hold and drinking away her tears with a quick raid of the mini-bar. She had cursed the fact that a repeat visit was out of the question if she was to retain the control required for the afternoon of glad-handing and polite conversation that Algers had warned lay ahead of her, when she had contacted him as per Lake's instructions. Now on her way to meet him, in as smart a set of clothes as she presently had with her – black jeans instead of blue, a simple Navy blue shirt with white trim and her ever present overcoat – she wished she had taken advantage of at least one more of the extortionately priced drinks

"I hope you didn't have any plans for the afternoon," Algers said as he met her at the tram stop and they began walking together into the cold afternoon air.

Lucie shrugged.

"Well nothing concrete but I was thinking of heading into town, seeing if any of the old gang were still knocking around…"

"Aww, gee," Algers interrupted, "unfortunately the old gang are all out of town today, though I believe they sent their best."

"Oh really?" Lucie answered, her amusement at Algers' manner outweighing her annoyance at his dismissal of her intentions – for now at least. "Well not to worry, I'm sure I can think of something else to pass the time."

"Oh, don't you worry yourself about that Lucie, I've saved you the trouble."

"How considerate of you!"

"How does an afternoon of tiny sandwiches, polite conversation and political bullshittery sound to you?"

"Slightly less fun than if Fostrow had succeeded in putting his blade through my chest, to be honest."

"I knew you'd be pleased," he said, grinning a wide grin of such insincerity it could likely rival the more fatuous statements made by some of those she was now expected to rub shoulders with that afternoon, and Lucie could no longer hide her grimace; an expression in which Algers soon joined her.

"Look, I'm sorry," the MP said, his default deadpan expression containing more honesty than had his political smile. "I'm sorry you're in this mess at all, but here we are. You passed Lake's little 'test' this morning and you've got Hartnell's attention in doing so, your invitation has come from him. He wants to thank you personally for saving him. Now it's time to follow through."

"Follow through how?" Lucie spat. "By eating cucumber sandwiches and ordering pink gin?"

She was being facetious, and she knew it. A personal invitation was of course a superb opportunity to ingratiate herself with Hartnell and find some way of digging around the now infamous death threat.

"You'll be lucky if that's all it is Lucie," Hartnell said as the pair reached the British Embassy steps, "if ever you've pined for the chance to swap meaningless anecdotes and weak handshakes with

Parliament's finest, then this is your lucky day."

"Hold me back," replied Lucie with a resigned grin, looking around at some of those mingling within the entrance hall before them, in all the cross-spectrum glory. A couple of Tory rebel MPs, regularly derided as 'traitors' in the media were drinking with an opposite number from the Labour benches and a former Lib Dem member turned activist, all of whom were laughing hard and bonding over their mutual antipathy towards Brexit. Across from them were various other faces of the political scene, some active, some not, but all joining Hartnell on his Pro European 'good will' tour, including several once loathed by the fickle public, only to be later embraced thanks to a charity single here and reality show appearance there.

"Bloody hell," Lucie exclaimed in surprise, "is that...?"

Algers followed her eyes to a small, cheery faced man in the corner, chatting happily to a grand, immaculately suited figure, a thinning mane of once wild hair swept back across his head.

"Oh, yeah…" Algers confirmed, "fuck, I hope that doesn't mean we have to do any ballroom dancing…"

"Well it might liven things up a little, but at least everyone seems to be on speaking terms."

"Oh, completely!" Algers nodded. "We're all friends here; this is to be an afternoon of cross-party bullshittery. At least it's in a good cause."

The inner doors to the reception room opened and people began to file obediently in, collecting glasses from the patiently waiting serving staff on the way, the chatter and buzz of the room following them as Lucie and Algers fell in behind.

"By the way, if anyone asks you now officially work on my staff, understand?"

"That was quick," Lucie joked, "when did this happen exactly?"

"A couple of hours ago," came the answer. "I heard what you'd done via the Ambassador and was so overcome with your heroism that I tracked you down and offered you a job on the spot, ok?"

"If you say so," Lucie shrugged, "but why the urgency, if you don't mind my asking?"

"Because we didn't want to run to the risk of Hartnell offering you a job first."

"But why would that be a problem," asked Lucie, confused. "I thought the whole point was to get close to him and dig deep for anything that might shed light on the Huxley letter?"

Algers nodded to accept Lucie's point before elaborating.

"Believe me, Hartnell will be far more interested in you if you remain just out of his reach; a hell of a lot more so than if you worked directly for him."

Lucie shivered. "That sounds a little ominous; I take it he fancies himself as a ladies' man, does he?"

"He might have the slightest of reputations," Algers concurred, "but nothing I'm sure you can't handle. Besides, if you and I are going to keep working together, I need you recognised as an independent, attached to me, not some Party hack desperate to get on the MP's nomination list."

Algers stepped ahead of her to handle introductions while Lucie hung back, just inside the room, a champagne flute almost pushed into her hand as she watched Algers go to work with handshakes here and warm smiles there. Despite the bitterness that had remained with her since the morning's debacle, she found herself warming quickly to the man and his interest and desire to work with her appeared genuine, but that was where she knew they would have a problem.

"Sorry Kasper," she whispered under her breath as she raised the glass to her lips and toasted her own determination that this was not the beginning of a long association. "But this girl's getting off at the next stop."

BLOOD, WHITE AND BLUE

TWELVE

"Nice to see someone under forty in the room."

The comment came from behind her and Lucie turned to see a young man standing there, with a martini glass in his hand and an immaculately sharp suit adorning him, of the type usually worn by supremely arrogant salespeople on some loathsome reality TV show, competing to be lauded as 'Top Twat' in the hope of forging a C-List celebrity career. In this case though, the suit served as a veneer, a distraction from a face that though trying to convey confidence and control, instead appeared only nervous and uncertain.

"And you know that how?" Lucie quizzed, sick to her back teeth of greetings based on her appearance, however 'complimentary' they were sometimes intended to be.

"You know," the struggling Lothario stammered, "everyone in here is pushing on a bit, there's only you and me flying the flag for the younger generation."

"Is that a fact?"

"Yeah, it is." The voice was shockingly nervous with a twist of condescension, as though its owner were fully aware that the conversation was not proceeding as intended, but equally surprised by as much and seemingly determined to press past this point and fast forward to the part where Lucie would succumb to his obvious charms.

Lucie, for her part was well used to such transparent attempts at courtship and equally well bored by them, and she briefly considered making a loud and embarrassing – at least for him – scene, but taking him in for a moment, she was struck with a surprising sense of what felt like pity. Looking at him, the only aspect of him that appeared genuine were his nerves. The rest, the expensive suit, the over-styled hair, didn't seem to belong to him, as though he were a little boy wearing his Dad's suit; even the words he spoke sounded like a script he'd been told to recite.

"What's your name?" Lucie asked him after a moment.

"I'm Eddie," he answered, "Eddie Underfoot."

"Well, Eddie," Lucie replied, her tone soft and seductive. "I'm probably a lot closer to your self-imposed cut off age than I am your own, and I've flown a lot of flags in that time. So many in fact that it would take somebody with a truly magnificent pole and the knowledge of how to properly raise it to get me interested in flying one again, and I'm sorry, but erm…" She cast her eyes quickly up and down him. "…it doesn't look to me like you've got the equipment."

Eddie squinted as though his brain were trying to process her comment to work out whether or not he had been insulted, and when after a moment he still hadn't spoken, Lucie gave him a huge smile and a wink.

"Have a good afternoon, Eddie," she said, "why don't you go home and practice raising your flag?"

She smiled to herself as she left him to his nervous ponderings. He didn't seem such a bad lad really she mused, but it was unquestionably better both for him and any women in his life that

BLOOD, WHITE AND BLUE

he learn his lesson now about how to speak to and generally treat them.

She caught Algers' eye as he made his way through the room and he quickly changed direction to catch her.

"Ready for the big moment?" he asked, and for a moment, Lucie wondered if she genuinely was.

Lucie was not a woman easily intimidated or impressed by grandeur and she could look back on a long list of officers and clergy whose pomposity she'd pricked with a raised eyebrow or a withering look. But this was different. *He* was different.

Sir Geoffrey Hartnell strode towards her, his hand outstretched, the arm shaking slightly she noticed, and effortlessly carrying the attention of the room. Classically tall and thin, he was dressed in an immaculate lounge suit, his fine silver hair sweeping back from a high forehead off which the light reflected, which leant him an altogether angelic quality. Hartnell's smile was sincerity itself as he took Lucie's palm in his grasp and beamed down at her from his great height.

"Miss Musilova," he beamed, *"Dovolte mi dát své poděkování za vaši pomoc dnes ráno."*

"Call me Lucie," she answered, a shade more deferentially than she would have preferred, "and please, English is fine."

"That bad was I?" the Statesman chuckled, "I'm afraid it's been a good few years since I used the language properly; I always found it beautiful to listen to but rather hard to wrap one's tongue around."

"Word perfect," she smiled back, "almost."

The clasped hand released her with expert timing having hung on just long enough for all the key figures in the room to acknowledge the greeting, before returning to the statesman's side, the shake in the arm she had presently noticed now a definite tremor. With his other arm, Hartnell took a champagne flute from a proffered silver tray and handed it to Lucie to replace the one she had emptied, taking another for himself as he continued what seemed a perfectly orchestrated charm offensive.

"Shame on you, Kasper," he jokingly admonished, "not providing the lady with a drink. Cheers, my dear, or should that be '*nastravi*'?"

He raised the glass to Lucie who smiled at the paternal condescension on display, giving him, for now at least, the benefit of the doubt that it was affectionately meant as she returned the salute.

"It seems I am in your debt, Lucie," Hartnell picked up after his toast. "My thanks for your timely intervention are, I assure you, most sincere. It's amazing you weren't hurt."

"Lucie spent some time in the military, Geoff," Algers interrupted, "Afghanistan."

"I see! So, you know how to handle yourself, eh?"

Rather than select one of several sarcastic responses currently working their way through her brain, she instead took a further drink from her glass and kept the smile affixed to her face.

"You could say that, Sir Geoffrey, you could say that."

"Oh, call me Geoff, please," he insisted. "Well military experience or not, I am deeply grateful for what you did for me and the lengths to which you went to do it."

"I'm just glad I was there to help," Lucie lied, the fresh memory of Fostrow's final expression threatening to remove the smile from hers.

"Well if he'd started firing into the street, who knows how many people might have been hurt or killed along with you, Geoff," Algers piped in, "you did damn well, Lucie."

"You certainly did," Hartnell echoed, "in fact my only regret is that Mr Algers here has beaten me to making you an offer of employment."

Lucie was temporarily lost for words and it took a moment for her to respond.

"Really? Thanks Sir… I mean, thank you, Geoff, that's exceptionally kind of you, but Kasper just got in ahead of you."

"Well should you find life under the dourest Scot this side of Hadrian's Wall unpleasant, you make sure you come and see me, alright?"

Lucie's grin returned at the gentle ribbing and she saw Algers' brow crease in mock offence.

"Ah, I doubt Lucie would want to be on your party's payroll, Geoff," Algers opined, "she's under eighty-five and speaks another language for a start."

Hartnell laughed heartily.

"I can't say I blame you, Lucie," he sighed, "God knows what's happened to my lot these last few years; they're allowing themselves to be dictated to by a handful of malcontents completely obsessed with Brexit at any cost, absolute madness. Still, no madder arguably than a certain Independent MP of our acquaintance, who used a full-page interview in the *Mail* to say that Brexiteers reminded him of the villain in *Indiana Jones and the Last Crusade*…"

"He didn't…?" Lucie laughed.

"He most certainly did," Hartnell confirmed with a chuckle. "What was it you called them, Kasper? Harmless elderly eccentrics to start with, who turn out to be closet Nazis, oblivious to the fact that their golden chalice is poisoned, before blaming everyone else as they crumble away to irrelevance…"

Lucie and Hartnell both turned to Algers with looks of amused faux accusation, the MP shrugging in return.

"Well none of them were exactly going to sign up to my fan club anyway," he protested, "why not at least be honest with them?"

"Engage, young man, engage! Belittling them will get neither you nor the rest of us opposed to this insanity anywhere at all."

"Easier said than done, Geoff," Algers smiled in faux humility.

"Tell me, Kasper," Hartnell grinned. "Is there anything in this life that angers you as much as the Brexiteers?"

"Oh yes," Algers nodded, "people who order coffee in Subway. You're already packed in there so close you're in danger of having to marry the guy behind you and then some string of cast offs from the Muppet Show order coffee and hang around the till waiting the thousand years for it to come, while everyone starts backing up like bowling pins in a broken alley."

A moment's silence followed the passionate outburst before the trio burst out in laughter, Hartnell gesturing to his counterpart and warning Lucie that this would be what to expect on a daily basis from the man. Excusing himself, Hartnell stepped away to circulate the room, leaving Lucie and her new employer with their thoughts.

"Charming man," Lucie observed.

"He is that," Algers agreed, "but be aware that it's all 'political charm'. I doubt the man's said a sincere word in fifty years."

"He's on our side, though, isn't he?" Lucie was puzzled.

"Oh yes," Algers agreed, "but that doesn't stop him from being a bullshitter. If someone had told me that a sniper had been watching me and lining up a shot before a stranger quite by chance stumbled into things and ended up killing the poor bastard, I'd have done a little more than raise an eyebrow and order another tea."

"Me too, but then we're not English," Lucie smiled in response.

Algers reciprocated but continued his train of thought.

"I mean it though; he was stoicism itself when the Ambassador told us what had happened. I know some people can take stuff like that in their stride, but he was casual to the point of being blithe."

"Maybe that's just his public face? You know, the stiff upper-lipped English Statesman? Bowling in the face of armadas and all that?"

"Maybe," Algers nodded, "but just as likely is he's trying to do a 'Boris'..."

"A what?" Lucie frowned at the expression, never having come across it before.

"You know," the MP began to elaborate, "manipulating events to present yourself to the public as an honourable, desirable figure, ready to take the reins if and when the Prime Minister falls. Just like Boris and the referendum."

"Ah," Lucie nodded in understanding. "But Boris screwed that one up, didn't he? And however high his ambitions stretch, I can't believe that Hartnell would be complicit in anything that could cost someone their life."

"No, perhaps not," Algers mused noncommittally, "but Lake wants to press a little deeper with him, get him to open up, just in case."

"Does he now? And how does he propose we do that?"

Algers shot her a sympathetic glance and sighed.

"I'm afraid that's your problem," he said apologetically, "I have several of my own."

"Well not to pile too much on your plate, but I might have one more for you..."

"Who?"

"That guy over there," Lucie gestured with her eyes towards the young man who had approached her as she entered, the rate of perspiration on his face presently masked by the extravagant rim of the martini glass he was draining. "Young Mr Underfoot; what is he exactly?"

Algers squinted over to see him replace his empty glass on the bar and wave for another.

"Oh, he'll be a Fast Tracker," he replied.

"A what?"

"You know the kind of thing; a graduate programme supposedly open to everyone with a degree but generally populated by posh kids. They're supposed to be the 'leaders of tomorrow', they get pushed up the ranks quickly with short spells across a few different departments. Mr Underfoot will be destined for big things at the Foreign Office and this will just be one of his stepping stones to fame and glory. Why, what's he done to you?"

"Oh, nothing," Lucie answered honestly, "it's just that, well... don't you think he looks a bit nervous for someone on that kind of career path?"

"Yeah... he doesn't look entirely comfortable, does he?" Algers thoughtfully concurred as the subject of their observations swiftly consumed another of the cocktails, the creases on his brow betraying his preoccupation with something, before he placed his glass on the bar and quickly hurried from the room. "Although, anyone who feels entirely comfortable in a roomful of politicians is worthy of suspicion in my book."

"Should I keep an eye on him?"

"No, you've got other priorities, I'll ask Della to look into him. Now speaking of other priorities, would you excuse me for a moment..."

Lucie opened her mouth to protest but knew at once it was pointless. Algers moved away to accept the smile and greeting of a sharply suited woman in her fifties, slim and certainly still attractive, who had beckoned him to come over. Watching the pair, Lucie understood only too well the type of 'problems' Algers intended to be dealing with that evening, seeing all the signs of a flirtatious exchange between them, the glint of Algers' wedding

BLOOD, WHITE AND BLUE

ring catching the light as he raised his glass to his lips disgusting her.

Damn the adulterous sod, and damn Lake, she thought to herself, as she walked to the grand, tall windows overlooking the city. A darker mood appeared to cling to the Old Town, aided by the thick grey clouds full of un-fallen snow which seemed so out of place for this time of year, while in the middle distance, the first of the lights began to flicker on across the houses below.

She looked back across the room and the cavalcade of sharp suits and designer dresses it contained; the people they adorned busying themselves with cocktails and light conversation as the Great British Statesman worked his way amongst them. She took Hartnell in again, her silent observations unnoticed in a room of noisy conversation.

Hartnell's reaction to the news of the foiled attack on his life and the fact the would-be assailant had been killed, had certainly been underwhelming to say the least, and not what Lucie had come to expect from the man's televisual persona, which made heavy play of thoroughness and attention to detail, but his readiness to offer employment had appeared genuine, as had his opposition to the bitter division Brexit had caused. In addition to the charm he possessed in abundance, he clearly too had cultivated the gift of being able to make each individual he encountered feel like the most important person in the room; a skill he was utilising presently, as he circulated the room with expert awareness, leaving a compliment here and a kind word there as he completed his individual interactions with each person or group in turn and moved on. This was a room of dignitaries and high-ranking officials, Lucie thought to herself, and they had surely encountered such behaviours before from a hundred visiting persons of importance, self-imagined or otherwise, but there was little routine about the reactions on their faces which to a person glowed with something approaching awe. Lucie found it difficult to criticise their reactions as she had felt the same herself when first she saw him striding towards her. Good luck to them, she thought to herself and turned back to the window and sea of snow dusted rooftops stretching out before her into the city. Lucie began to ponder how the hell she could 'press' this man who inspired such reactions into telling her anything.

It was a curiously metallic flicker that caught Lucie's eye as she was beginning to move from the window, causing her to stop in her tracks and look out once more. The French windows she stood in front of was set above a garden terrace, now closed off from the cold weather, but which itself was only feet away from its neighbour, the angled orange slate peeking in patches through the snow as the heat from the rooms inside rose incessantly upwards. An aerial and flag pole towered skywards from the roof, but neither had been the source of the distracting blink of light, and Lucie squinted to focus better.

It flashed again, and Lucie's eyes moved sharply to follow it. It was next to a large, square skylight, that something had moved, and she squinted to try and make it out. The paned glass stood open, but she was sure that it had not been the source of the light…

She cursed her idiocy and frowned in frustration. Why the hell would a skylight, and a large one at that, be open to the elements in the middle of a snowfall, however unseasonal it may be? What was more, snow had been piled against it, clearly by hand as evidenced by the uneven patches where it had been scraped and massed, creating what was in effect, a large, square 'shield', just large enough for an average sized person to hide unseen behind; at least, that was how Lucie's military experience taught her to see it.

BLOOD, WHITE AND BLUE

She was still staring hard, unsure of what she was looking for when she heard Hartnell's voice behind her.

"Ah, Lucie, good news," she heard him say, "the Ambassador has been kind enough to extend you an invitation to the official dinner this evening. Do you perhaps have any more appropriate attire you'd like to change …"

The question remained unfinished as Lucie's patience was finally rewarded and the source of the tell-tale glint revealed itself.

"Get down!" she hollered commandingly to the room as she gripped Hartnell by his immaculate lapels and forced him to the floor, covering him with her own body as they landed and shielding him from the falling shattered glass that rained over them.

Even before they had landed, the bullet which had been heading for Hartnell's forehead had sliced through the room and embedded itself in the far wall, accompanied by a chaotic concerto of screaming guests and fallen beverages.

"What the…?"

Hartnell, shock on his face struggled to rise under Lucie's weight and she held him down as another shot whistled into the room.

"Keep down!"

Algers scrambled across to them, the glass crunching under his shoes as he squatted next to Lucie with his back against the wall.

"Where's the shooter?" he hissed at Lucie.

"Next roof over," she gestured with her head, "behind the skylight."

"Stay here and keep him safe." Algers slipped his hand towards his inner pocket and Lucie, wide eyed, leapt from her position atop Hartnell and grabbed his arm before he could complete the movement.

"Are you mad?" she whispered in haste, "you can't get your gun out and play the action hero here! Your cover would be blown for good!"

"I need to get the sniper!" Algers retorted, in equal frustration.

"Not you," Lucie corrected, "we."

Risking straightening up, Lucie looked through the shattered pane and saw the shooter, clad in white ski suit and balaclava, fleeing at pace across the rooftop. Rising fully to her feet, she took a deep breath and looked again at Algers.

"Look after Hartnell," she said.

Whatever profanities Algers may have shouted in response would have to be repeated later, as by then, Lucie had already pushed her fears to one side and leapt through the window, and she hoped, possibly against all reason, that should she even be able to catch up to the sniper, she would have even the slightest idea what to do next.

THIRTEEN

Lucie struggled to retain her balance as she leapt through the shattered window, jarring her bad knee as her soles struggled to grip to the snow underfoot. The crisp, white blanket was spread unevenly before her, with ancient spires and the occasional flash of red and orange slate punctuating it, and Lucie struggled to see the edge of the roof she stood on against the pale sky. It was the Shooter's jump across the divide from one rooftop to another that focussed Lucie's vision and she set off in pursuit of the white, ski suit clad figure, ignoring the pain in her knee and taking the gap between buildings in a running leap; the people below looking up in shocked surprise.

She whispered a silent prayer of thanks that a flatter rooftop greeted her landing, and she felt herself gathering speed as her feet got used to the slippery surface, narrowing the gap between herself and the shooter and passing the abandoned rifle her quarry had dropped. She was almost upon the assailant as she launched into another jump, but the sight of the shooter standing atop her slanted destination, gun pointed squarely in her direction, caused Lucie to twist in mid-air, narrowly avoiding the bullet which whooshed past her right ear, and turning her landing into a desperate thump.

Struggling for balance, Lucie straightened up directly into a powerful backhand across her jaw from the assailant, stunning her and sending her slipping down the acutely angled rooftop, snow scraping underneath her as she slid, exposing the bright slate as though her fall were smearing blood over white paper.

Grasping her rapidly freezing pink fingers down onto the rim of decades old guttering, Lucie squeezed tightly, ignoring the pain and the jolt to her shoulders as the weight of her body slipped from the edge and she hung precariously above the ancient cobbles of the street far below. Filling her lungs with the cold, biting air she swung her legs to the wall she hung against and pushed, shuffling her elbows onto the ridge and scrambling desperately for the next finger hold along the wet, slippery orange slate. Before she could dig down into her next grip, the crunch of a snow boot on disturbed and broken flakes told her that the additional threat had not taken the opportunity to flee. Looking slowly up, Lucie saw the figure, white suited and foreboding, standing over her; its face covered and its gun ominously in its hand.

The eye holes of the ski mask were veiled and dark, as though worn by some malign spirit staring quizzically down at her, toying maliciously with her fate as she clung helplessly to her ancient support. Slowly, the figure raised the gun towards her head, Lucie stared defiantly into the barrel, indignation rising in her gut alongside an unexpected but not entirely unwelcome mirth; a mischievous smile lightening the tension on her face. Death had not frightened Lucie before now; her sins had been confessed, her soul prepared, but that had been before today, with the blood she had spilled still on her hands and the final words of the life she had taken still taunting her in the cold breeze. Her lips moved rapidly in silent prayer, as though her soul were akin to boots she had failed to polish before inspection parade, and to which she was now hastily applying a thin veneer of quick shine before the Group Captain appeared. The bullet was surely on its way she thought, and her eyes remained fixed on the expressionless mask above her. Do not fear those with the power to destroy the body, she had oft been told, but rather the One who decides the fate of the soul, and Lucie was determined to honour this in her final moments and not give any satisfaction to her murderer.

The figure's trigger finger was growing tighter and Lucie strained to defy the tightening of her gut; yearning for serenity on her face to be the last her killer saw of her, but try as she might, the serenity and peace she craved would not come and she felt tell-tale beads of sweat begin to break out on her brow as a grim mockery of her attempted stoicism in death and the freezing weather it was to happen in. As the mask of mischievousness on her face slipped away to reveal the panic that had forced its way to the forefront, she noticed a slight movement in the gun arm raised and pointed at her.

The sound of the shot was excruciating, but Lucie felt absolutely no pain. Opening her eyes which had clamped shut in instinct, Lucie saw the smoke rising from the gun which the shooter now held nonchalantly by the side and wondered if not her, who or what had been the victim of the shot.

She did not wonder for long. The guttering she hung from, already struggling under her weight began to inch, slowly at first, away from the ancient wall to which it had clung, the bullet having struck the downpipe a few short feet from her, forcing the entire framework into slow collapse. Brick dust and powder peppered the snow as the collapse began to hasten under her weight and Lucie looked around in desperation for something, anything to slow the descent or break the fall. The shooter still stood at the edge of the roof, ready, Lucie was sure, to stamp down on her hands should she try to make a leap onto the wet slate, and in any case, she had no leverage with which to make the jump.

The clips broke away from the wall like a row of poppers on a hurriedly discarded coat and Lucie found herself falling backwards, still clinging pathetically to the metal, her weight increasing her rate of descent. Fighting back the panic, she settled on her sole option and threw herself the short distance to the down pipe, barely managing to wrap her arms around the smooth, cold metal, her grip-less shoes sliding from it and leaving her still dangling. Though at a slower pace than the gutter, the pipe too would fall before long and Lucie began to shimmy down it as it dropped, stretching her fingers around the frigid tubing until her flesh was numb and her bones began to ache.

Looking up as she half climbed/half fell, she could see the wannabe murderer still standing, looking back at her and she saw the gun rise again. Hoping more than reasoning that the pipe had fallen far enough for her to make the rest of the drop without injury, Lucie pushed herself away from the chute and let herself plunge. Remembering what her Dad had always told her about the luck of falling drunks stemming from their unwittingly relaxed postures, Lucie tried to avoid the tensing of her body as she waited for impact, almost breaking out in laughter as she felt herself drop into the rough, canvas embrace of a well-worn but still sturdy restaurant canopy.

She had prayed more these last few minutes than in any day in as long as she cared to remember, but she silently and gladly offered one more as she took air deeply into her lungs. The thought of the attacker again though filled her mind and she opened her eyes to see the figure still standing far above, looking down at her through the expressionless mask. Lucie was safe from falling, yes, but there was no way she could move in time to avoid a bullet. Rather than raise the gun again though, the shooter merely turned and backed away from the edge of the roof, soon disappearing.

A myriad of voices called up to her in as many languages as Prague had to offer but busy berating herself for her rash display and ultimate failure in capturing the assailant, she ignored them all. All except one. Rolling over in the canopy and leaning out, she saw Algers standing below, breathless and flustered and wearing an expression of anger diluted with genuine concern on his wrinkled features. And as she levered herself to the edge of the canvas and dropped the remaining few feet to the cobbles, the look in his eyes mirrored the voice in her head, and each mirroring the words of her former Commander barely a couple of weeks earlier: that this time, once again, she had really fucked up.

FOURTEEN

The furious admonishing she had expected did not come as ferociously as expected, with it transpiring that the assembled guests had simply thought Lucie a brave, if foolishly impulsive young woman. With the Czech security refusing to discuss talk of a rooftop chase of the attempted assassin, Lucie's cover remained, for now, intact. Instead, Algers' criticisms were stern and to the point, warning her not to risk her cover so blithely again, but that if she felt circumstances dictated an extreme response, to make damn sure she backed them up in future with results.

The rebel within her had wanted to object and point out that she had in fact saved Algers from breaking his own, far more consequential cover by going after the attacker, but she stayed silent this time. She did not yet know much about Algers, but from what she had seen he was as unwillingly involved in this situation as she and was for now at least unwilling to kick a prisoner sharing her cell.

The dinner to her surprise was to go ahead, rapidly rehoused at the Castle itself, and Algers had quickly sent her out into town with his credit card and instructions to find something appropriate to wear for a formal, if unofficial, diplomatic function. The sleeveless, knee length black retro cut dress, and shining black shoes she returned in seemed to match her colleague's expectations, as did her styled and tied hair.

"You scrub up well," Algers had opined as he straightened his black bow tie and offered her his arm before they entered. "We've managed to keep you out of the news, all anyone's focussing on are the shots through the window, your Wonder Woman impression hasn't got a mention."

He imparted the developments softly, and she accepted them in the same unpretentious manner.

"Good. Just as long as I don't show up on YouTube this time next week."

"We think we've got all that contained," he reassured her. "There weren't that many people around and Della's already hacked into the CCTV system. If anyone does say they saw something the Czechs are happy for us to spin it was one of them."

"Well that's half right at least," Lucie smiled.

"Yeah, well don't get too comfortable. Some of Parliament's more moronic minds are using the incident to spout off their border control bollocks again; an idea to introduce a travel ban on EU countries if the talks fail is the topic of many a late-night discussion show tonight."

"You're joking!"

"Nope, I don't have the face for comedy. The proponents say it's in response to the increased threat from Euro Federalist fanatics, and nothing less than a complete, if temporary, ban is necessary until Britain can 'figure out what's going on'…"

Lucie's anger rose once more to the fore and she struggled to retain her dignified posture adorning Algers' arm.

"That's ludicrous!"

"Travel bans usually are."

"Who's behind it?"

"I'm sure you can guess. All the usual suspects plus one or two who should know better. You can imagine how the news has gone down with the public; there are all manner of demonstrations and counter demonstrations brewing, tensions are running pretty high right now. Anyway, mind back on the game, here comes your Wild Card."

She looked ahead to see Hartnell striding once more towards her, greeting her as she entered the hall and displaying anything but displeasure at her new look. Her trusty black overcoat over her arm and her face delicately and untypically made up, Hartnell was so taken he commented under his breath that she had succeeded in bringing some life to the dead, and she hoped that he was referencing the tired blend of dinner suits and elegant gowns that otherwise populated the room, rather than any more vulgar interpretation.

There were no compliments and precious little conversation during the dinner itself, during which Lucie was very much on the periphery, save for one cringeworthy moment just before the entrée, when Hartnell stood and led the room in a toast to Lucie and her remarkable efforts throughout the day. All around her were bright smiles and warm expressions while the glasses were in the air, but they disappeared as quickly as the drinks were drained and posteriors returned to chairs; all and sundry immediately resuming their own private conversations. More than once Lucie looked over to Algers on the other side of the table, who offered sympathetic smiles but who was clearly occupied in an interaction of his own with the woman from earlier.

When finally the coffee cups were empty, Lucie stood as quickly as etiquette allowed. There was to be music and light conversation following the meal and she wished no part of that, having spent perhaps the most boring couple of hours of her life at the table. Wondering why the hell she had bothered attending in the first place, Lucie had almost reached the door when a voice behind her stopped her.

"Leaving already?" Hartnell asked. "I was hoping to properly thank you for everything you've done today."

"Oh, it's fine, I mean it was nothing, really," Lucie answered, immediately annoyed at her flustered response.

"Rooftop acrobatics are hardly 'nothing'," replied Hartnell, "and coming only hours after you wrestled a rifle away from a man wanting to kill me, too. I'd be very interested to see what it is you define as 'something', I think."

The pair laughed together and Hartnell opened the door, gesturing for her to walk through. Despite his charm and apparently genuine interest in her, Lucie felt a sudden and peculiar sense of unease tease her instincts; a feeling she couldn't quite put her finger on, and she quickly looked behind her, searching out Algers, looking for some sort of reassurance. Algers was there, at the far end of the room, glass in hand, still locked in conversation with his female dining companion. He raised his head though towards her and nodded.

As gestures went it was ambiguous to say the least, but Lucie drew sufficient encouragement from it to go through the door and allow Hartnell to lead her to a separate room containing a further long, oak table next to which stood a large, silver ice bucket, with three bottles of champagne resting within it.

Lucie knew she was supposed to be impressed, though her long and extraordinary day was fast catching up with her and her true reaction was one of resignation, brought on as much by her disappointment at Hartnell's unsubtlety as anything else. She allowed herself a wry smile as she sat down opposite him; in truth she liked the man, who for all his archaic paternalism seemed genuinely charming and to have the best interests of the country at heart. Plus, she was all too aware of Lake's instruction to delve deeper into his motivations and now presented the perfect opportunity to do so, and if being honest with herself, she was anyway curious about him after her earlier conversation with Algers.

Hartnell was a man ageing in as elegant a way as anyone Lucie could recall meeting; the thinning, silver hair brushed back over the high forehead afforded him an air of natural authority, complimented by his high cheekbones and the seemingly perpetual gentle smile he wore beneath them. A look of sincere concern drifted over the kind, old face as Lucie winced from the sudden twinge of pain that raced through her leg as she drew her chair closer to the table.

"Are you alright?" he quizzed as he popped open a bottle from the ice bucket and poured glasses for Lucie and himself.

"I will be," she smiled back, "It's an old knee injury from my RAF days, I'm used to it now."

"Ah, your further heroics in Afghanistan that Kasper alluded to?"

"Again, I wouldn't call them heroics," Lucie replied, keeping her smile polite in the sudden onslaught of unwelcome memories.

"And I again would suspect that you are likely being too modest in your recollections."

The pair sat alone in the luxurious splendour of the State Room deep within Prague Castle, to where the reception had been hastily rearranged, both as a display of generosity from the Czech government, and as a notice to the press that the actions of one criminal could not deter a Czech or his guest from raising glasses together.

BLOOD, WHITE AND BLUE

Hartnell sat across from Lucie, the pair of them seated at the top end of a long, gleamingly polished conference table in the centre of the ornately decorated room; two exuberantly large, golden chandeliers hanging above them, and the cream walls similarly trimmed with golden craftwork and intricately patterned designs. It was a room like none other Lucie had ever sat in, and in truth, it was not one in which she could feel herself relaxing, except that the natural charm of the gentleman across from her countered the feelings of discomfort that had arisen. Despite herself, she could not help but warm to him and enjoy the attention he was affording her now, when across the hallway was a roomful of people waiting to lavish him with political honour.

"What did you do to it, may I ask?" Hartnell queried, continuing his investigation into the state of her knee.

"It's the cruciate ligament," she replied, "I ruptured it a few years back and it needed reconstructing."

"Sounds painful," Hartnell reacted, wincing playfully.

"It's not as bad as all that most days, it just doesn't enjoy exercise too much, and I gave it a hell of a knock jumping out of the window. I think it's just reminding me who's in charge..."

The Statesman's smile widened.

"Well please pass on to your offended joint the heartfelt thanks of at least one Member of Parliament."

"Shortly to be a member of the government too, if the rumours are anything to go by."

Hartnell seemed to blush, if only for a second, and shrugged away the comment.

"One shouldn't always believe what one reads in the papers, Ms. Musilova," he smiled. "I am content to serve as MP for my constituents; should the Good Lord decree that He wishes me to serve elsewhere than I should be only too happy to listen to His offer."

He reached across and picked up a bottle of champagne standing between them, his arm shaking and nearly giving way as he went to pour it into Lucie's glass, causing him to steady it with his other hand. Both glasses full, he set the bottle back down and raised his own glass to her, the ever-present smile firmly in place.

"For the second time today, Ms. Musilova, I am indebted to you."

"I'm sure I told you to call me Lucie," she grinned back.

"Well, Lucie, you have my sincere gratitude. The redoubtable Mr Algers may have beaten me to securing your services, but please do remember, if there's ever anything you need…"

"Thanks," Lucie muttered shyly, possessing no inclination to hang the memory of favours owed over Hartnell's, nor anyone's head, "but there's really no need."

"A gentleman always repays his debts," Hartnell protested.

"There are no debts between friends," Lucie countered, immediately worrying that she had overstepped the unseen boundary between them. She needn't have worried as after the briefest of pauses, Hartnell nodded silently and took a deep sip from his glass, pulling up in obvious discomfort as he returned it to the table.

"It looks like I'm not the only one carrying an injury," Lucie said, unable to ignore the weakness in Hartnell's arm, and desperate to find a way to steer the conversation towards his capture in the sixties.

"Yes," he chuckled slightly, "look at the two of us, the walking wounded!"

"What happened?"

Hartnell stopped chuckling and his eyes dropped for a moment while he silently massaged the muscles in his bad arm with his left hand. It seemed for a moment that Lucie would not get an answer, until he raised his face to her once more and spoke in almost a whisper.

"It was a long time ago. It's not a memory I particularly enjoy re-living."

Lucie's gut wrenched as she took in his answer. She knew only too well the pain of reliving torturous memories and had no wish to make him go through those days again, or speak of his time with Huxley, except that she had to. Learning more of the details of that time was about her only hope of unravelling the mystery behind the letters, the leaks and the figure taking pot shots in the snow. But it would also clearly cause him anguish, and while it was completely unintended, Lucie had found herself respecting the man, even enjoying his company, and now here she was ready to exploit his feelings and cheapening the offer of friendship between them, all to satisfy a hunch. And if she was to do that, she thought, she must offer something in return.

She drained her own glass of the exquisite champagne within, picked up the bottle and refilled both their glasses. If she was to make him relive his own personal hell, then she was damned if she was going to let him be the only one in the room to do so. Raising her glass back towards him, she offered the only quid pro quo available to her.

"I'll tell you mine, if you tell me yours," she said, her face suddenly serious and completely devoid of the warmth that had hitherto defined their conversation. Hartnell's own features reflected her change in tone and he reached towards his own glass, his arm shaking once more before he could grasp it, causing him to rest it upon the table where he clenched and unclenched his fist time and again.

"Why not?" he mused quietly, his eyes fixed unflinchingly on hers. "Why not?"

FIFTEEN

They remained quiet for a few moments, considering the stories ahead of them, as a climber might contemplate the mountain before ascent. Through the closed double doors Lucie could hear the noise of laughter and polite conversation and momentarily longed to be among them, swapping harmless tales of unseasonal weather and excellent canapés. But that was not her lot this night, and neither his. When she finally spoke, it was without exuberant deep breath or grandiose preamble.

"It was in Afghanistan, a few years back. I was a Chaplain assigned to Camp Bastion; that was the main British airbase in Helmand before we handed it over to the Afghan government in October 2014. I had a number of different duties but at the time, I was attached to the RAF Regiment, and our job was to aggressively repel incursions or attacks on the base, and on a base, twenty square miles in size, that's a pretty big job and skirmishes were commonplace…"

She heard her voice tail off for a moment as she recounted the memory and cursed herself at the display of weakness in front of him. She shook her head free of self-doubt and allowed her typical veneer of confidence to clothe her once more as she continued.

"One day, a couple of the lads got caught up in a skirmish some distance out from the base with a small group of rogue fighters, God knows what they were doing out that far. I was there when they radioed in for back-up. One of the lads had been hit pretty badly; I'd been around injured troops a long time and I knew from the description of the wound that he wouldn't make it, and so did he. I could hear him screaming for a priest over the airwaves…"

She paused again, the veneer once more slipping down, like a poorly tucked napkin. Her eyes dropped with it as she searched for the strength to continue. Her hand, hitherto wrapped around the stem of her glass, felt suddenly warm, and she looked up to see Hartnell's own, covering it in support.

"Do you want to go on?" the charming voice softly intoned.

The gesture brought a smile back to Lucie's face and she gently pulled her hand away, lifting her glass to her lips and draining it.

"They were sending in a Puma for support and recovery, but I knew he wouldn't make it back to base, so I insisted I go out with the team to give him comfort in his last moments. It was against regulations, but I can be quite insistent when I want to be. Seven of us went out in the Puma, not counting the pilot. Four of us crawled out of the wreckage; the official report said we'd been in the air less than three minutes before the mortar struck. Before we knew what was happening we'd spun in and Alfie, Leroy and the pilot were dead. I never could remember the pilot's name… We'd only crawled out a few yards when we each got a cosh to the back of the head and blacked out."

"You were taken?"

"Into the mountains," she nodded slowly, "five days, we were there…"

"They tortured you?"

"I was a woman and a Chaplain," she snapped back, "what do you think they did to me?"

"I'm sorry," Hartnell softly replied.

"No, no," Lucie responded, regretting her impatience with him, "don't be. It's hardly your fault."

She absent-mindedly picked up a pen from the table, twisting and turning it between her fingers as her mind picked up its journey again.

"Pete was the CO, he put up a fight on the first day, and by the third he showed no sign of giving in so they shot him once in each limb… they told him they wouldn't put one between his eyes until he swore allegiance to them. It took him hours to bleed out…"

She dropped the pen. Shifting her gaze to the wall behind Hartnell, she took a deeper sip from her re-filled glass and continued.

"That left me as ranking officer, a Reverend Flight Lieutenant with three years of field experience trying to lead a breakout…"

"You managed it, clearly."

"Eventually," she acknowledged, "after a couple of days."

"How?" A hint of hitherto absent intensity clung to Hartnell's voice, enough to momentarily chink his armour of paternal care and betray his curiosity.

A cynical half smile, half grimace crept onto Lucie's face as she answered.

"When your captor thinks he's broken you," she began, "that's when he's at his weakest. After five days of doing what they wanted with me and beating the resistance out of us all, one of them got sloppy. While the others were out on reconnaissance, this one thought he could handle us… handle me… alone. He unchained me, pushed me down onto my knees on the rocks, just like they'd done time and again those past days, he dropped his pants and…"

She paused, her eyes clamping involuntarily shut, the grimace fully replacing the half smile on her face.

"You know? I might not have had much dignity left by the time he came to me that morning, but what I did have left was my teeth. I swear you could have heard him screaming all the way to Kabul… While he was writhing around the place, I picked up a rock and did what I'd always promised myself, what I'd promised God, I'd never do."

"You had no choice," Hartnell assured her, "none."

"I could have stopped," she countered, her eyes beginning to glisten and her throat crack. "I didn't just kill him. I kept on hitting and hitting…by the time I snapped out of it, not even his Mother would have recognised him. Every humiliation, every insult, every unwanted touch from those past few days, they went into every blow. In the end, it took Steve, one of the surviving lads shouting my name to bring me round, otherwise we might still all be there."

"But you did snap out of it, and you rescued your comrades."

Lucie nodded, still refusing eye contact.

"It took us another two days to find our way across the desert and back to base, hiding during the day and travelling at night, trying to avoid the militants and rogue fighters out there. I knew the desert was cold at night, but you've never… at least I'd never felt anything like that before in my life and I hope I never do again; dragging myself and my busted knee across sand, me and Steve, carrying Digzzy between us most of the way. The bastards had broken his leg and given the other one a fair beating; he wanted us to leave him behind but there was no way we'd do that. We managed to get a few supplies from the cave before we ran, but we were running on fumes when we finally came into sight of one of our patrols and were picked up. I don't know how much longer we could have held out for."

"It sounds like you performed a miracle in getting your group home," Hartnell said in admiration. The warmth in his voice though was not matched in Lucie's as she explained further.

"Only three of us made it back," she retorted, "I was no hero."

"That's three more than would have made it back if you hadn't taken control and done what you did. Even if none of you had made it back, you stood up to be counted, you tried to make a difference; in the end that's all any hero can do."

Lucie shrugged, determined to cast off any notion of heroism.

"Yeah, well," she answered. "When they got us back to base, examined us and cleaned us up, they found that amongst other things I'd torn my cruciate ligament in the cave and then completely snapped it during the trudge through the desert. I had reconstruction surgery to replace the ligament with one of my tendons, and then screwed back in place, and they took a load of the torn cartilage out at the same time. The knee's stable enough most of the time but it doesn't half ache in the cold, and with the cartilage gone I suppose it'll be arthritic before too much longer. But I can still run and jump with the best of them for now."

She offered a slight smile and met his eyes for the first time since the re-telling of her tale had begun to overwhelm her but knew from the look in his eyes that Hartnell wanted more, perhaps from sincere interest, perhaps only to delay his own re-telling. Whatever his motivation though, she was content for now to indulge it.

"Anyway, Digzzy was in a right state, his leg was a mess and ended up needing amputation. He was pensioned off and I never saw him after that. Steve eventually recovered enough physically to return to duty, but he was rotated home not long after. He's still in the RAF, so far as I know and has regular counselling to cope with the nightmares and stuff."

"And you?"

"Me?" She stayed quiet a moment longer. "They pinned a medal on my chest and offered me promotion to Squadron Leader. I turned them down and took sick leave for a while then resigned from the Church and handed back my commission; I just needed out of the Service."

Hartnell nodded sagely, narrowing his eyes as he assimilated her words.

"You lost your faith?" he quizzed, only for Lucie to laugh out loud and shake her head in frustration.

"Why does everyone always assume that?"

"Forgive me," Hartnell replied, "I assumed, after what had happened to you in the cave, that you'd either abandoned your faith or felt abandoned by it."

"If God had abandoned me in that cave, I'd have died in it," Lucie answered. "No, it was just that… I needed a break, some time for myself."

"I see."

Lucie exhaled, relieved it was over and drained the last vestiges of champagne from her glass.

"So," she breathed, a smile restored to her face, "that's me. Your turn, Sir Geoffrey."

The Statesman's already pale flesh turned a whiter shade still, the warmth dropping from his features as she spoke. Standing up, he moved from the table to the grand window overlooking the city, whose illuminated rooftops and spires seemed to stare back up at him.

"Lucie, forgive me," he began hesitantly, not taking his eyes from the window. "I'm afraid our conversation was somewhat unexpected, and I find myself ill-prepared for it. Would you join me tomorrow? After my engagements I'll be better placed to recount the tale. I feel tonight I should rest."

Lucie suppressed the urge to object; if she wanted to know Hartnell's history then she had no choice but to accept his offer, although doing so stirred embarrassed resentment within her, as though she had exposed her nakedness to a new partner for the first time, only for them to decline to disrobe and leave her alone and unfulfilled in the room.

"Oh, sure," she answered, as casually as she was able, "no problem. I just thought that, you know, while we're sharing things…"

"Impossible, I'm afraid," Hartnell cut her off, a certain confidence returned to his voice as he stepped away from the window and turned to her. "I'm an old man, it takes more out of me to go over such things than it used to."

Though the charming smile was returning to his face, his words contained just the slightest hint of coldness, but enough to make Lucie feel she was in a business negotiation rather than a friendly chat and she cursed herself for the ease with which she had played the only card she had.

"Perhaps as some small recompense I could offer you a lift back to the hotel?"

Hartnell's offer seemed genuine but she shook her head anyway, trying to avoid allowing the frustration in her voice to show through.

"No," she replied, "no thank you. My apartment is on the other side of town, I'll jump on a tram."

"Nonsense," he replied, "did Algers not tell you? You've been moved to the King's Court Hotel along with the rest of my group. I do hope that's not an inconvenience?"

Once more she found herself outmanoeuvred by the politician and once more she swallowed back the temptation to object to his actions and berate him for his paternalistic presumptuousness.

She would have to find some way of countering him, she thought to herself, for at least as long as she needed him, anyway.

"Really? That's lovely of you, thank you," she lied, "when do we leave?"

"Now, if you've finished your drink? I've a busy schedule in the morning, breakfasting with the President and at my age I need a good sleep beforehand. You don't mind?"

"Not at all."

Lucie rose from the table and collected her black overcoat from the chair where she had deposited it and relished the familiarity of it slipping over her shoulders, as though it were a shield offering her some form of protection against this new world she had been thrust into. Her ensemble complete, she faced him again, her emotions contained and her professionalism intact.

"It'll be my pleasure," she said.

SIXTEEN

The journey was short in distance but long in atmosphere, Hartnell's demeanour seeming to cool further still with each yard the car travelled; perhaps, Lucie pondered, due in part to her having pressed herself against the door of the vehicle, rather than taking the seat next to him.

The limousine was elegant but strictly formal, no bottles of champagne or romantic music had awaited their arrival in it, much to Lucie's relief, but she was conscious of the need not to alienate Hartnell or be seen to reject whatever courtesies he threw at her, no matter how clumsily he did so.

As the car pulled into the hotel's expansive grounds and a smartly suited valet hurried to open their doors, Lucie linked her arm into the politician's, who seemed surprised but welcomed the gesture by placing his hand over hers as they stepped into the reception. Collecting a key from the receptionist, Hartnell passed it to her.

"Your room's just down the corridor from mine," he informed her, "your bag has already been moved there, I hope you don't mind?"

"No, that's fine," she answered, cynically smirking inside at the nonchalant manner he employed to exercise the control he seemed to presently enjoy.

"Then we may as well head up together, the lift is this way."

He held out a hand to direct her, Lucie noticing how it brushed against her rear as he let it drop once she had passed him, a sickening sensation gripping her stomach as she realised properly for the first time what his intentions were for the evening. He knew she was probing him for something, that much was obvious, and now Lucie had shot her only bolt and had nothing left with which to bargain except…

She shook her head silently, clenching her eyes. She had been naïve, had assumed that Hartnell's gratitude was genuine, when in fact it was, as it was always likely to be, political. They walked together in silence along the brightly lit and golden wallpapered corridor, Lucie feeling sicker with each step, until Hartnell stood outside one gleaming white door and slipped a key card into the locking device affixed to the door. It swung open and Lucie looked past him to the luxurious room inside, its splendour crowned by the opulent King-sized bed which on any other day would have looked heavenly to her, but this night brought merely unease.

"You're just down there," Hartnell gestured further down the corridor, "but if you don't mind coming in for a moment, we can make our arrangements for tomorrow."

Without waiting for an answer, he stepped inside, leaving Lucie in the doorway where she felt more powerless than at any time since she'd crawled to freedom from the Afghan mountains. Without choice, she stepped through, slipping off her coat and throwing it onto one of the chairs arranged so curiously in hotels the world over.

"Help yourself to a drink," Hartnell shouted from the bathroom he had disappeared to, and Lucie gave serious thought to doing so, reasoning that the experience may pass quicker if she added to the alcohol already in her system. Instead though she picked up a remote from the bedside table and flicked on the flat screen television, hung onto the wall opposite the bed. Finding an English-speaking news channel, she scoured the headline for any details of the political controversies and protestations of the day, and to see quite how the rifle shots through the Embassy window were being reported. By then though, the immediacy of the situation was over and Lucie found only the same sensationalised, and endlessly recycled infotainment regurgitated ad infinitum by presenters bored of even their own baseless speculation. Clicking it back off, Lucie turned to see Sir Geoffrey standing before her, his legs bare and his chest showing through the gap in the black silk dressing gown he wore.

Lucie refused to allow her distaste to show on her face, determined instead to appear as in control of the situation as he seemed to be.

"Haven't you ever heard of *#metoo?*" Lucie quizzed, only half joking. Hartnell laughed off the implied admonishing and sat on the bed looking up at her.

"There's no harassment here," he protested, "we're both adults and we're both curious about each other."

"Maybe our curiosity is directed differently," Lucie replied, "I find your history fascinating but that doesn't mean…"

"No, it's more than that," he interrupted." You don't just want the official history, you want the unabridged version. You're a journalist, aren't you?"

Lucie didn't know whether to laugh out loud or let the arrogant bastard know how wrong he was and watch him squirm as she told him the truth, but in the end her sense of 'duty', however she chose to define it, demanded she play along.

"And just how did you figure that one out?

"Oh, come on," he scoffed. "It's all rather coincidental isn't it? You arriving in Prague just in time to save me? I must admit I was surprised to see you go after the shooter as you did, though with your military background I suppose you had the skills for it and we all know what lengths journos will go to for a story. You think I'm being lined up for Cabinet, don't you? That the PM wants me to take over the Foreign Office from the clowns we have around the table now, am I right?"

Lucie couldn't believe her luck, the old man or rather his ego, it seemed was about to succeed where she had failed and open up to her, but not, she was sure, without a price, and the thought of paying it still filled her with nausea. The charade though needed to be played out and she moved to sit next to him on the bed, crossing her legs and hoping against hope that his hands would not wander too quickly.

"Go on," she said softly, neither confirming nor denying the politician's theory.

"Well you don't know the half of it Ms. Musilova, not even one half."

The champagne they had consumed together was clearly affecting him more than her, boosting his ego and aiding him in relishing his moment of power, and combined with the tiredness gnawing at his ageing body, he perhaps wasn't as in control as he thought. Lucie rolled over to where the drinks table stood and poured two generous measures of Scotch from a crystal decanter, handing one to Hartnell in the hope that not only would it loosen further his tongue, but would ensure his other plans for the evening would have difficulty in standing.

She clinked her glass against his and took a sip. It had been a while since she had drunk Scotch and the instant heat, lacking the flavour of her usual rum, burned her throat. She inhaled with wide eyes, intentionally exaggerating her reaction; Hartnell's lip curling just a little at the reaction as he knocked back his own drink in one, in what came across as a somewhat pathetically tribal display of potency.

"Go on then," she smiled, "enlighten me."

"Well let's just say," Hartnell began, the edge of his words just beginning to slur, "that it isn't just the pin striped idiots and free market ideologues in the Cabinet who should be worried about the next reshuffle."

"No?"

"No. You see…" he paused for a moment, a look of sudden concern spreading across his face, "this is all Charterhouse Rules, by the way."

"Of course," Lucie nodded, amused by the certainty with which Hartnell invested in his belief.

"Good, that's alright then. Yes, you see if all goes well, it won't just be the buffoons who get shuffled out, the PM may well find that someone else has already stacked the deck and is getting ready to play their hand."

Whether the words were born from drink, bravado or both, Lucie saw the truth behind them and felt another twist in her already knitted stomach. Hartnell had no interest in holding a Cabinet brief, he wanted to hold the Cabinet itself.

"A leadership challenge?" Lucie quizzed. "You're going to take down the Prime Minister?"

"I?" Hartnell looked shocked at such a suggestion, "I have absolutely no intention of launching anything or taking anybody down. No, my dear, others will tear down the walls and then turn to me to rebuild them. There won't be any 'leadership challenge', it'll be a damn coronation!"

Lucie raised her own glass to her lips as she assimilated the tale. Perhaps there was merit to Algers' theory that Hartnell was, after all, 'doing a Boris' and trying to set himself up as a perverse martyr and use that to ride the crest of a wave of sympathy all the way to Number Ten. Damn it, she needed to talk to Algers or Della, fuck, even Lake would do now; where the hell was this 'team' she was supposed to be in when she needed it?

"So, it's not just the story of your past that's of interest," Lucie teased, continuing the façade, "it's the tale of your rise to power?"

She poured and handed him another drink which his ego prevented him from refusing. Her flattery was taken by Hartnell and worn clearly on his face; the charming, gentle smile which Lucie had seen so often on front pages and bulletins, now, up close, devoid of its warmth and invested almost with maliciousness, twisting what once was a welcome beam into a cruel sneer.

"My rise to power, eh?" he nodded, as though replaying the description over and over in his head. "I like the sound of that. Of course, there would be a lot of competition in your industry for the right to chronicle that journey from a, shall we say, 'up close and personal' perspective…"

He slowly drained the Scotch glass of its contents, the effects of the strong spirit growing more obvious with each sip, not least in the lust in his eyes, now displayed openly and without veneer.

"And it goes without saying that whomever I chose to chronicle my future – and the future of the country – would also be invited to tell the tale of my past."

He moved closer on the bed to Lucie, who stifled her revulsion as the Statesman's hand found its way to her knee. In her mind she began to panic, there was no way out of this that she could see. Here he was, on the verge of admitting a carefully stage-managed plan to elevate himself to the Premiership, and to reject him now would scupper her chances of exposing what she knew. But the deeper pain she felt was the sense of betrayal that this man, who had seemed to embody the political salvation of people like her, cast aside and castigated by the legitimised trolls of the referendum, was just as much a monster as any of them. After having saved his life, after having opened her past to him, even after he had learned of the trauma she had suffered at the hands of the rapists and torturers in the desert, his sole intent was still to barter career advancement, so far as he knew, for some 'up close and personal attention'.

Well fuck that. Lake would admonish her for it, but she was no whore. They would just have to get their information some other way.

Hartnell was busying himself kissing her neck in the rough, uncomfortable manner that alcohol and ego often promoted, and she could bear the unwelcome touch no more, pushing him away and standing up.

"I'm sorry," she said, composing herself, "I can't."

The change in Hartnell's tone was immediate, lust replaced by coldness, lechery by embarrassment.

"I see," he said, sitting upright and pulling the gown tighter around his chest. "I must have misunderstood your intentions. Naturally, there will be no need for a repeat engagement tomorrow and I'd remind you that everything which occurred here tonight occurred under Charterhouse Rule, and if you choose to break that convention your story will be denied…"

He had stood and moved to the door at lightening pace, holding it open for Lucie without looking at her. Lucie had almost reached it when another thought stopped her from stepping through.

Her mother.

Damn it, this was why Lake had played that card so early. He knew exoneration would ultimately mean little to her, that she wouldn't put herself through hell for any misplaced notion of 'patriotism' or fight to save a country that hated her simply to spare herself from prison. But her mum… her matka… for her she would do anything. Damn him.

"No, it's nothing like that!" Lucie shocked herself as well as Hartnell with the commanding tone of her interruption. "I'm sorry," she quickly corrected, "it's nothing like that, it's just that it's my…"

She did her best to look embarrassed and nodded downwards, hoping that he could both translate her unsubtle code, and mistake the cause of her obvious discomfort.

"Oh!" The statesman eventually spluttered, his usual tone restored as instantly as it had disappeared, "I see, forgive me!"

"Even I can't fight nature," Lucie nervously laughed.

Shutting the door, Lucie adopted a look of fierce seduction and pressed her finger against Hartnell's chest, walking him backwards until he fell back on the bed, where he scrambled to a comfortable position, the look on his own face turned into that of a naughty school boy.

"But that doesn't mean we can't have a little fun," she whispered commandingly. Her determination to find her mother's killer might well have compelled her into this position, but she was damned if it was going to happen under anyone else's conditions but her own; the situation was hers to control now.

"Turn out the light."

Lucie turned her head from him and swallowed her revulsion as she pulled open Hartnell's silk robe and reached inside, the politician letting out a slight gasp as she closed her hand around him and began to softly stroke

The celebrated political giant was now a mere pygmy, governed by his lust, writhing and wriggling beneath her touch, pathetic murmurs of pleasure sounding as he gripped and clawed at her with his closest hand, sending her mind racing back to the night on the boat when her fellow cooks had cornered her, a fresh wave of repugnance washing over her as the memory flashed by. Reaching behind herself with her other hand, she eased her dress partly down, allowing her to let it slip from her shoulder. She then pulled down the left cup of her bra, exposing her breast to his lustful yearnings and clamping his hand to it, his typically weak arm suddenly galvanised with excitement. Better she sacrifice one part of herself than give the lecherous old bastard free reign over the rest of her.

"So, you'll tell me all about it tomorrow, Sir Geoffrey?" Her voice was soft and velveteen and met with an immediate nodding from the old man.

"Yes, yes, of course!" he consented, an obvious fear in his voice that his refusal may result in her stopping.

The politician began bucking his hips to her movements, the hand on her breast tightening, the fingers pinching unwantedly at her nipple while she grimaced hard and quickened her pace. Before long, the murmuring became an exultant cry of release, and Lucie shut her eyes hard and carried on, thankful at least that the end was near.

Finally, the hips relaxed, and the ageing hand released her breast from its clutch, dropping to the bed in contented exhaustion. The moment it was over, Lucie pulled her bra back over herself and stood up, holding her soiled hand away from her as though the whole limb were contaminated and alien.

"You can stay if you like" sighed Hartnell in sleepy nonchalance, "it's no problem."

"You need your rest," Lucie responded, almost too quickly, bending forward and planting the obligatory kiss on his forehead before turning to leave, "you have to be up and with a clear head before your breakfast with the President. I'll see you here at the hotel afterwards."

"There'll be more tomorrow night?"

"Why not?" she stammered, fighting the revulsion from her voice as she opened the door. "It's better than Horlicks."

Without another word she was through the door, and moments later through that of her own room, instantly more comfortable in its modest surroundings than the grander counterpart she had just departed. Her bag from the apartment had been left unopened on the bed, but Lucie didn't even register it at first, instead letting the door swing behind her as she rushed straight through to the bathroom. She thrust her soiled hand under the hot tap until it turned pink in the scalding stream, scrubbing at it with Lady Macbeth-like fury until she could bear the heat no more.

With her loathing and anger refusing to turn off with the tap, Lucie sunk miserably to her knees by the side of the bed, clasping her wet hands together and bowing her head as the day's utter exhaustion reached her soul and the first tears broke through her tightly shut eyes.

"Help me," she whispered softly in prayer, "help me please."

For what felt like an age she knelt there, at once exposing her soul to Divine inspection and breathing calmness back into it, until a voice, soft and understanding sounded behind her.

"The door was open," Della quietly said, "am I intruding?"

Before Lucie could answer, the woman's hands slid delicately onto her shoulders, her thumbs expertly beginning to ease the tension and stress of Lucie's life into temporary submission.

"What are you doing?" Lucie asked, almost reluctantly as she began to succumb to the magic in her friend's fingertips.

"Shush now," Della whispered, "It'll be alright soon."

And Lucie thought, as her resistance began to crumble, that Della was right and that soon, quite soon now and for tonight at least, things would indeed be alright.

SEVENTEEN

Lucie woke with the sunrise the next morning and pulled herself up promptly from the sofa she had slept on, looking across to the bed she had insisted Della sleep in, alone, to the older woman's obvious disappointment, and where she still lay, sleeping soundly.

Della's presence had helped the previous night, it really had. She had soaked up Lucie's resentment of the previous day's horrors, culminating in her sordid encounter with Hartnell, like a sponge, and without resentment. She had listened intently to what Lucie had learned from the libidinous old toff and offered sincere compliments on her ability to stay focussed and get the information while under such obvious pressure. When Lucie's tears had led to the accusatory question of why she, Algers and Lake hadn't told her what to expect, she had smiled and answered simply that there are three constants to life in the field espionage: sooner or later it's kill or be killed, women make better liars than men and are never to be trusted, and there is never any shortage of people who can be bought off with a quick wank and the promise of an 'SSS', or State Sanctioned Shag, and it's up to each Newbie to learn those lessons for themselves. When Lucie questioned why, she was told bluntly that only once an operative had learned to count on themselves and not rely on a non-existent cavalry to ride to the rescue could she reach her true potential. The answer was honest and after the day she had endured, that was as much as she could have hoped for.

Della had kept up her massage of Lucie's neck while they had talked, and she'd been grateful for it and the relaxation it had brought her. Only when she had gone to remove the cross and chain from Lucie's neck had the younger woman resisted, getting up from the floor and placing her hand protectively over it, before insisting on settling down for the night.

Instinctively now she touched it again and stood up from the sofa, stretching the cricks from her neck and heading to the bathroom. Surrendering herself to the hot water, she hoped her frequent hope that if she stood beneath it long enough, the stresses and anxieties which so often allowed the darkness in would flow off her body with the previous day's grime. Thus far, they hadn't.

Finishing her morning routine, she pulled fresh underwear from her bag, along with a pair of navy, flared jeans and a black polo shirt with white trim, dressing quickly and brushing the tangles from her long hair, which she tied back in a ponytail. She had always eschewed make-up, and by the time she had slipped on her shoes, Della was awaking in the bed, straining to focus on the clock resting on the cabinet beside her.

"Did you get your worm?" she smiled at Lucie, looking at her through puffy, still-tired eyes.

"You know what they say about early birds," she smiled back as she tightened her laces, her cross dangling from her neck as she did so.

"You still won't take that off?"

"Why would I?"

Della sighed and shook her head. "I don't know," she mused.

"It just seems like you're holding yourself to impossible standards and limiting how useful an agent you could turn out to be, all for an ancient myth that's rejected you..."

"You think God's rejected me?" Lucie queried, content for the moment to play along with Della's game, the experienced spy looking back at her with one of her trademark naughty smiles.

"No," she finally answered, "no, not God, maybe not Him. But a pretty sizeable chunk of the people who claim to follow Him wouldn't care too much for you or what you get up to. Or who you might fall for..."

The last words were sharper, and Lucie supposed they were intended to be; a blush spreading across her face as she dropped her stare to her final lace.

"Other people's relationships with God are their own concern," she shrugged, "I can't live them for them. All I can do is focus on my own and hope I let it influence how I live my life."

"And doing that makes you uncomfortable with this kind of work?"

"Killing people I've never exchanged two words with makes me uncomfortable with this kind of work," Lucie snapped as she rose from the sofa and moved to the full length mirror on the wall, brushing herself down and choosing to dilute her friend's remarks by conversing with her reflection. "Getting felt up by an old man who thinks just because he's got the keys to Number Ten within reach he can put his hands and his dick wherever he wants, makes me uncomfortable with this work. The faith you're so merrily taking the piss out of me for, believe me, is not in any way responsible for my 'discomfort.'"

Della took a sip of the water from the table beside the bed.

"It isn't me you need to convince," she said, her voice containing a hint of mockery that instinctively brought resentment to Lucie's belly. "It sounds to me like you gave up on all that when you resigned the Chaplaincy and your mind hasn't caught up with the rest of you yet…"

Lucie spun around now, her emotion more and more difficult to control.

"I didn't quit the Chaplaincy because I lost my faith!"

"Then why did you?"

"Because I didn't know how to use it anymore!"

She bellowed the words at Della, who sat back in the bed, the goading expression she had worn now instantly replaced with one of concerned understanding. Lucie herself stood silently, tears in her eyes and her ears ringing with the words it had taken years to hear herself admit.

"I was a Minister," she said softly, her voice cracking, "who didn't know how to Minister anymore… what good was I to anyone?"

Della's voice turned as soft as her expression had become and her questions sounded now as though they were born from genuine concern, instead of malicious taunting.

"What do you mean, you didn't know how to use it?"

Lucie shook her head in frustration, struggling to articulate precisely what she meant in a way her friend could understand; uncertain and perhaps on some level unwilling to divulge such personal and unresolved troubles.

"I found I couldn't *help* people the same as I used to," she blustered, "oh, I don't know, it's… it's hard to explain."

"Hey, it isn't your fault," Della attempted to persuade her. "I'm not much of a theologian but I'm guessing souls don't just stop making it to the afterlife because of one priest who's forgotten how to save people."

"Priests are Catholic," Lucie answered, allowing a slight smile to show on her face in response to Della's words, "and it's God who does the saving, not His representatives on earth. If the saving was down to us you'd be first on my list."

"Oh, you want to save me, do you?" The mischievous grin was back on Della's face and Lucie allowed her smile to grow wider in response, the hollow feeling within her beginning to fade.

"It's an idea."

"Well perhaps," Della replied, her grin suddenly fading, "you need to focus on saving yourself first. Don't waste your time on lost causes like us."

"Lost causes?"

"Don't waste your affections on us, Lucie. Not on Lake, Algers, even me... we're all bastards. None of us are worth saving."

"Everyone is worth saving," Lucie defiantly answered. "Everyone."

Della looked unconvinced. "Maybe," she half whispered, "maybe not. You might think I'm teasing you Lucie, but the truth is I admire your spiritual side; I mean it confuses the crap out of me but if there's anything that stops you getting dragged down to our level then take it, even if it's your imaginary friend in the sky. Just don't let it stop you doing your job as an agent; you're too good to let anything hold you back."

Lucie didn't answer, she couldn't. To Della, her faith was a curiosity at best and an inconvenience all other times that while giving her a useful moral focus, was also keeping her from embracing the role of an agent of the 'Overlappers' as fully as she should. Well Lucie had only just now finally admitted out loud the reasons she had abandoned her former career and there was no way she could explain the intricacies of her spirituality, however tarnished it might have been, to someone to whom it was all simply an eccentric curiosity. Likewise, Della seemed to be entertaining notions of a long working relationship with Lucie

– and had made it clear she was prepared to cross professional and personal boundaries – and Lucie didn't have the heart to tell her that this was strictly a short-term arrangement. Instead, she simply offered a half-smile and moved to the corner of the room into which she had thrown her bag the previous night.

Lucie took the strip of tiny pills from its place in her bag and popped one through the foil, washing it down with the now warm glass of water she had placed on the floor next to the sofa the previous night.

"Not going in for it at the moment, eh?" Della teased, the familiar edge of naughtiness in her voice, referencing Lucie's explanation the previous night that she was staying away from carnal misadventures for the time being, at least, it seemed, ones that didn't involve septuagenarian politicians.

"It's not the Pill," Lucie corrected, "I mean it's *a* pill, but not *the* Pill."

"I get it, ok," her friend laughed, "for the knee, are they?"

"No, not the knee," Lucie answered, pushing the strip back into the recesses of her still unpacked bag. "They're for my, erm… brain."

"Ah."

"They help, that's all, just to keep me on an even keel, you know."

Lucie jabbered out the explanation and immediately regretted doing so. It was no-one else's damn business what she was taking or why, and anyway she wouldn't feel the need to explain away an ibuprofen or a tube of haemorrhoid cream, why the hell did she always feel as though she had to justify this?

"Please," Della interrupted her thinking, her voice instantly switched to its soothing setting, "there's no need to explain. Believe me, you're not the only one who needs a little help to stare the world down sometimes."

BLOOD, WHITE AND BLUE

"Really? You mean…?"

"Oh, God yes," Della confirmed, "and to be honest I think I'm going to have to go back for something stronger; things are a bit tougher to cope with than usual right now for some reason…"

"There's peaks and troughs, aren't there?" Lucie smiled in sympathy. "I've been trying to keep off them for a while, but after yesterday…"

Not wishing to delve too deeply into a topic that could well leave her affected for the whole day, Lucie examined herself in the mirror, properly this time, brushing the odd stray crease and piece of fluff from her top and pondering the ever-growing dark lines beneath her eyes which once more shouted their resentment of poor quality sleep into the glass. Again, she ignored them. Catching her attention instead was the reflection of Della, throwing the covers from her body and rising naked from the bed.

She had been and was a beautiful woman, the slight imperfections and hallmarks of age displayed on her body only serving to heighten her magnetism, and Lucie at first found it difficult to look away, especially as she paused on her way from bed to bathroom and came to stand behind Lucie, who blushed in response to the experienced woman's touch on her shoulder.

"You're a beautiful woman, Lucie," Della said in apparent honesty, looking at their reflections. "Not just physically but on the inside. Don't let us take that away from you."

She moved her hand slowly from shoulder to cheek, brushing, ever so slightly her fingers down it, goose bumps rising on Lucie's flesh as she finished the movement, leaving her, for once, speechless and unable to reply. With what looked like sadness in her eyes, Della stepped away and moved again toward the bathroom, pausing as she opened the door.

"You know, it's a shame you weren't quite ready last night," she said, not just in mischievousness but discernible sincerity. "You should never be afraid of your first time doing something new."

It wasn't until she turned away and went into the bathroom, closing the door behind her that Lucie looked across to where she had stood and breathed out a long and deep breath.

"I didn't say it'd be my first time," she quietly said.

BLOOD, WHITE AND BLUE

EIGHTEEN

Della opted against breakfast, insisting that she needed to go and report to Lake while the information was fresh, and she quickly departed into the city, a quick peck on Lucie's cheek her only nod to her politely refused pass of the night before. Refused, or perhaps just deferred, Lucie was as yet unsure. Physical attention was not something she had craved from anybody since her experience in the Forces and recent events had done nothing to sway her from that position. She was no prude, nor had she entered Holy Service chaste, pure and dressed in virginal white, but she held to the belief that the most intimate of acts was something that should be reserved for those with whom one had a special bond, and to have that intimacy abused was as close to unforgiveable as Lucie could imagine herself being. She needed time, space, and a much clearer mind before deciding if it was an intimacy she wished to share with anyone again.

With her friend gone, she made her way downstairs to the voluminous restaurant, the edges of which were laid out with all manner of breakfast items, from cooked meals, cold meats and cereals to fruit, yogurts and pastries; a smart, white clad line cook stood behind each display, ready to assist the queues of guests in filling their plates and bowls.

Taking a pastry and a coffee, Lucie spied Algers, sitting alone and contemplating a plate of bacon and eggs with his usual intensity.

"Is this seat taken?" she asked him as she drew level with his table, "Or don't you like to eat with your staff?"

Looking up at her underneath his bushy eyebrows, his lined face wrinkled into a brief smile and he gestured her to sit down.

"I bumped into Della on her way out," Algers said, "you did well last night."

"Yeah? Well Hartnell seemed to think so; so much for the movies, eh?" Lucie smiled sadly. "I thought the world of espionage was supposed to be all first-class dining, fast cars and glamorous sex."

"The dinners are boring, the cars are older than my Mother-in-Law's prejudices and the sex, believe me, is never 'glamorous,'" Algers replied, with a bitterness and sorrow in his voice so profound it made Lucie regret her small attempt at humour. She raised her eyes as he continued, his own stare fixed into his coffee cup in such a way to make Lucie ponder if he actually ate his food, or ingested it via a process of aggressive glaring.

"Last night, apparently, my duty to protect the national interest was best served by accepting the advances of Mrs. Phillipa Brown, diary secretary to our Ambassador here, and the person, aside from the Ambassador himself, with the easiest access to the stationary used in the death threat."

"You think it could have come from her?"

"No," Algers shook his head, "I don't."

"Ah," acknowledged Lucie.

"Brown is a career civil servant, and a damn good one by all accounts," Algers expanded. "Her only vice as far as I can see is the occasional dalliance with visiting dignitaries and after having made it clear she was prepared to add me to her quite impressive and sizeable list, my instructions last night were to let her."

BLOOD, WHITE AND BLUE

"Maybe," Lucie began in an effort to thaw the conversation, "maybe if any of these 'dalliances' were recent she could give you a lead as to who could be behind it."

"Mr. Lake's thoughts precisely!"

Algers turned to her, the coffee cup raised in mock salute and his eyes tired and sad. He knocked back the contents and slammed the cup down to the table, rattling the spoon against his saucer as he did so.

"Don't take this the wrong way," Lucie began through a mouthful of pastry, "but you seemed to be enjoying Mrs Brown's attentions at the ball last night. She's an attractive woman and…"

"Just like you were enjoying Hartnell's?"

Algers snapped his interruption and almost at once looked apologetic.

"I'm sorry," he said, "that was a cheap remark."

"It's ok," Lucie muttered, suddenly embarrassed.

Algers pushed away his largely untouched breakfast and sat back in his chair, looking across at Lucie.

"Believe it or not but not every guy out there is a sex crazed predator waiting for a chance to get his end away," Algers spat, resentment clearly gnawing at him. "Don't get me wrong, plenty of them are, but I'm a married man, happily so for over thirty years, do you think I enjoy cheating on my wife, whether it's in the 'National Interest' or not? Most days I can't even look at myself in the mirror."

Lucie dropped her eyes from his, unsure of what comfort she could offer and feeling a slight twinge of guilt that she had assumed this man – most men – would jump at the chance for what Della had called 'State Sanctioned Shags'. She took a sip from her coffee and finally offered a totally inadequate but at least sincere, "I'm sorry."

"Ah, don't be," Algers answered softly.

"Couldn't you refuse, you know, walk away?"

Algers raised an impressive eyebrow and Lucie knew, of course, that there was no way he could. That wasn't how Lake operated.

"He's got me by the balls, Lucie," the MP confirmed. "Any defiance, any insubordination from me and that's it, it's over. Not just my political career which I give less than a rat's arsehole about, but my marriage, my reputation… and then, before I know it one or two mistakes I may have made in the past find their way into the papers and I'm left with no choice but to step out in front of the 7:25 from Euston, and no hope except that they bury me upside down so Lake can kiss my arse."

Lucie grinned at the exaggerated fatalism but was curious at the finality of it.

"Isn't there a part of you still 'doing it for Britain' anymore?" she quizzed. "It's not all just down to whatever hold Lake has on you is it?"

Algers sighed deeply and shook his head.

"In the early days, maybe," he answered. "But I don't recognise Britain anymore. If our job was to save it, then we fucked that rather royally a couple of years ago and ended up granting credence to a bunch of extremist clowns who just wanted an excuse to be nasty to foreigners."

"That's democracy for you," Lucie lamented.

"If you think that withholding the ballot from the people the outcome affects most, be they ex-pats, people who've set up home with you or the future generations we're supposed to be fighting for, most of whom have been happily paying their taxes, just to appease a handful of right wing nut jobs constitutes 'democracy' then you and I have very different dictionaries."

It was a speech Algers had made many times in Parliament and which had brought an army of social media warriors to his side and just as many in opposition, and Lucie grinned at the passion with which he still made it.

"So, you do still have something to fight for," she smiled, drawing a short, reluctant laugh from her colleague.

"Aye, maybe," he exhaled. "And what about you, Lucie Musilova? What are you fighting for?"

She dropped her eyes at the question, but instinct told her she could trust Algers, certainly more than she should have Hartnell, and she took another bite of her pastry while she pondered the question.

"My Mum, mainly," she answered, honestly. "She was murdered, a few years back; Lake says if I do the job he'll re-open the case."

"Admirable reason," Algers nodded, "but what about the rest? You said 'mainly.'"

This was harder to answer, and Lucie shook her head.

"Honestly? I don't bloody know. I grew up between here and the UK, but neither feels like home anymore. Here, people resent the treatment of the EU nationals in Britain and don't entirely trust that I'm not part of that, and back there I get looked at like I'm hybrid and get the very same treatment myself…"

"Well another reason for you might be that if we don't get to the bottom of this, that 'treatment' is only going to get worse. I've seen some of the documents the government are hiding."

"How?"

"I've seen them," Algers repeated. "And believe me, the negotiations are not going well. Between you, me and the portrait of Vaclav Havel over there, if things go on as they are, Britain will be crashing out without a deal and the EU nationals will be thrown under the fucking bus. You think they're being treated badly now? It's not too much of a stretch from where we are now to see them made to wear special badges when they use the NHS and have their places of work publicly listed outside of Jobcentres."

"You're joking."

"Do I look like the fucking ghost of Ken Dodd to you? The hard right have total control of the PM now and so if there's any possibility that Hartnell is behind his own death threat, then painful as it may be and lecherous arsehole that he may be, it may well be in the country's best interests to let him succeed and steer us back to somewhere approaching the Centre and maybe even knock Brexit on the head in the process."

Lucie chewed on Algers' words, her brow furrowing as she licked the last bits of pastry from her teeth. After her experience of the previous night and the realisation that Hartnell was far from the near perfect figure she had allowed herself to see, the thought of his elevation to the Premiership was hardly one that filled her with joy. But that said, if anyone was going to pluck the country from the jaws of Brexit...

"Maybe," she finally agreed, "although whether Hartnell is 'doing a Boris' or not, somebody still took a shot at him yesterday."

"They did indeed," Algers nodded, "and there were no theatrics there, did you see Hartnell's face? Whatever else he might have known about, that wasn't one of them; that bullet was live... Which means..."

"Which means," Lucie picked up, "we're back to square one, because someone out there really is trying to kill him."

NINETEEN

If there had been one positive, however slight, from her assignation with Hartnell the previous night, it was his demeanour upon greeting her as she arrived for their conversation. His car had returned to the hotel for her, driving some distance from the centre of the city and to a secluded area of woodland, the banks of the Vltava running through it. Though nervous at first that she would be facing a repeat of his lecherous behaviour of the previous night, his reaction to her arrival was devoid entirely of lustfulness and his manners were those of a gentleman. While she was pleased that his behaviour today was of a higher standard, she also inwardly wept for the countless victims of violence, sexual or otherwise, who stayed with their abusers because of who they were without the bottle or whatever it was they hid their true selves behind. Today though, for the sake of the mission and her Mum, Lucie would smile and bear the boorishness.

"Good morning, Lucie," he beamed at her, his voice once again bursting with charm and what yesterday had felt like sincerity. "I trust you slept well? Have you breakfasted?"

"Yes, and yes," Lucie smiled back, seeking to match his casual display and avoid mention of how their evening together had ended. "How was your breakfast with the High and Mighty?"

"Oh, as boring as one expected. The President is a fine man but rather poor company I'm afraid. I'm pleased to see you came, Lucie."

"Well who am I to miss a good story?" she answered, playing on his suspicion of her as a journalist as she looked around a place she didn't immediately recognise. "Where are we?"

The car had stopped on a narrow road beneath a hillside resplendent with evergreen trees, some still sporting their dusting of snow and others brazenly defying the weather's efforts to decorate them. Looking up the hill, Lucie could see occasional slanted orange roofs peeking through the branches, while beneath them, the hill continued down through more trees to the muddy banks of the Vltava. They weren't that far from the city, she reasoned, but far enough away to be as sure as one could be of not running into dog walkers, joggers or curious passers-by.

"Somewhere I wanted to show you," Hartnell replied, "if you're interested in telling my story, that is."

Lucie was interested indeed and confirmed as much.

Dressed in his typical business suit and tie, navy overcoat and red scarf, Hartnell stood at the head of a thin, dusty path that led through the trees and down to the river, his hand outstretched in invitation to Lucie.

"Good," he said, satisfied. "Perhaps you'd care to walk this way?"

Lucie raised an eyebrow at Hartnell's enigmatic manner and caught up with him on the path, though she pointedly refused his offer to link arms, instead keeping one hand in her pocket and the other swinging loosely beside her ready for action if the politician tried for a repeat of last night's fun and games.

"It seems an odd place to come for a walk down memory lane," Lucie pondered as they brushed branches from their faces and pushed on towards the river.

"Ah, but this is memory lane, Lucie, very much so," the old man replied, suddenly whimsical, "and in a moment I'll explain why."

They pushed through a final set of branches and emerged onto the river bank, the water only feet away from them, rushing through the Bohemian valleys to merge finally with the river Elbe at Mělník. In the distance, Lucie could make out the towers and bridges of central Prague, while more woodland and occasional houses punctuated this portion of the waterway.

Hartnell stood at the water's edge taking in the ambience of their surroundings, his face unreadable as though he were struggling with conflicting emotions. After taking in a deep lungful of the river air he turned back to Lucie, his expression suddenly one of sadness.

"You haven't asked about the letter."

His words were unexpected, but which letter he was referring to was obvious and Lucie raised her eyebrow in anticipation of what might follow.

"There's no time like the present," she answered.

"It's a forgery, of course."

"You seem very certain of that."

"As certain as I am that you are standing here now."

"How can you be so absolute?"

"Because," Hartnell sighed as either emotion or the cold air brought water to his eyes, "you and I are standing on his grave."

Lucie looked around in horror, half expecting to see some crumbling Headstone tucked beneath the branches, before more rational thoughts took back hold of her mind.

"You mean, under here…?"

Hartnell nodded sadly. If there any theatrical intent behind his revelation to her then it was exceedingly well hidden, Lucie thought, the emotion of the man quite genuine, at least as far as she could tell.

Behind her lay a large and long fallen tree trunk, its upturned roots reaching into the woodland and its dead branches sliding beneath the water. Brushing as much dirt as she could see from the bark, she sat down and readied herself for the explanation Hartnell clearly wanted to give, offering him as much sympathy as her eyes could muster.

"What happened?" she softly asked.

Hartnell was not really looking at her as he spoke, but rather just past her, his gaze following the waters flowing on their unstoppable journey onwards.

"Alexander was my friend, you know?" he began, his voice devoid of confidence, like a child seeking to explain itself to an angry parent. "He was my best friend. In fact, we would fish together not too far from here sometimes, when the weather allowed us. The StB knew who we were and we knew them; there was little posturing between the sides in those days, at least not here. That's why discovering his treachery was so difficult to accept."

"It was you who exposed him?" Lucie asked, hoping he would fill in the blanks around what little she did know of that era. Hartnell simply nodded in reply, pausing a moment before continuing.

"When finally I was posted back to Britain I assumed that would be the last I saw of Czechoslovakia, and indeed the last I would hear of Alexander. Intelligence quickly ascertained that after his brief moment of celebrity when he was paraded as a prize catch by the new hard-line regime, his life wasn't exactly one of luxury; he was given a token job, a modest flat and a regular enough income to develop and feed his alcohol problems. He was broadly forgotten other than for occasional use as a bogeyman figure by our own side now and then, until that is, the Velvet Revolution."

Lucie didn't need reminding of the details of that moment in history, those few days in November of 1989 when mass uprisings led by a collection of students and actors swept the Communists from power in a largely bloodless show of unrest and elevated the world-renowned Vaclav Havel to leadership.

"With the Old Guard falling around him, Huxley had no-one to protect him anymore?" Lucie hypothesised, earning a nod of agreement from Hartnell.

"Russia didn't want him, they'd made that clear and Gorbachev had too many of his own problems by then to be concerned with the fate of one British traitor. And although the Revolution turned out to be bloodless, no-one knew for sure that would be the case and those figures of the old regime had every right to fear reprisals. Alexander would have nowhere to run to, so the theory went, except back to us."

"You came to take him home…" Lucie guessed, following the trail of the story.

"It was thought that because of our previous friendship he would respond to my offer."

"Which was?"

"Nothing much in reality; safe passage home is all. It was an opportunity too good to miss; Communism was collapsing right before our eyes and suddenly here was a chance to snatch back one of our most infamous defectors. I imagine the thought of parading him in chains for the *Ten o'clock news* was too much for the government to resist."

"They wanted a show trial?" Lucie quizzed, the distaste in her voice obvious but met with a blithe nod of the head from Hartnell.

"Well, I can't really blame them, to be fair," he gently sighed. "After all the publicity over the Cambridge ring, plus the fact that Stonehouse and Mawby both got away scot free with spying for the Czechs in the sixties – and Mawby being a Tory to boot – here was a chance to make someone pay for the embarrassment. Someone of Mrs T's resolve wasn't about to pass up an opportunity like that."

Hartnell played his memories like an intoxicating melody to an eagerly listening Lucie, pausing only to pull his maroon scarf tighter around his neck to guard against the biting cold.

"We'd missed our chance of getting Philby," he continued, "and in any case, making a move for him would only have antagonised Moscow just as relations were thawing. But Huxley was a different kettle of fish; he found himself very suddenly caught with his trousers down, so to speak."

"I bet he was thrilled to see you again," Lucie said, only half joking.

"I wasn't exactly thrilled with being handed the assignment either," the Statesman shrugged, a hint of regret invading his hitherto gentle recollections, "but it made sense. We were friends, as I said. When my wife left and went back to England, Alex was there to pick up the pieces. I was supposed to use the relationship to make the retrieval go more smoothly, and from a purely strategic viewpoint it was the right choice. But that didn't make it any easier for me to reconcile myself to the fact I was on my way to betray him."

Though he had settled into a stride, Hartnell hesitated for a moment, as though it were a struggle to vocalise what came next.

Taking advantage of the pause, Lucie stood up from the trunk and crossed over to him, gently touching his cheek and bringing his eyes back from the river and into contact with her own.

"What happened, Geoff?" she asked, "What was Huxley's answer?"

"I never found out," Huxley whispered, almost in fear of the memory he was conveying.

"Why?"

"They'd killed him."

"Who? Who killed him, Geoff?" Lucie repeated the question, her voice harder than she would have liked, as she strived to stop him from falling into introspection.

"I arranged to meet him, here, but when I arrived there was only his StB Handler. I demanded to know where Alexander was, but he just laughed and pointed to the ground. I knew then what he'd done. Something came over me then… I can only describe it as a rage, something I'd never felt before and certainly never since. I struggled with the man, he'd hoped to take me and use me as leverage to get out of the country, but it's fair to say I wasn't keen on accompanying him. We were both scrambling for a weapon, gouging, clawing, fighting like animals in the dirt. My arm was still weak in those days and he overpowered me, sitting on my chest with his hands around my throat… Eventually I managed to grab hold of a rock and I swung. He was bleeding profusely but we were in the middle of nowhere and I had no medical supplies of any kind with me, so I…"

The pause again, this time accompanied by clamped eyes and a cracked voice of regret.

"I dragged him to the water and held his head underneath until the breathing stopped. It was late at night, nobody was around, and so I filled his pockets with as many rocks as I could find and waded out into the river with him as far as I could go and I… let him sink."

He blinked back the tears that danced in his eyes and inhaled a lungful of cold air, stepping away from her as though fearful of her reaction.

Lucie herself stepped back, to give him the space such memories evoked. She knew only too well the despair that taking a life could bring, however justified the act might have been.

"Geoff, why have you told me this?" she asked softly.

"To be honest, I'm not entirely sure," Hartnell admitted as he dabbed at his eyes with his silk handkerchief. "Partly perhaps in recompense for my behaviour last night, partly just so I can hear from someone else's mouth that I'm not going crazy. While Alexander had every reason to be angry with me, it's impossible for him to be behind the note; dead men tell no tales, so the saying goes, and neither do they pen letters."

"Or pull triggers," Lucie picked up, earning a worried glance from her companion. "Geoff, somebody took a shot at you yesterday, not to mention the other guy that tried to, and whoever it was they're going to great lengths to make it look like Huxley. Now think, who knew it was you who exposed him in the sixties?"

"That could be anyone in the service with access to the files," Hartnell answered, his frustration rising.

"Ok, then who knew about your friendship?"

"Nobody!" he insisted, "At least nobody still alive, it was fifty years ago, Lucie... No, no I cannot accept that this is anything other than an elaborate hoax."

"Every hoax needs a motivation, and if you can't think of anyone else who has one, then maybe Huxley isn't as dead as you think?"

Hartnell looked back out across the water, his frown emphatic and his eyes flicking back and forth and side to side, as though searching frantically for answers.

"That's impossible," he hissed. "It's just impossible!"

His voice was strained with confusion, as though he were desperately attempting to convince not just Lucie, but himself, doubt creeping into his inflection as he spoke, something tripping up his logic and eroding his certainty, Lucie picking up on his hesitancy.

"Except?"

Hartnell looked to her, shaking his head as though the words he yearned to speak were not worthy of consideration.

"Nothing."

"Geoff!"

"Except," he reluctantly began, "that man…"

"What man?"

"There was a man yesterday, near Fostrow's apartment when I'd stopped to address the reporters."

"And?"

Hartnell looked irritated to distraction as he struggled to bring forth and articulate the memory clearly.

"He wasn't doing anything of note, just walking past, but… it was the way he was dressed. He was normally dressed for the time of year, but he wore a trilby…"

"A trilby?" Lucie repeated, Hartnell nodding in answer as his hand subconsciously rose above his head, as though silently adorning himself in headwear of his own.

"Yes. Brown with a narrow brim, just like the one Alexander used to wear…"

Lucie narrowed her eyes as she took in the information.

"Did you see his face?"

"No… But I saw him again, this morning, outside the hotel. I didn't register him at first but now…"

Lucie finished the words he seemed unable to say.

"And now you're not so sure if Huxley is really dead after all."

She stood close to him, the loathing she had felt the previous night replaced with sympathy for a logical mind wrestling with the wholly illogical notion that his past had quite literally come to haunt him. His face pale and his usually charismatic eyes hanging heavy with worry, he silently mouthed his affirmation, even vocalising the notion proving too much for him to accept.

"Well then," Lucie said before taking his hand and leading him back up the path to civilisation, "I suppose there's only one way to find out."

BLOOD, WHITE AND BLUE

TWENTY

"I've alerted the Czech police," Lucie informed Hartnell as she came to the table bearing coffees. "I've called it in as an anonymous tip that there's a body by the river bank and given them the GPS reference, so it shouldn't be long before they check it out."

The pair sat alone in a small coffee shop not far from the river bank they had occupied a couple of hours earlier, sitting across an unstable wooden table beside a window, being peppered and pelted with the suddenly falling rain.

"I suppose we should keep our eyes peeled to the news then," Hartnell mused, gratefully accepting the cup and saucer. "Thank you for your confidence, Lucie."

Lucie smiled an acknowledgement of his thanks and inwardly chastised herself for having already betrayed it. While she had indeed phoned in a tip as to the whereabouts of a mystery body to the police, her first call had been to inform Algers of every word Hartnell had said and to ensure that Lake's vaunted 'contacts' within the force would be on hand to provide regular updates as to the search's progress.

"You're welcome," she said, before adding with a nod to her journalistic pretences, "but you owe me an equally juicy story when I write your memoirs, deal?"

"Deal," Hartnell smiled in agreement, "and believe me there are plenty to choose from, precious few though I could reveal to the public without kissing goodbye to my political career."

"Oh, I don't know," Lucie mused. "I think a few stories about a former agent who put his life on the line for his country before turning to politics would win you quite a few admirers back in Blighty."

There was a slight hesitation before Hartnell answered, one which Lucie had hoped to elicit, as though she had touched a nerve or at least given him pause for thought. When he did speak, a hint of suspicion touched his voice.

"Is that a journalistic opinion, Ms. Musilova?"

Lucie matched his expression and his sudden formality, leaning back in her seat and raising her coffee cup to her lips.

"An observation, Sir Geoffrey, that's all."

"And is this the first time you've made such an 'observation'?" He mirrored her movement, drinking from his own cup and keeping his eyes intransigently on hers.

"Truthfully? No," she admitted, "In fact I must admit that's one of the reasons I came to Prague."

"Really?"

"The letter threatening your life, on official notepaper no less, and being released to the press just before your visit to Prague? I must admit I found it all rather convenient."

Lucie had learned long ago that the best lies were those shrouded in truth and that knowledge alongside Lake's advice that the best covers were those applied minimally, she toyed with the politician before her. Judging by Hartnell's reaction it was clearly a tactic worth pursuing.

"Convenient in what sense?" he asked, his voice growing colder with each syllable.

"In the sense that a politician, bravely facing down a threat from an infamous traitor to the Crown, however unrealistic that threat was…? Well it's all rather romantic isn't it? Stuff like that would play well in Britain today, even amongst the hardcore nutters on your back benches. That'd be just the kind of shot in the arm you'd need if you were planning on changing jobs anytime soon…"

She let her musings hang in the air between them as she drained her black as night coffee from her cup, her eyes as immovable as his.

"Are you suggesting," he eventually began once he clinked his own empty ceramic cup to its saucer, "that I had some prior knowledge of the Huxley letter and its origins?"

"I need to know, Geoff," she said in earnest. "I've got the Czech police digging up a river bank looking for a thirty-year-old corpse on the back of this. I can tell you're scared and I would be too if some nutter was shooting at me; but if any part of this is a PR stunt gone wrong, I need to know now."

Hartnell merely looked straight back at her, his gaze wavering not even for a second.

"I can understand your predicament," he finally answered.

"Did you know about the letter?" she asked directly. "Off the record."

"Off the record?" he replied. "No. Machinations of that kind I leave to people like Boris and his little chums; plotting seems to be the only thing they spend any time doing, not that they're particularly good at it."

Lucie sat up straight, not entirely believing his answer but lacking any detail with which to challenge it.

"And is my biographer content with my answer?" Hartnell quizzed, a hint of his usual smile returning to his face.

"Absolutely," she lied, mirroring his smile. "Frankly I'd have been amazed if you'd said yes. Even if you'd somehow managed to send the letter that doesn't explain who was shooting bullets at you last night, or who your mystery man in the trilby is."

"Well," Hartnell grinned, "precisely. Would you care for another?"

*

The moment of tension between them was over as soon as it had begun, though Lucie knew that he would now be even more suspicious of her, despite his having shared his secret by the river. His reasons for doing so still confused her and she wondered what so secretive a man would have to gain from being so open with her that morning.

They enjoyed another coffee before heading back to the city where Hartnell dropped her in the majestic Old Town before heading to his next engagement with Algers, among others, arranging to meet for a drink later. Losing herself in the ancient beauty of the city, she managed to keep her mind from all thought of conspiracies, gunmen and age-old feuds for a precious few hours before heading back to the hotel to freshen up and meet again with Hartnell to see what else if anything she could learn from him.

It was as she walked back towards the hotel that she saw him. A man, the same manner of man Hartnell had described; nonchalantly leaning against the lamppost on the other side of the street to the hotel's main entrance. The demeanour was casual, the dress was typical, only the narrow brimmed brown trilby pulled low over the face gave the figure an air of the unusual. As she laid eyes on him, she knew that he had been waiting to be seen, and

BLOOD, WHITE AND BLUE

she shouted, running towards him at pace, not caring about the twinge in her knee as she went.

Unmoved, the figure remained, casually watching, until as Lucie finally neared, he shifted swiftly from the post and into the backseat of a waiting yellow taxi, which sped dangerously into traffic and was away.

"Shit," Lucie heaved as she caught her breath and pulled her phone from her pocket. Crossing the road, she went into the hotel and quickly got in the lift up to her floor, dialling Algers' number as the doors slid open.

"Listen, Kasper," she began when he answered, "I've seen him, Huxley, or whoever is pretending to be Huxley; he was outside the hotel waiting for me…"

"Never mind about that now," Algers interrupted, "it looks like you've been played."

"What?"

"The river Lucie; Lake's heard from his contacts in the Czech police, they've turned the place upside down, dug up every square inch of the area you gave them and nothing."

"No body?" Lucie quizzed incredulously as she started down the corridor.

"No body, no remains, nothing," his voice explained through the phone.

"But that's impossible," she protested, "he told me!"

"He tells a lot of people lots of things Lucie, he's a politician…"

"No, Kasper, you weren't there," she was rapidly becoming angry, though whether it was directed towards the mystery of a missing body or Hartnell for his apparent lies she had yet to work out. "I'm telling you, the man was in pieces, something was troubling him and not in a small way."

"Look, Lucie, I don't know what to tell you," Algers insisted.

"I'm not saying he's lying for sure, but there's nothing there to back up his story; all I'm saying for now is that if Huxley's body was there, then it isn't now."

"Well that's just rubbish," she replied in anger, "if it's not there, where can it be?"

She shouted the question down the phone just as she reached the door to Hartnell's room, but before Algers could offer an answer, their conversation was interrupted by a hellish, banshee-like scream coming from within.

"Geoff?" she shouted through the door, "Are you alright? Geoff!"

No answer came except the continued scream and Algers' demands through the phone to know what was happening. Taking a step back, Lucie ran to the door, slamming her foot against the lock and smashing the door wide open to a sight born straight from the depths of a nightmarish mind.

Hartnell had collapsed, half on the bed, half on the floor, his feet lying inside the open closet, out of which had toppled the putrid and rotting frame of a years-dead cadaver, its fleshless jaw gaping open in a silent scream as it stared in sightless accusation at the horrified man pinned beneath it. Hartnell screamed and railed against the gruesome embrace in which the withered, decayed arms had claimed him, while Lucie, frozen in shock and almost overcome, knew that the answer to her questions of seconds earlier lay sickeningly before her.

BLOOD, WHITE AND BLUE

TWENTY-ONE

The Scotch failed emphatically to bring the colour back to Hartnell's cheeks, even after two large measures, though that did not stop him continuing to attempt the remedy. He perched precariously on the edge of a voluminous chair in the hotel lounge, his fingers tightly wrapped around his glass and his eyes staring forward, his high forehead glistening with the cold sweat that had broken out the instant the cadaver began to fall.

He shuddered for the hundredth time, unable to escape the memory of the corpse as it pressed down upon him; the scent of the rotted flesh, the silent accusation behind the empty eye sockets as its weight began to lie heavy on his chest, as though trying to replace the life in its own putrid frame by letting the air leak from Hartnell's own.

"He came for me," Hartnell whispered, unable to stop the shaking. "He warned me he'd come for me..."

Beside him, her chair tucked closely in, sat Lucie, though her stare was directed through the lounge doors to reception, where Algers was busily quizzing the Front Desk Manager.

His questions were interrupted by the passage through reception of two masked and sombre stretcher bearers, a twisted shape ominously present beneath a white sheet on the precariously borne gurney between them. A trio of uniformed officers followed in a macabre procession, two of them peeling off to speak themselves to the flustered and overwhelmed staff.

As Algers returned to the lounge, his wrinkled brow furrowed to new depths in a tell-tale sign of a lack of information.

"Nobody saw anything?" Lucie asked in incredulity, standing to meet him at the entrance to the room.

"No-one who's saying anything, anyway," Algers confirmed. "And there's not even any luck with the CCTV; all the cameras between the front entrance to Hartnell's room are down. Likewise, the key entry system so we can't even tell which card was used to swipe in."

"A professional job then?"

"Aye, or at least a very keen amateur who knows exactly what they're doing…"

Lucie shook her head and cursed under her breath.

"Until he opened that wardrobe door I was all set to accuse Hartnell of setting Fostrow up to be killed… but this can't be a put-up job, can it?"

"You tell me," came Algers' exasperated response. "On the one hand secrets you'd think only Hartnell could know are being bandied about the internet, and on the other, someone's taking pot shots at the guy and making sure that if there are no skeletons in his closet they'll damn well rectify the situation. Maybe he's a better actor than we give him credit for? Maybe he's behind the whole thing?"

Lucie shook her head.

"No. You know what fear looks like, Kasper; that is a frightened man."

Lucie turned to look again at Hartnell, who still sat shaking on his chair, and could not imagine anyone would willingly put themselves through such hell as this.

"Well then," she said, "there's only one way we're going to get to the bottom of this."

The pair returned to the seats alongside the fearful politician, who raised his eyes at their arrival and tried once more to speak.

"He came for me, "Hartnell repeated, weakly. "Came to take me to hell…"

Algers sighed in frustration, shaking his head, but Lucie moved herself closer, taking the Scotch glass from the politician and covering his shaking white hands with the warmth of her own.

"Look, it's time for you to start talking, Geoff," Lucie pressed, "and not the sanitised version, warts and all. What happened between you and Huxley? If you don't tell us now, then God knows who will be able to help you."

Whether it was the tone of Lucie's voice or her empathetic body language, something seemed to register inside the ageing MP and he turned to her, offering something approaching a half smile and the gentlest of nods.

"Yes," he said faintly, "yes, you're right, but it was all so long ago… I don't know how much of it I can remember."

Algers placed a hand on his shoulder and Hartnell offered the pair a faint smile which was presumably, Lucie thought, as much thanks as they were likely to get for having rescued him from his own personal 'terror from beyond the grave' barely a couple of hours before. With the body – whoever's it may have been - now having been removed for testing and identification by police, and Hartnell at least temporarily calmed, it was perhaps the only opportunity they would have to get to the bottom of Hartnell's relationship with the man who seemed to be quite literally haunting him.

"Geoff," Algers piped up, "whether that body belongs to Huxley or whether it's Norman bloody Bates's mum on a package tour, somebody put it there, in your wardrobe, to scare the living shit out of you. Now if we're going to help the authorities get to the bottom of this, we need to know what happened between you and Huxley and maybe then we can figure out who would have anything to gain by this and why."

"Just think back, Geoff," Lucie picked up softly, surprised by the concern she genuinely felt for him even after his behaviour the previous evening. "You told me that you and Huxley were friends, yes?"

"Oh yes," Hartnell nodded, "the very best."

"Ok," said Algers," let's start there. Two friends attached to the intelligence service and posted to the British Embassy in Communist Czechoslovakia."

Hartnell's shaking was slowing and his breathing becoming more regular, his demeanour too approaching something close to relaxed as he eased himself back from the edge of the chair and settled deeper into it.

"Two friends," he repeated faintly. "Yes, that's where I'll begin…"

BLOOD, WHITE AND BLUE

TWENTY-TWO

The strength in Hartnell's voice seemed to grow with each syllable, taking him in no time from frightened husk to master storyteller, as though recounting his memories imbibed him with some regenerative vigour. Lucie in turn felt herself turn from curious investigator to eager listener as the old man continued down the neglected track of his memory.

He began, as promised, with two friends beavering away at the embassy in Czechoslovakia. It was the late 1960s, the Dubček regime was in power and the world famous 'Prague Spring' at the height of its glory.

Hartnell's wife, unhappy at the reality of her husband's long-term secondment to this part of the globe, had reluctantly joined him in his sparse Prague quarters only the week before. She survived for four days before, after a miserable evening of unappetising local cuisine, poor conversation and passionless sex, she had demanded to be returned home. Hartnell had lamented her loss, but only briefly; Alexander had been there to raise his spirits, and his soon to be former wife's departure had once more freed up his evenings to indulge in the many excitements the city, and Alexander, had to offer.

Top of their more recent list was a discreet address just on the outskirts of Old Town. Ostensibly a bar, the venue prided itself in catering for gentlemen of more discerning tastes, be they directed towards each other or the many young ladies only too willing to make themselves 'available' to entertain visiting professionals. Such visits were entirely against procedure of course, but what was good for the goose was good for the gander, and both Hartnell and Huxley well knew that their superiors at the embassy, and in the Service at large, regularly indulged in similar pleasures, not least their own direct controller, Brigadier Sir Barrington Hurndall, a man who in later years would prove one of the House of Lords' more belligerent and ultra conservative members. Content that any attempt at discipline or exposure would result in a mutually destructive fall out, all parties continued to pursue their more hedonistic vices by night while, by day, maintaining the gentlemanly cloak so important in keeping up appearances.

It was on one such evening sojourn that the 'incident' occurred. The injury to Hartnell's arm which pained and weakened him to this day did not, if truth be told, have the noble origins ascribed to it by his service personnel file. While it was most certainly caused through torture, Hartnell's capture had not been during a night time raid on the offices of hard line, coup plotting Communists on the government's outer rim, but rather during a night time excursion to an altogether more pleasurable destination, fuelled not by patriotism, but marijuana, and inspired by lust rather than the National Interest. After being told that the building in which they indulged their excess had, two years earlier, played home to none other than Che Guevara during one of his many secretive visits to the country, Huxley and Hartnell, both as high as could be and recharging their batteries from the orgy's latest round, were persuaded by one of the women – a new girl neither

168   BLOOD, WHITE AND BLUE

had seen before – to go and view what had been the infamous man's bedroom. It had been upon entering the small, unfurnished room that Hartnell had felt the cosh to his head; his last sight upon falling to the creaky wooden floor being the fallen body of Alexander, who had entered the room just before him.

Hartnell had paused at this point to gather his thoughts and Lucie also paused to assimilate the volume of information he was spewing forth. The man who only the previous evening had guarded his secrets jealously, now spoke freely.

She had no time to properly process the irony before Hartnell began again, a further mouthful of Scotch aiding his flow.

He had awoken to sightlessness, his hands roughly bound to the chair he had been placed upon, and crude, coarse material wrapped so tightly over his eyes he could feel them pressing into his skull. He had called out for Alexander, but no response came, save for the laughter of his captors, a shrill cacophony of mocking derision which haunted every minute of his time there and which even years later, Hartnell insisted he could still hear, goading him and cackling at his impotence. As an ailing doctor is cursed to know the intricacies of the disease killing him, so too was Hartnell, even despite his youth, experienced enough to know who his captors belonged to and where he in all probability was, and he had guessed his own reality would prove equally fatal. He was almost certainly secured in Domeček, a name which quite literally translated to 'little house' and served as a prison in the Hradčany district of the city, which the StB, following the example of their former Gestapo occupiers, used for their more secretive interrogations.

Alas, Hartnell's awareness had brought him little comfort, only the dread of knowing what to expect. Torture had been an inherent feature of StB operations ever since the Communists took control back in '48, and since then they had only increased their expertise under the watchful tutelage of their more nuanced Soviet 'advisors'. While Hartnell would not have presumed to call himself a brave man, neither had he considered himself a coward, but he could now freely admit to having been terrified as he had sat there, anticipating the horrors of what was surely to come with such a nervous intensity that he had almost begged the torture to begin simply to relieve it. But it did not begin, at least not for that first day when all he had heard was the cruel laughter and the absence of Alexander's replies. Likewise passed the second day with not so much as a finger laid on him and the laughter further away, coming from what sounded like a different cell in the building but still, he had no doubt, intended for his benefit.

By the end of the third day, he had been approaching delirium, deprived of food, water and rest. He had taken to shouting ever less coherent profanities in as many tongues as he could muster at the walls of his cell, until the strength in his body was finally spent. Sitting there, offended and embarrassed by the stench of his own soiled body and the tears he had wept for the friend he now presumed dead – for surely he would have shouted back from wherever in the small house he was – he had drifted in and out of painful consciousness before the door to his cell finally creaked open at what felt like the end of the third day.

As the footsteps had entered the room, Hartnell remembered that he had smiled, no, in fact he had even laughed out loud, because it was then that he had realised that the torture had begun from the moment he had come to from the blow, days before. It made perfect sense to him now; why waste time and energy on interrogating a resistant and angered mind? Not only did every operative on both sides of the iron curtain know that if captured they would eventually talk – the legends of 'super spies' impervious to maltreatment were all simply that – so too did the interrogators know it. Why spend the early days battling intransigence when solitude, hunger and the fear of what was coming would do the 'softening up' work for them. It was genius in its way, compounded by the fact that when the real pain began, no questions had accompanied it. Hartnell had screamed, begged to know what it was his attendant had wanted to know, and he would have told them anything, but despite his pleading, the pain had only intensified, interspersed with short breaks where water and thin broth were fed to him like an infant.

It had only been after two days of the abuse that his questioner spoke to him. By then, Hartnell had given up on ever hearing another word spoken in what remained of his life, but the voice was polite and accompanied by the sensation of the cloth being removed from his face. The throbbing of his eyes as they eased themselves open, scared of and yet desperate for light of any kind, was one that Hartnell had never forgotten, and when they had finally readjusted to sight they had settled on the frame of a small, inoffensive looking man in late middle age, with greying black hair and a thoughtful, contemplative face. He would not give his name but Hartnell remembered that he had claimed to be a one-time student of Mikhail Dmitrievich Ryumin, the infamous Soviet torture master who had honed his skills during the war with SMERSH, before taking control of internal matters. If the statement had been intended as a threat it had been entirely unnecessary as by that time Hartnell had no fight at all left in him. Neither was it followed with any questioning; instead the newcomer wanted to discuss philosophy and political thought, which Hartnell could just remember sufficiently from his University days.

It had been only when his spirits appeared suitably lifted, however slightly, that his fellow had turned to leave before stopping to ask whether Hartnell was right or left handed. When he had answered right, the man produced a small baton which he then took to Hartnell's right arm, beating it repeatedly until it was blackened and limp, still tied behind him to the chair. Standing in the doorway until Hartnell's howls had subsided, the torturer had apologised for the inconvenience and explained that Hartnell was shortly to be exchanged and rendering his arm useless ensured that he would never be able to fire an accurate shot in revenge. With that he was gone, and the agony had consumed Hartnell so completely that it had followed him into unconsciousness.

He did not know how much longer he had stayed in that chair, but it had been sufficient time for his delirium to return, so much so that when he first felt Alexander's hand stroking his cheek, he had thought himself dead and in paradise. The brightness in the room had been as intolerable as the attempt to move his stiffened and tortured limbs, his right arm sending trauma through his body with even the slightest of movements, though he had pushed his weakened frame beyond its limits to greet his friend, who had wept profuse apologies as he embraced Hartnell in his bed, safely back within the embassy compound.

Alexander had explained it all. The pair had been targeted weeks before, their regular trips to their favourite haunt common knowledge among the 'other lot'. With the Dubček regime in place, there had been a general 'truce' and lack of hostilities between the two sides; each, for the most part, knew who each other's key players were, and each were left alone. Huxley and Hartnell though had not been targeted by the regime, but by a hardline faction within the Czech government. When the embassy protested their capture, Dubček had got to hear of the situation and ordered their immediate release.

BLOOD, WHITE AND BLUE

Hartnell had queried why Alexander had not been similarly injured and his friend had explained that while Hartnell had been deprived of sight, he had been deprived of speech. Each day he had heard Hartnell's screams for him but could not answer back, and when the physical torture had begun, he was wheeled in each morning, strapped to his own chair, and made to watch what Hartnell had to endure. He had fully expected to watch Hartnell tortured to death and that he was being afforded the sight of it merely as a foretaste of what was to come when it was his turn to fall victim to the agonies. A few days into his recovery, Hartnell had dared to ask the one question plaguing him since regaining consciousness: was Alexander glad that it was not he who had been tormented, but his friend. When he answered with an eventual, simple 'yes', Hartnell had at least been grateful for the honesty.

Hartnell's recovery had begun slowly but quickly gathered pace, the indignities stemming from his injuries proving more difficult for his pride to overcome than the physical ailments themselves. He had never forgotten, he explained, the humiliation that came with asking others to help him dress or cut his food or having to teach himself how to wipe his damn backside again now the arm he'd used his whole life would no longer reach. Brigadier Hurndall had wanted to transfer him straight back to London but Hartnell had insisted on remaining; he had to show them, all of them, that he was stronger than what they had thrown at him, that the best efforts of the StB had been but an 'occupational hazard' to him. It had been all bluster of course, borne of a foolish youthful desire to 'prove' to his superior, who had always suspected and treated Hartnell as the weaker of the pair, that he was as strong and as capable as Huxley was. In later years Hartnell would often ponder when the precise moment was that he had begun to resent Huxley, but it had definitely, and perhaps understandably been somewhere around then.

Such resentment was though at that point merely a seed, and Hartnell had eventually been cleared to return to duties. Tensions between the Dubček regime and that of Leonid Brezhnev of the Soviet Union were high that summer, and June had already seen Soviet forces present in Czechoslovakia on 'manoeuvres'. While they had for now withdrawn past the border, their continued proximity had made a bad situation worse, culminating in the Russian invasion of August '68 and the removal of Dubček from power.

The events of the Prague Spring and its destruction were common knowledge, but what few outside the intelligence community had been aware of was the incident which preceded the Russian response. A coded message had been intercepted by Soviet intelligence, detailing NATO's acceptance of Czechoslovakia's invitation to fly armoured units into Prague, Brno and Bratislava, and open the border with Austria to allow free movement of military personnel to support the liberalising regime and deter the Soviets from further incursions.

The whole thing had been farcical, of course. There never was such a plan and even if an invitation of that nature had been made, it could never have been accepted. To do so would have meant war. But it put Brezhnev in an impossible situation: did he run the risk of the message being true and see thousands of Western troops crawl through a gap in the Curtain and gain a foothold deep within Warsaw Pact territory, or did he call time on Dubček's experiment? It soon became clear that he had but one option.

Pausing for a moment to refill his glass and take another deep drink, Hartnell's voice dropped a little, retreating just a touch back

BLOOD, WHITE AND BLUE

into the shell they had coaxed him from as he mulled over the crescendo of his evocation, before finally voicing the memory causing so much obvious pain.

Alexander, he told them, had been the one responsible for the message. He had fabricated it, coded it and ensured it would be picked up by the relevant parties. Hartnell had discovered this and challenged him, only for his friend to pull a gun on him. Hartnell had realised straight away that this had been the reason for their abduction; to choose one of them to bring about the end of the Dubček regime by proxy, and that Alexander had been chosen to do the deed. Hartnell could remember feeling a curious pride that despite Hurndall's opinions of the pair, it had been Hartnell with the strength to retain his loyalties under pressure. This was tempered by anger that his friend had not shown a similar resolve and was overwhelmed by the horror of what Alexander had been doing, after having caught him in the act of preparing another counterfeit memorandum.

After a brief struggle, Hartnell had been able to disarm Huxley, who fled the embassy, presumably into the arms of his Czech contacts, while becoming known for evermore in intelligence circles as 'the man who murdered Spring', a fitting if somewhat grandiose pseudonym. And that, Hartnell sighed, had been that. Their friendship in tatters and Huxley's reputation in ruins, the pair never laid eyes on each other again and their relationship, to Hartnell's lasting regret, would remain unrepaired for good.

The tale was over and Hartnell, his mind rejoining his body in the present finished what was left in his glass, Algers moving the bottle surreptitiously out of reach, while Lucie stared at the old man, her eyes narrow and her brow creased.

"And that was it?" she asked, her voice unencumbered with gentleness or sympathy.

"Yes," Hartnell nodded. "As I told you this morning I was eventually sent out to bring him back for trial, but that's when I learned that his handlers had killed him. We'd always suspected that Vasil' Bil'ak was behind our kidnapping and Alexander's brainwashing; he was one of Dubček's key opponents in '68 and was still very much active in 1989. The last thing he would have wanted was questions being asked about his involvement with us when his government and party were collapsing around him."

"It makes sense," Algers chewed the information over, "but it doesn't give us a clue as to who's behind all this; it has to be someone who knew what you've just told us. Can you think of anyone it could be?"

Hartnell shook his silver haired head slowly.

"I only wish I could. Hurndall was our controller and aside from his absolute patriotism he's practically an invalid these days; he just sits in his rooms near the House of Lords, ancient and decaying, just like his politics."

"It doesn't sound like there's any love lost between you," Lucie noted.

"None at all," Hartnell concurred, "but even if he wanted to do something like this he couldn't."

"Nonetheless, I think I'd like to pay him a house call when we get back to London."

"Good idea," Algers agreed, "and in the meantime I'll see what I can find out about who else would have access to the records of your time here, Geoff, ok?"

Hartnell nodded, once more becoming worse the wear for drink.

"Absolutely," he said, beginning to ever so slightly slur, "if you think it'll help?"

"We'll see. Meanwhile, Geoff, Lucie, the last thing we need is any more headlines, bulletins or web logs from tinfoil hat wearing virgins, so for God's sake, let's be discreet. Lucie, I'm going to ask Della to hang on here another day and keep her ear to the ground; maybe people will find it easier to talk when the circus has left town."

"Fine," Lucie nodded as the trio stood up, Hartnell's limousine to his new accommodation ahead of the group's return to Britain the next day having pulled in beyond the main doors. Hartnell caught her eye as he moved past her, dropping his glance suddenly, like a child caught with their hand in the sweetie jar, and she continued to watch him as he moved to the door.

"Mum's the word," she said.

TWENTY-THREE

Mum, as it turned out, was far from the word when it came to keeping the story under wraps, as Lucie discovered when she, Algers and Hartnell were stood together in the departure lounge of vaclav havel airport the next morning, and the elder Statesman's mobile began to ring.

Hartnell tutted and reached inside his jacket to retrieve the phone, the scowl on his face giving way to a softer expression not wholly dissimilar to shock, giving Lucie and Algers cause for concern.

"What is it, Geoff?" Algers quizzed.

"It's from the Embassy," he almost silently replied, "a young staffer there named Edward…"

"Underfoot?" Lucie pressed closer in, concern on her face, "Eddie Underfoot?"

"Yes, that's him," Hartnell confirmed. "He's dead."

"What?" the pair exclaimed in unison, the shock on Hartnell's face now spreading to theirs.

"Yes, I'm very afraid so… he was found in his office this morning, hanging by his tie from the ceiling fan. He'd left a note apparently…"

"Saying what?" demanded Lucie.

A second message alert sounded and this time it was Algers who reached into his pocket and swiped open his phone.

"It's from Della," he said, his tone serious, "It's confirmed. Suicide by hanging, the note says he found the Huxley case in the files when he arrived on secondment and sent the letter in the diplomatic bag as a joke, a joke that very quickly got out of hand. When he saw people were beginning to close in on him he saw this as the only way out."

Lucie was silent, abhorred both at the death of a young and essentially harmless boy, but also the things of which he was now accused.

"Poor boy," Hartnell said with a crack again in his voice. "Most of us at some point play the fool in our youthful exuberance, very few of us pay for it with our lives. If only he'd owned up, perhaps we could have worked something out."

Lucie's head was still turned away and her eyes shut as she mouthed her silent prayer for the fallen young man. Hartnell's voice broke her concentration, his sympathetic inflection suggesting he had mistaken her posture for a more personal grief.

"I'm so sorry, I didn't realise you knew him so well."

"I didn't," Lucie corrected, shaking her head back to the present, "I'd barely met him, but it's just another young life snuffed out before its time; that's something I'd hoped I'd seen the end of."

"Indeed," Hartnell concurred, before a brief silence fell on the group.

The quietude lasted barely a moment before Hartnell spoke again, his voice this time chipper and jovial, devoid completely of the emotion that had seemingly claimed him upon news of Underfoot's death.

"Well, at least that solves our little mystery!"

"Does it?" Algers frowned.

"Oh, come now, of course it does, of course it does," the Statesman insisted, his demeanour returned to its imperious best. "Young Underfoot sent the threat as a practical joke and got caught up in the lie, that's all. Tragic of course, but there we are… I should send flowers to the funeral."

Algers already creased brow furrowed further still not just at Hartnell's reasoning but the speed at which his demeanour changed.

"I don't think we can put it all down to him, Geoff," he insisted, struggling to keep the volume of his voice in check. "There's still the shooting, your mystery man in the trilby and the quite literal skeleton in your closet; are we going to pin all of that on this kid's head?"

"Why not, if the cap fits?" Hartnell hissed back, his own temper clearly rising. "Look, I realise you distrust those of us who take party whips, Kasper, whichever side of the House they sit on, or maybe it's that you consider yourself superior to those of use prepared to pledge loyalty to something? But kindly take your conspiratorial glasses off for a moment and witness the truth as it actually is. I never took the threat seriously and now it's proven to be nothing more than a practical joke gone tragically wrong; we have a body that tells us as much and more than that, a confession. Now I'd remind you that our Czech partners are keen to keep this incident contained and I see no reason to interfere with their investigation. The matter is closed, and I'd thank you to remember that."

His glare switched from Algers to Lucie, and she both understood and resented the added warning to her that it contained, but she could feel eyes beginning to fall upon the trio and for the moment at least, her head was in sufficient control of her heart for her to bite back the retort she could feel brewing inside.

"I don't think I'm superior to anyone, Geoff," Algers responded quietly but with steel. "And I'd like to think that my loyalty didn't simply extend to the well-being of one party or another, but the good of the country as a whole."

"An admirable sentiment," Hartnell retorted, unblinking, "see that you remain true to it and stop looking for ghosts in the dark that aren't there."

He turned on his heel and with his posture fully restored to its typical state of self-assured total confidence he moved to stand by the desk, his company immediately sought by several other of the politicians present.

"Arsehole," Lucie whispered, just loud enough for Algers to overhear and nod in agreement.

"I'm afraid you might be right, Lucie," he concurred, watching how the famed international figure was being again fawned over by those who had flocked to be seen with him at the gate. "You might well be very right. And that means you and I have a problem."

TWENTY-FOUR

The opaqueness of Hartnell's actions aside, what was abundantly clear was how greatly the trip had bolstered his personal image, the surge in his popularity emphatic and obvious as soon as he stepped from the plane onto British soil. It was exactly as Lucie had suggested to him, only more so, with even the right-wing dailies applauding his stoicism in the face of death and the stiffness of his upper lip in continuing his mission of goodwill while under the fire of an uncaptured sniper. The fate of the late Eddie Underfoot was largely relegated to the inner columns and comprised of a few short paragraphs scant on detail and paying lip service to the tragedy of a practical joke gone wrong, while former friends and colleagues queued up to tell stories of his mental health difficulties and the pressures he was under. The suggestion that the letter and shooting had been down to him was never explicitly made, but this would not be the first time that the media would allow innuendo to do its worst. And with so much of what occurred unreported, the facts dependent on the outcome of the Czech police's investigation, it was easy for minds to leap to casual and convenient conclusions. Fostrow, and the body in the cupboard, received no mention at all.

The main focus of the press though was not on Hartnell, as he discovered before the plane had even dipped its wings to land, courtesy once more of the loathsome Steven Nelson and his commitment to alternative news. The final act of the leaker – whether Underfoot or someone else – had been to light the touch paper and run; their firework of choice taking the form of a decades old cipher sent from the British Embassy. But this was not the message Hartnell had spoken of the previous day, offering support and solidarity with Czechoslovakia's liberalising regime. Rather it was a communiqué direct to the Soviet Politburo in Russia, conveying the compliments of British Prime Minister Harold Wilson and his dire warnings of communism's collapse in Prague unless Brezhnev took decisive action.

The uproar as Nelson spewed his revelations onto the web engulfed the Westminster bubble and the country en masse, with the Czech and Slovak community in the UK outraged by the evidence of betrayal and the hard right jubilant that their long-held smears of Wilson as a communist sympathiser now apparently had substance. Demonstrations met counter-demonstrations as social media scrambled to take sides and commentators stirred up passions, with Parliament Square, where a statue of Wilson had only recently been unveiled, now home to a mass encampment of EU and other nationals, using the bronze figure of Wilson as a symbol of the betrayal by Brexit of each and every voter in the land. The government for its part refused to comment on the veracity of the cipher, but subsequent actions made clear how true it considered it to be, as calls for stricter border controls and the curtailing of rights grew louder by the day.

It was into this chaos that Lucie and Algers landed, no closer in either of their views to getting to the heart of the matter. Lucie requested access to the original intelligence file, opining that they had missed something obvious and a fresh pair of eyes on the background info could prove fruitful. Lake agreed, arranging to have the relevant documents delivered to her flat in Camden the following evening. With Algers occupied with gathering data on the venerated peer Lord Barrington Hurndall, Lucie lacked an immediate project with which to occupy her mind and wary of allowing herself to slip into a depressive episode before this matter was resolved, she rattled off a text to Della, due to be following from Prague the next morning.

At least, Lucie thought, she could spend the next day wrestling with conundrums of an altogether more pleasant nature before it was time to wade through files once again.

TWENTY-FIVE

Lucie had long since abandoned the dubious pleasures of social media and the venom so incessantly spewed upon such platforms, and the briefest of glances at the threads scrolling alongside the repetitious news coverage on the screens dotted around the room was enough to convince her she had been right to do so.

Countless avatars of flag adorned lions and victorious knights sat above wilfully malicious and poorly spelled diatribes, condemning the sheer brass neck of bloody foreigners, daring to object to the way proper Brits spoke to them, shared, liked and re-tweeted by innumerable like-minded – or half minded, Lucie thought – 'patriots'.

The largest wide screen TV at the far end of the bar beamed the image of a mirthless, willowy MP, his bespectacled face devoid of compassion and reason to all who cared to watch. Announcing his intent to introduce an amendment to the government's Home Security Bill, calling for the right to protest for British nationals only to be enshrined in law, he expressed his dismay at the blatant ingratitude of those now occupying Parliament Square, adding that they should think themselves lucky they were not being cleared by water cannon, rubber bullets or worse.

When one or two started banging their tables in drunken support of the MP's words, Lucie stood and removed herself to a vacant table outside on the terrace, where the view of Parliament across the Thames was better, even if the words being spoken within and around it continued to poison the atmosphere.

The freshly arrived Della, returning from the bar carrying drinks, had spotted her move and followed her out, her face twisting in disgust at the sight and sound of the offending politician on the screen she passed.

"Yuck," she grimaced as the coverage continued. "More wise words from people who think 'good old British pluck' is enough to make up for crashing out of Europe and over the cliff edge."

Lucie forced a reluctant laugh at her friend's attempt to lighten the mood.

"What, you don't think a touch of Dunkirk Spirit and blood, toil, tears and sweat will get us through?"

Della raised an eyebrow in mock ridicule.

"Even if it did, there's precious little of that left," she replied, taking a sip from her tequila and lemonade. "Where once Britain had Dunkirk Spirit, it now has a beer belly, a Union Jack tattoo on its arse and a penchant for calling the police when it runs out of *KFC*. Believe me, some people are in for a rude awakening…"

Lucie drank deeply from her own glass and sat back, relishing the all too rare appearance of the sun and pondering the fears and worries that must lead people to get behind such agendas as those she so often saw peddled today.

"I don't know," she sighed resignedly. "Ordinary people have been getting screwed over for so long I suppose I can't blame them for lashing out at the establishment. And if enough voices pick out a group or a section of society to blame, it must be the easiest thing in the world to fall in with that; to become part of the mob…"

"Then they deserve everything that's coming to them," Della replied, clearly in no mood or mind to understand the motivations of the Right. "If people can't see that they're still being manipulated by elites then I've no sympathy for them; sooner or later they'll realise that all this has done is legitimise the kind of people who beat people up for speaking two languages and think it's 'political correctness gone mad' that you can't call it the 'Paki Shop' anymore."

Once again, Della's bluntness brought a smile to Lucie's face

"Heart-warming isn't it?" replied Lucie. "Makes you proud to be British, or a half British arsehole in my case like someone called me the last time I went on Twitter."

"Excuse me, madam," Della answered feigning indignation, "I happen to only be part British myself."

"Really? Which part?

"My arsehole."

The women laughed and drank together, as relaxed in each other's company as they were uncomfortable in the tense, uncertain atmosphere of the city. There they stayed, watching the sun set and the yellow, electric lights of civilisation flickered on as though competing with the stars in a contest they could never win. As midnight approached, the absence of the chimes of Big Ben, silenced in the wake of urgent repairs, was compensated for by the tuneless efforts of an intoxicated group of young men, bellowing their efforts to all, before losing track of how many 'bongs' were required and staggering off to find somewhere else to drink. The brief moment brought a smile to Lucie's face, accompanied by the strangely welcoming caress of midnight melancholia, so often experienced when she had drunk just the right amount, or allowed herself a precise level of introspection.

"That's what hurts so much," she said softly, watching the harmless drunkards stagger on. "I can remember so clearly when

I loved my British half. It was never pride, how the hell can anyone claim pride over where they were born like it was some sort of planned and strived for achievement? It was just love, love for what I thought the country was. I'd always thought that people were smart enough to see through the papers' lies, that they accepted those of us with mixed or different heritage. But then that moron called his stupid referendum, and all of a sudden, the place I'd loved and respected as part of me turned on me and everyone like me, and without so much as a 'thanks for coming' or a 'kiss my arse', told us we weren't welcome anymore. Perhaps we never were. Perhaps all that British eccentricity known the world over, all that tea loving, self-deprecating, cricket and warm beer reserve was all just bollocks all along; a mask to hide a deep and cold-hearted xenophobia and a superiority complex that refused to die with the Empire. I cried the morning after the vote, I actually sat down and wept. People I'd thought were my friends wouldn't make eye contact with me; others would smile at me and tell me I was alright, and that it was the rest of 'them' that they wanted rid of, as though I was their token bloody foreigner..."

She drained the last vestiges of alcohol from her glass, tapping the bottom so that the ice dropped into her mouth, to be crunched and crushed between her teeth.

"It doesn't hurt so much because I hated Britain," she said, placing her glass back on the table. "It hurts because I loved it, and it broke my heart."

Lucie stood, her balance slightly off and her bad knee a little unsteady after the evening's drinking. Della rose with her, having likewise tipped over into mild intoxication.

"I don't suppose I can interest you in a nightcap?" she asked with a cheeky wink as she wrapped her coat around her.

Lucie laughed. "You know, you really need to stop that," she

BLOOD, WHITE AND BLUE

jokingly admonished, burying herself snugly within her trusted and tattered black overcoat. "How are you getting home?"

"Oh, I'll grab a taxi," Della answered as the two women embraced warmly and said their goodnights.

Lucie was through the door, pondering the mechanics of how to return to her chip shop flat in Camden, before she turned back to wave to her friend, only to see that instead of a cab, she had ordered another drink and was now sat at the almost empty bar, alone, her face devoid of its characteristic mischievousness, and her features now reflecting the same signs of anguish that Lucie herself felt daily. She hovered for a moment, torn between whether to go back inside or respect her privacy, only for her colleague to look up and meet her eyes with her own, her face reverting in a heartbeat to its typically cheeky expression as she waved to Lucie, mouthing what looked like the words 'just waiting for an Uber' to her through the glass doors.

Lucie nodded and smiled back. Della had surely seen the concern on Lucie's face and elected to ignore it, and Lucie knew from managing her own condition that had she wanted further company, she would have asked for it. In any case, Lucie was in no shape to stage any sort of intervention tonight. Satisfied, at least for the moment, Lucie stepped to the kerb and waved her arm to the black cab passing on the other side of the road, which turned at once and pulled into the side of the pavement beside her.

Stepping in and settling back into the clicking, clunking motor, Lucie gave her address to the driver, nodding and smiling at his regurgitated banter while mentally tuning out. And as the heavens began to delicately spatter the ground beneath them with rain, Lucie preoccupied herself with half drunk ruminations, and worry that perhaps Della's mask, like Britain's, was in danger of falling away.

TWENTY-SIX

Becoming steadily if reluctantly more familiar with the London transport network, Lucie was pleasantly surprised how quickly she had made it back to her home, although the strong coffee she had downed to steady herself before going to bed proved to be a mistake, leaving her wide awake and counting the cracks in her ceiling. After an age of sleepless boredom, she peeled herself from the bed and went into the sparse living room, in which the wad of papers Lake had sent awaited her and which she hoped would bring about an end to her insomnia.

It was as her eyelids dropped on the brink of slumber that she spotted it; not so much a smoking gun as a struck match, but something which through carelessness or wilful intent, had not been mentioned in the briefing in this very flat days earlier. It was still there when she double checked the files the following morning before slipping a fresh polo shirt above her usual jeans and heading to the South Bank Walk by Tower Bridge, where she had told Della to meet her.

She found her by the railings, her clothes the same as those she had worn the previous evening and her features pale and barren, as though all joy, mischief and humour had been soaked up by the knowledge of what Lucie had come to discuss. This was not a conversation Lucie wanted to have with anyone, least of all a friend, and Della had very quickly become very much more than just a friend. As though sensing Lucie's discomfort, it was Della who spoke first as she drew up alongside her, under the shadow of Tower Bridge.

"Will you tell Lake?" She asked through unbrushed teeth, her dry eyes staring.

"I wanted to talk to you first," Lucie replied.

"Why?"

"Because I need to know if it was an error, or something else."

"So, what? You don't trust me now?"

"It was you who told me not to."

Della let out a cynical laugh, the previous night's stale alcohol evident on her breath.

"Why didn't you go home last night, Della?"

"Because I'm in my fifties and don't have a bed time anymore," she spat. "But it seems I do have competition from a newbie who claimed to be my friend and who thinks she knows all there is to know about espionage after a couple of days on the job."

"I'm not competing with you," Lucie responded in as calm a voice as she could muster while keeping her eyes fixed on the small boat chugging along towards the bridge. "But I need to ask you how it happened."

"How what happened?"

"You know."

"I don't," Della insisted, clamping her eyes tightly shut, leaving Lucie no choice but to press home her interrogation.

"Fostrow," she said, simply and firmly. "He'd been tweeting all kinds of disgusting comments to Hartnell for years and he never batted an eyelid, never blocked or reported him, he even answered a couple of them with a joke or two here and there. But then this one, this last tweet from Fostrow to Hartnell, sent a couple of weeks before the threat arrived, you see?"

Lucie selected the picture she'd taken of the offending tweet from her mobile and held it up to Della, who stared at it for a moment before closing her eyes and turning her head away.

"What does it say, Della?" Lucie pressed, her voice stern and steady.

Della refused to look again at the offending comment, reciting its content from memory, every drop of her usual impish joie de vivre drained from her exhausted and pale face.

"It says 'So much for Operation Triple H, Geoff. See you in Prague, love from all at the CPR.'"

"Right," Lucie answered, pocketing the phone. "And right after that tweet was sent, Hartnell blocked Fostrow. Now he was totally within his rights to do so, but it wouldn't be churlish of anyone to think that a man who had laughed off abuse from this guy that would make the SAS blush was maybe being a little touchy to block him for a largely inoffensive message like that."

"There was an implied threat in that Tweet," Della retorted, defensively, "See you in Prague? That could have meant anything, Hartnell had every right to block him!"

"True. But that was when you noticed this Fostrow character and started to look into him," Lucie picked up. "You made a few enquiries, found out he'd booked a flight to Prague when Hartnell would be there, you found out where he was staying, dug out his plan to coat Hartnell in paint, and then you took all that to Lake. Only you didn't bother to tell him about the 'CPR', 'Project Triple H' or that paint was the last thing on Fostrow's mind, you didn't dig deep enough to find out what he was really up to! The truth was you pieced together a rough sketch of what this guy might get up to from a few social media posts and old blogs and hoped for the best!"

Lucie's patience was eroding now, her anger growing with each word she vocalised and she fought with herself to keep her furious words out of the ears of passers-by.

"Della, I killed this man, for fuck's sake! I put a blade to his chest and I pushed!"

"You had no ch–"

"I wouldn't have needed a choice if I'd known what he was up to in there! That last minute intelligence you uncovered, you would have known before I stepped on the plane if you'd bothered to properly look!"

Della's defensive resolve sapped further away with each word Lucie spoke, until her typically playful face creased into an avatar for despair and she wept, quietly but with profound depth, shaking her head and refusing to look Lucie in the eye.

"It shouldn't have happened," she insisted through her tears, "I'm so sorry Lucie, I had no idea you'd be in danger, really. I just needed a quick win, something to impress Lake with, and I thought Fostrow was it; just another keyboard warrior out for his five minutes of fame, like those people who throw eggs at Ministers. I thought he was harmless."

Lucie's anger at once dissipated. Despite her errors, Della was her friend and she wasn't merely apologetic, she was in despair. She stood closer alongside her and put an arm around her shoulders, the chaplain in her coming to the fore and her desire to forgive and support impossible to resist.

"Hey," she soothed, "It's ok, I'm still here, so's Hartnell. It worked out fine in the end."

"And at what price?" Della retorted, apparently determined not to be let off the hook so easily. "You had to kill him Lucie, after all the promises you'd made to yourself and to that god of yours."

"You let Him and me worry about that," she answered, knowing that was another of the tough conversations she was putting off. "But Della, you're a professional, you've been doing this job a long time, years now; how could you miss it?"

Della took a deep breath and composed herself, placing her hand atop Lucie's in a gesture of thanks for her understanding and patience.

"Like I said, I needed something for Lake. It's a hard job, Lucie, the demands are extraordinary, and your shelf life isn't so long, you know? You start making mistakes, you give someone reason to question your effectiveness and your days are numbered. Well, our dear Mr. Lake has been questioning my effectiveness of late, my value to the team. I needed something tangible, concrete to remind him of what I could do, and I thought Fostrow would be an easy win. I knew Lake wanted a way to ingratiate his new agent with Hartnell, and I thought I'd given it to him."

Lucie nodded, understanding the pressure her friend had been under and her desperation to come up with the goods, and how that kind of situation could lead one to take their eye off the ball.

"And you had," Lucie said, stroking her tearful friend's shoulder.

"Yes, and I almost got you killed too."

Della had long-since given up on trying to contain the dampness in her eyes and the pair stood there for a moment as the grey clouds rolled in overhead, Lucie's arm protectively around her friend.

"Do you know what it's like to spend every second of the day holding back tears that you'd give anything to cry?" Della asked as the cold pitter patter began to tickle and tease from high above. "Keeping your damn 'upper lip' so stiff for so long that you're

BLOOD, WHITE AND BLUE

scared that when what's trapped inside does finally break you, and you know it will, you might never be able to put the pieces back together again?"

Lucie had no answer to give other than to tighten her embrace and lean her ear closer, knowing all too well that some questions had no answers, at least none that would be understood in this world. All she could do was listen as her friend finally released the years of torment within her.

"Do you know what it's like to watch bulletins, read headlines, telling you all about some innocent kid or some local hero stricken with the most insidious of illnesses and just screaming to the world 'let it be me! Take all of the filth out of those innocent, beautiful people and put it on me!' You go through everything, every motion of the day, getting up, going to bed, washing, cooking, drinking, fucking... and seeing every day how you feel just that little bit worse than the day before. Watching joy turn into apathy, apathy to irritation, irritation to loathing and despair and knowing that there's nothing, nothing you can do to make it go back the other way. Knowing that friends, family, lovers... everyone who gives two shits about you deserves so much more than the nightmare you're putting them through but knowing that you'll continue putting them through it because that's who you are and the disease in your head won't let you be anything else. You're like a fucking repentant alcoholic, flinging around apologies so often they lose all meaning and making promises of bright futures and bread tomorrow that you know damn well you'll never ever keep, until everyone you've ever cared about stops reaching into the shadows for you, just to protect their own emotions and their own minds. And rightly so..."

Lucie stood, her face etched in sympathy and her arm around her friend, but could offer no other movement to comfort her, no magic words or comforting smile. Not through any callousness on her part, but simply because she did know what Della was talking about, she understood intimately well the pain of which she spoke, and she knew that no offer of comfort, no shoulder to cry on was ever big enough for the tears that needed to flow; at least no shoulder this side of Heaven. The medication could maybe help, so too perhaps the counselling, but after that it came down to Della herself; others could light the way for her, but it was up to her to walk towards it. It was a battle Lucie had faced many times, sometimes daily, and though, with the help of her doctor and medication – and her faith – she had defeated it for now, she knew that it was an ever-present danger; addiction-like in its capacity to trick you into one more indulgence.

Lucie turned Della towards her as the rain began to grow stronger, cupping her face in her hands and stroking her white, pale cheeks until she opened up her eyes in silent apology.

"I understand why you'd want to make Lake eat his words," Lucie said as the boats chugged under Tower Bridge sounding their horns as they went. "I'll try and keep all this away from him if I can, maybe Algers and me can sort things without him finding out."

"I'm so sorry about what happened to you, Lucie…"

"Hey, hey, that's over now, you don't owe me any apologies. I suppose I'm just trying to say that you don't need to be on edge because of me; I'm not in this for the long haul. I'm doing this one job for my Mum and then I'm out, ok?"

A smile cracked its way onto Della's face at Lucie's casual end to her words and the younger woman was glad to see the anguish lift at least temporarily from her friend's face.

"Ok," Della smiled, "I never wanted to be 'spy of the month' or anything like that, God knows I'm so ashamed of myself for cutting corners like that. I suppose I didn't realise how much the job means to me."

"Well don't worry," Lucie replied with a chuckle of her own, "I don't intend to stick around long enough for that to happen to me."

Lucie moved to leave and the pair embraced warmly.

"I know it's not your cup of tea," Lucie said to Della, "but I know what you're going through, and I'll say a prayer for you tonight, if that's ok with you?"

"Asking the magic cloud fairy to make my head better?" Della grinned, before her mischievous smile gave way to a look of sincere gratitude. "You know? I think I might like that. It's good to know I have a friend who still wants to save me."

"Somebody's got to," Lucie smiled as the heavens opened completely and the two friends were doused in the sky's tears. "See you later?"

"Later," Della concurred, before clutching at Lucie who paused, knowing what the other woman wanted. With so many conflicting priorities, pressures and emotions swirling in her head, this was exactly the last thing she needed right now, but against all her expectations, the thought of it brought a calming hand to the turmoil within her, and she leant slowly forward, the two friends' lips meeting in a soft and delicate kiss.

It lasted just a moment before Lucie broke away with a smile and turned, heading back to find whichever damn tube station she was nearest to and take a few hours rest. The empyrean weeping intensified, as though washing the dirty city in a diluted grey paint, and she turned back to see if her friend had taken shelter, only to see her returned to her statuesque position at the railings, her gaze once more upon the scurrying boats, as though hoping that her pain, and perhaps even herself, could be washed away with the grime and rejection the city was shedding, and be lost with them forever in the waters.

Lucie remembered the feelings as though they were a part of her, and she noted to herself as she turned back, her eyes stinging in the rain, to say an extra prayer not just for Della and her battle with her demons, but that Lucie's own would never again return to haunt her.

TWENTY-SEVEN

"Any news?"

"None that you'll like," came the dour response as Algers caught up to her, the fresh puddles splashing around his ankles as he jogged, spattering his suit trousers and creeping over the edge of his shoes.

Lucie had been grateful that Algers had agreed to keep Della's error under wraps as much as he could. Though she knew nothing of the details of their working relationship and whether or not it had ever been social, it was clear that he understood the pressures she'd been under and was in no hurry to add to them. As he'd said in his typically blunt and less than complimentary style, the three of them were considered by Lake to be trapped rats in a sewer, and Algers was in no way inclined to give him the pleasure of watching them turn on each other. Instead, he had set about the reference to 'CPR' and 'Project Triple H' as a fresh lead, scouring records and files for any and all references of what either acronym stood for. Now, after leading the charge against the government's proposed *'Emergency Powers Act'*, designed to contain the fall out of any post-exit day catastrophes, he had headed straight from Parliament to meet with Lucie and discuss their findings in detail.

"There really isn't very much at all to be honest. This 'CPR' of yours," he began, "it most likely refers to the Centre for Policy Review – a Right Wing policy research group in the late sixties and early seventies."

"What, so they'd produce papers, influence policy, that sort of thing?"

"Well that's what you would have expected them to do, but…"

"Yes?"

Algers frowned down at her.

"But I can't find any record of any report they produced, any committees they advised, any speeches they made, nothing. It's as if they never really existed in anything but name. Kind of a paper exercise it seems, but Huxley and this Lord Barrington Hurndall both belonged to it at one time or another."

"And Hartnell?"

"Seems pretty unlikely," he mused, "it was a pretty right-wing group, not really his scene."

"You wouldn't have thought it was Huxley's either but…"

"True," Algers mused. "Anyway, they disbanded in '72 and while a few of the Members are still around, they don't have any influence or reach anymore, not that they ever did."

"Suppose not… how about Project Triple H?"

Algers huffed as they reached the edge of the pavement and waited for the lights to change.

"Even less luck, I'm afraid. I can't find a parliamentary record although I asked Lake to check the Service's files and he did manage to find one reference."

"He did?"

"Aye," the MP confirmed as they reached the other side of the road and began to cut through the wet and worsening Victoria Gardens, the mud joining in the assault of the pairs' footwear. "It was one obscure reference in one of the old embassy folders from the Cold War."

"Which Embassy?" Lucie asked, her heart ready to sink should the word she feared be spoken. Her preparations would not go to waste.

"Guess," hissed Algers.

"Don't tell me…"

"Yep. One reference recorded in 1968: 'Project Triple H – Failed - of no continued interest."

Lucie swore, then composed herself and swore again, attracting the condescending glances of a dozen scurrying passers-by, all of whom were busy protecting hairdos and clothing underneath copious umbrellas. Lucie and Algers had come to a halt at the edge of the gardens, unprotected from the rain and content, or at least disinterested in it enough to allow themselves to be soaked as they pondered; a look probably not helped, Lucie thought, by her sudden and loudly pitched profanities.

"Well that's that, then! I don't know, Kasper, I'd convinced myself that Fostrow using those words then turning up in Prague with a rifle in his hand was the key to all this."

"I know," Algers sympathised, "but if this was all one big conspiracy it's a fifty-year-old one, and like I said, most people in the CPR have died and any that are left are far closer to the levers of their stair lifts than they ever were to the levers of power."

"But why mention it if it wasn't relevant?" Lucie persisted. "Look, I don't trust Geoff, not one bit. He's had shit dumped on him yes, but he's come up smelling far too sweet for him not to have been involved somehow, and that shooter on the embassy roof was real, not some screwed up kid."

"Can you be sure of that, Lucie?" Algers gently quizzed, "Maybe the shot was staged, maybe Hartnell was never in any real danger?

He didn't kill you when he the chance after all..."

"Nah, come off it, Kasper," she said, shaking her head. "You've seen front line action, we both know what a sniper looks like; if I hadn't have pushed him out of the way that bullet would have gone straight through his heart. As for why I wasn't killed, who knows? Maybe the shooter has some code of ethics he subscribes to."

"It'd be a curious one if he does," Algers pondered. "But we're still no closer to learning who it was."

"Well if it isn't some decades old conspiracy, could one of his political enemies in the Commons be behind it? Someone who sees him as a block to Brexit and wants him out of the way?"

Algers laughed and pushed his rain-soaked hair from his eyes.

"I might have a low opinion of my parliamentary colleagues, Lucie, but I can't see any of them are ideological enough to go through with something like that."

"Why? If he stands in the way of their 'Grand Vision'?"

Algers smiled and with the rain showing no sign of stopping, gestured to her that they at least move under a tree while it persisted.

"What you have to remember, Lucie," he began, "is that the key players in all this aren't all simply a collection of racists and xenophobes. Some of them are and they'll play those cards of course, they're not afraid of getting their dog whistles out because they know that's what gets the hounds wound up, but they're more casual racists then actual ideologues, they don't really believe in all that racial purity crap. Most of them don't even believe in Brexit."

"How can you be so sure?"

"Because they don't really believe in anything except the continuation of their own wealth and power. The Tories for example will change their position in a heartbeat and swear night is day to you that they'd held that view all along. Straight out of a

BLOOD, WHITE AND BLUE

damn Orwell novel, that lot. They long ago stopped standing for anything except their own survival and it's a mentality that's spread into the other parties too. Look around the Commons today, you can count on one hand the number of MPs who'll put country before Party, and one of them is standing with you right now."

Lucie frowned as she took in Algers' comments, dismayed as much by the suggestion that a party would espouse such views without even holding those convictions, as she was that anyone genuinely held them at all.

"But what about the ones who say it's all about the economy? That we're financially better off outside of Europe and doing some kind of deal with the U.S?"

"Well, it's the same again. There's a small handful of people who genuinely believe that, but they're usually the same ones who need their heads feeling and think Elvis is still alive and working on the bin lorries in Cleethorpes. In the main these people are interested in their own money, how to make more of it and how to stop other people from looking into how it's been made; the good of the country is a long way down their list of priorities. So, they count their cash in private while muttering about mongrel races and the legalisation of buggery, yearning for the country to maximise what they laughably still see as the 'Special Relationship.'"

"What, the 'Special Relationship' isn't really very special?"

"Only in the sense that America thinks we must be pretty fucking special ourselves to still believe in it," came the response, dripping in sarcasm. "And anyone who genuinely believes getting into bed with the current ape in the Oval Office will benefit Britain is three pages short of a White Paper. Don't get me wrong, America has always enjoyed screwing us, but this guy will screw us while pulling our hair, slapping our face with his stumpy little cock and calling us his bitch."

Lucie guffawed out loud at Alger's crass description and the deadpan nature of his delivery. It was a welcome relief from the frustration of their talk thus far.

"So, your back up profession as a stand-up comedian aside, we still have nothing concrete to go on?"

Algers squinted, as though weighing something up in his mind.

"Well, there might be something…"

Algers reached into his inner pocket and pulled from it a brown paper bag which instantly fell victim to the drips of rain which found their way through the branches they sheltered under.

"I got you a present," he smiled, Lucie taking the package from him and turning her body to the rain to better shield it.

"What is it?"

"The last chance," Algers sighed. "At least, I can't think of anything else."

Lucie peeled the remnants of bag away and found herself staring down at the laminated features of a grandly dressed military figure, his uniform resplendent with decorations and his face fiercely unapologetic and staring with such ferocity from the cover that one could be forgiven for thinking the man himself was condemning the reader by proxy through some literary avatar. He was positioned against an impressively full bookcase, against which rested a Union Flag, wrapped neatly around its pole. In bold, white letters juxtaposed against the black background which took up the lower half of the cover, the words 'The Right Man – The life and struggles of General Sir Barrington Hurndall'.

The book, evidently written after his time in Prague, as evidenced by his promotion, but before his elevation to the peerage, was stained with age and the jacket creased and torn in parts, giving way to the rough, hard cover beneath.

"I thought it might help you sleep," Algers joked.

"How? By reading it or dropping it on my head?" She weighed it up in her hand as she spoke. "Seriously that's a pretty weighty tome for a book about a guy nobody's ever heard of."

"Aye, you're not wrong," Algers agreed, "and it's pretty dry subject matter to say the least, but a lot of that's down to the author."

Lucie followed the cover to the smaller words, tucked underneath the grand title as though as an afterthought.

"Professor Martin J. Hyde?" she quizzed, "Never heard of him either."

"No reason why you should have," replied Algers, "but he's pretty widely known in his own circles. He's an academic, pretty far left in his politics but surprisingly conservative in the way he conducts himself. Before he retired he'd had stints teaching at most of the big universities and is surprisingly well respected across the spectrum for a guy as Bolshie as he is. That's probably why a guy as right wing as Hurndall was content for him to write his biography; well, that and nobody else was asking I suppose."

Lucie laughed. "So aside from a cure for insomnia, what do you want me to do with this?"

Algers took the book back from her and flicked it open to the index, running his finger down the 'P' column before stopping and handing it back.

"Look," he said simply.

Lucie did look and there, obscure and unnoticed, alongside a time-worn tea stain and a faded page reference lay a simple phrase that lifted her spirit and caused her to raise her eyes to Algers and smile, before slipping the book into her trusty black overcoat and setting off at a jog.

'Page 373,' the index had read, 'Project Triple H'.

TWENTY-EIGHT

It was the next morning when Lucie approached the address of Professor Martin J. Hyde, which turned out to be a top floor flat in a row of properties on Swains Lane, overlooking Highgate Cemetery, not at all far from the sightings of the infamous 'Vampire' decades earlier. Lucie hoped that the answer to her mystery would not continue to prove as elusive as the fanged monstrosity of popular legend.

The weather was its usual dull grey, although thus far it had not made good on its implied threat to continue the downpours of the previous day, and Lucie was grateful that she could at least attend the meeting dry.

Dressed in her typical ensemble of flared jeans and one of her seemingly endless supply of paisley shirts worn untucked, she flicked her hair from her ear to answer Algers' call, briefly regretting her choice not to tie it back today and let it hang long over her shoulders.

"Yeah, I'm there now, just about to go in," she confirmed. "There was no mobile number, but I managed to get hold of his landline. I asked him to scan me the file, but he flat out refused, insisted that I come to meet with him. Yeah, I'll check in when I finish up, bye."

While it hadn't taken long for her to Google the Professor's address and a potted outline of his career, more difficult was getting him to consent to release the information. Having accepted her story that she was a journalist researching a book about Hartnell, he had refused to even consider emailing any information of any kind to her, insisting instead that she come to see him, as 'that's what journalists are supposed to do'. Now, having found her way to Highgate she stood outside the building and pressed the buzzer for the professor's flat, waiting a small age for his voice to come through the intercom, devoid entirely of welcome and focussing it seemed strictly on business.

"That's you is it?" came the voice, Lucie confirming awkwardly. "Well up you come."

The door creaked open, revealing an unlit and formidable set of steps, which she headed up with a curious feeling of nervousness rising inside her, as though she were visiting a neglected elderly relative who suspected the call was simply to ensure inclusion in whatever will was eventually left behind. At the top of the stairs stood doors to two apartments and Lucie selected the appropriate number and knocked, the door opening as soon as her knuckles rapped against the wood.

There before her stood the professor. Not especially tall, his hair had fully whitened and was matched by a full beard which had been left perhaps a little too long. A check shirt was worn open collared beneath a pea green cardigan with beige corduroy trousers and sandals adding to his somewhat eccentric look. His flesh was almost deathly pale and his eyes wide, as though Lucie's visit had confused more than irritated him.

"Yes?" he asked, slowly and quizzically, the staring eyes now firmly and immovably upon her.

"Professor Hyde?"

"Yes."

"I'm Lucie Musilova, I just rang your intercom, you buzzed me in."

The eyes grew wider still, accompanied by an apologetic cry.

"Oh, I'm sorry!" he declared, apparently sincerely, "I thought you were the milkman!"

Lucie furrowed her brow, choosing not to ponder too deeply how he could have come to that conclusion.

"Right… well, I'm all out of gold tops but I'd appreciate it if I could come in and see the file we discussed on the phone yesterday?"

"The file?" The professor's voice had an otherworldly quality to it and a significant part of Lucie began to wonder whether he was entirely well, his manner being eccentric to the point of erraticism and his expressions apparently channelled entirely through his admittedly impressively wide eyes.

"Yes, the file," Lucie persisted having come this far. "On Project Triple H?"

The words provoked something akin to a Damascene conversion in the ageing man, his demeanour changing at once from scatter brained to attentive.

"You're the journalist?" he asked, his deep voice suddenly more serious.

"That's right."

"Please, come in."

He stood back and beckoned her inside, closing the door behind her. The hall space was small and, while not exactly poorly decorated, was nonetheless devoid of warmth and caked in an atmosphere of dust and age. All the doors leading off from the hall were closed bar one, which stood open to what looked like a small study or office, into which the professor ushered her.

Nowhere within the cramped and dusty room sat a computer, rather pile upon pile of folders, papers and charts, towering high upon the reliably solid oak desk which stood beneath the window ledge. Lining the wall was a row of archaic, heavy duty filing cabinets, built as though to withstand a bomb blast, while on the opposite side hung an antediluvian blackboard, upon which was scrawled all manner of commentary and exposition in writing so impossibly small Lucie could not begin to decipher it. The professor picked up the cane he walked with and used it to push a collection of folders from a wooden chair in the corner onto the floor, then hooking one of the legs with it and dragging it closer to the desk and what was obviously his preferred seat.

The set up amused Lucie who smiled warmly at the old man.

"I can see now why you wouldn't email the file to me," she said, earning a hawkish stare in response.

"In a world of spy-ware, viruses and smart phones, the man with a paper and pen is King," The Professor explained, easing himself into the aged leather and oak of his chair. "At least I know my notebook won't threaten to release copies of my browsing history to friends and colleagues unless I pay up with, what do you call them? Bitcoins?"

The smile remained on Lucie's face and despite herself she found she was warming to the elderly academic, although it remained to be seen whether or not he would deliver the goods.

"I'd offer you a cup of tea but I'm afraid I've misplaced my kettle."

"That's fine," Lucie grinned, "I'm fine, really."

The professor sat for a moment observing her, his thin fingers rapping on his desk.

"So, you're a journalist, are you?" he eventually queried. "Which paper do you write for?"

"I'm freelance," Lucie answered having anticipated a degree of questioning. "I usually do work for the Guardian and the New European, the Indie sometimes too."

"Ah," came the booming response, "anti-Brexit publications, then."

"Yes. I'm half Czech so Brexit is a very important issue for people like me. Sir Geoffrey Hartnell is being tipped for High Office at last and he's probably the best hope for EU nationals and their families in this country who are being handed the arse end of the stick right now. If he's going to be our champion then I want to be the one who writes the definitive article on him."

"An ambitious target for your first report," mused the professor, to which Lucie found herself struggling to reply.

"I, ah, it isn't my first report, Professor," she answered unconvincingly.

The old academic spun on his chair and gestured with his cane to several piles of newspapers, stacked according to title against the side of his towering cabinets.

"The Guardian, the New European and the Independent, or 'the i' or whatever it calls itself these days," he said, pointing to each title in turn. A paper for every day over the past three months; your name appears in none of them."

Lucie knew her cover, such as it was, had been blown with apparent nonchalance by the aged academic, but pride refused to acknowledge the fact just yet, scrambling instead for some counter-point that may yet salvage a conversation still in its infancy.

"Perhaps I'm a staff writer?" she posited.

It was a weak attempt at best and Professor Hyde looked a little disappointed she had made it.

"And perhaps you are wasting my time?" he replied.

"No. No, I assure you, I really do want to see that file."

BLOOD, WHITE AND BLUE

"Then let's be honest with each other," the Professor suggested. "I am Professor Martin J. Hyde, late of several universities, known for an extensive back catalogue of biographies and sporadic televisual appearances. These have been made all the rarer since my last appearance on *Question Time*, when I described Nigel Farage as a malignant tumour on the perineum of society and told Dimbleby he was talking out of his arse. Since then I haven't been as welcome on television, although I was invited to spend a week in a jungle somewhere with a snooker player, a celebrity cook, and that man who used to play a detective on Jersey..."

The Professor's words were spoken genuinely and utterly unforced, with apparently no concern or understanding given to the possibility that they or the stories behind them may amuse the listener. They were delivered instead simply as a statement of what Professor Hyde appeared to consider were the salient facts at the time. Lucie found herself grinning widely at the refreshing sincerity of the man before her.

"Which brings us on to you." His voice was at once deep and stern but gentle and honest as well, aspects reflected in his still wide but now tamer eyes. "You're not a journalist, not even a staff writer. You have no writing credentials that I have ever heard of and while it's possible you could be a television or internet journalist, were either of those true you would have introduced yourself as such. But as your desire for the case file appears genuine, that suggests an investigation of some sort. If you were from the police, again that would have been apparent in your opening statement to me, which it wasn't. Now that leaves us with one of two possibilities: either you think the file may hold some secret information which may aid you with any blackmail you have in mind, or..."

"Or?" Lucie repeated, impressed if not a little annoyed at the old man's reasoning.

"Or else, you're a spy."

Lucie remained silent, though she was sure her eyes gave her away and he looked at her with unfeigned sympathy.

"Oh, come now, don't let it bother you," came the baritone voice. "You're by no means the first in your industry to pick my considerable brains over the years you know. You all start off from the same angle, pretending to be this, that or the other, all of which tends to be easily verifiable yet never verified. Really, this whole thing would be far simpler if you were just honest with me from the start."

There was no point at all in prolonging the charade. Lucie could either walk out, or she could concede and perhaps come out with the file. Only by doing the latter could she complete her investigation.

"Alright," she smiled, "you win. Yes, I'm a spy, at least for the time being."

"Five or Six?"

"Neither."

"Ah," came the profound response, "you're one of *that* lot. Unless you're Russian of course. Are you Russian?"

"No, I'm not Russian," she smiled at his apparent disappointment. "You've no need to worry, I'm on our side."

"Whose?"

"Britain's."

"Ah. You'll forgive me if I'm surprised to hear that, with your surname, if indeed it's real, it doesn't seem as though Britain is altogether on your side right now."

"Well, maybe not – and yes, my name is real by the way - but perhaps Hartnell can change all that."

"Why? Because he'll throw his weight behind you and those like you?"

"Why not? He's pro-European and reasonably progressive, at least for someone in that party."

"Says who?"

"Everyone," Lucie answered, becoming confused and a little flustered with the endless interrogation. "The papers say it, the TV says it, it's conventional wisdom."

Professor Hyde nodded sagely, considering her words as he would a student's thesis.

"Well, progressively pro-European he must be then," he continued to nod, "if you accept conventional wisdom, that is."

"You don't?"

"I accept nothing, Ms. Musilova, nothing at all that I cannot evidence with my own eyes, or at the very least assess evidence from as unbiased a source as I am able to find."

"Really?" smiled Lucie. "I didn't think there were many of those left.

"Regrettably few," the scribe concurred, "which is a tragedy for those with independent minds and a joy to those who despise them. Do you want to know another word for 'conventional wisdom'? Laziness."

"Laziness?"

"Of course! What else would you call a refusal to independently examine the facts and form one's own conclusions? 'Conventional wisdom' gave us witch burnings, slavery, Iraq and the career of Danny Dyer, all because people were unprepared to engage their brains and challenge the status quo."

"You have a point," Lucie conceded, amused, the academic harrumphing in acknowledgement of her concession, before rising from his desk and crossing to the first of the ancient, chipped dull-green filing cabinets bracketed against the wall.

"It's one of the curiosities of evolution," he continued as he fished in his pocket for the small key and began wrestling with the aged, weary lock. "One would have expected the species' capacity for gullibility to decrease as civilisation grew, but if anything, humanity is more susceptible now to the influence of the powerful than it ever has been, and thanks to, what do you call it? 'Social Media', the very victims of manipulation vociferously increase its promulgation ten thousand-fold!"

He succeeded in heaving open a stiff, reluctant drawer which creaked its displeasure, as though resentful of its owner waking it. The papers it contained were yellowing and dry, and upon which were written the memories of decades long passed and mostly forgotten.

"You all share your little stories, swap news reports and web site fallacies, never once stopping to check if what you spread is the truth, and woe betide anyone who dares to stand up and criticise; that mob behind their keyboards will be on them like MPs on an intern for daring to hold an evidenced, contrary opinion."

His rough, dry fingers pinched around the edge of a brown file, plucking it upwards where he could grab it properly. Pulling the file out he hobbled back to the desk, picking up his rant as he went.

"And that, young lady, is where 'conventional wisdom' has got us."

He slapped the file down on his desk in an apparent display of triumph in a debate Lucie hadn't realised she had entered.

"I don't know though," she mused teasingly as she eased herself forward on the rickety old chair beside him. "I've never studied electricity, but I trust them when they say not to put my kettle in the bath."

She couldn't resist the joke, though she began to wonder whether it was worth it as he turned to stare at her through those distracting eyes of his, his white whiskers twitching above his lip.

BLOOD, WHITE AND BLUE

"The bath!" He cried the word as though it were a magical incantation, the irritation on his face replaced by the delight of his obvious 'eureka' moment. Pushing himself up once more he creaked out of the room in something approaching haste, returning moments later with a kettle, as antiquated and tarnished as everything else Lucie had thus far experienced under his roof.

"I'd left it in the bath, of course!" He grinned excitedly.

"Right…" Lucie responded from her chair, her eyes wide. "Because you were planning an elaborate suicide?"

His frown returned, probably more at her failure to follow his reasoning she thought than at her distasteful remark.

"The water and gas rates are increasingly extortionate young lady," he explained, sitting back down, "I find it more cost effective to source my bath water from the kettle. Anyway, I can offer you that drink now after all…"

"I'm, er, ok thanks," Lucie interrupted, not relishing the thought of what else he might us his teacups for, "do you mind if we take a look at the file?"

Hyde deposited his freshly retrieved vessel behind a wavering tower of paperbacks and flipped the file open. It was thin, containing barely a few sheets, most of which written in the professor's own hand and he began speed reading through them, clearly searching for something in particular.

Wary of being directed towards a further rant about the inadequacies of modern critical thought, Lucie quizzed the professor on how he had found about this 'Project Triple H' which seemed to have avoided any other mention as far as she could tell.

"By looking, Miss Musilova," came the grunted response, which was not in Lucie's mind entirely fair.

"I have looked, Professor," she calmly replied, "yours was the only mention out there."

"When you say 'looked' do you mean you typed something into, what is it? Goggle? Or did you actually bother to read any books?"

"I bothered to read yours, professor," her voice was sterner now, reflecting her tiredness of games. "And I bothered to follow up what I found, is that good enough?"

The change in her tone was enough to break the professor's self-indulgence and lift his gaze back towards her, Lucie noticing at once that it now contained a glimmer of what appeared to be admiration.

"We'll make a journalist of you yet," he grinned. "No, there are no mentions of Project Triple H anywhere else, at least in any of the source material I studied."

"So where did you get the information?"

"From the horse's mouth," Hyde confirmed, "or rather from the ass... I was granted extensive interviews with Sir Barrington, now My Lord Hurndall, over several months while writing his biography. And may I say it was the worst job of my life; the man's an idiot."

"And he told you about it willingly?"

"Not quite."

The Professor shifted a little in his seat.

"You'll have noticed that our former Premier, Harold Wilson has been back in the news recently?"

"I'll say," Lucie confirmed, the reaction to his newly revealed apparent support for the Russian invasion dominating events since the news broke.

"Well suggestions of his alleged communist sympathies are far from new and, I would have said until this cipher emerged, far from true."

"And now?"

Professor Hyde squinted, investing the proper thought into his reply.

BLOOD, WHITE AND BLUE

"Impossible to say yet," he eventually answered, "I'd need to see the cipher itself, or at least an independent report on its authenticity. It wouldn't be the first time the course of history had been influenced by inaccurate or even false communication."

"But if I pressed you for an answer based on your considered opinion of Wilson?"

"Then I would say the cipher is nonsense. Wilson was no communist, and if he appeared as such to anyone then my first instinct would be to question precisely how far right their own opinions reached."

Lucie warmed more to the elderly academic with each word he spoke, and even if he was going somewhat around the houses in his explanations, it was a journey she was willing to take.

"But, I've heard rumours of a plot against Wilson when he was in charge," Lucie remembered, "so presumably a few people had their suspicions about him."

Hyde's sagacious nod returned, his brow furrowing over those extraordinary eyes.

"Wilson always suspected that plots against him were brewing in the background, eventually the worry of them led to his stepping down and Callaghan taking office."

"So?"

"So, he believed that there were two specific plots against him, one in '68 and the other in '74."

"And these were real? They weren't just paranoia on his part?"

"He wasn't entirely correct in his assumptions," the professor replied. "In actual fact there were three…"

Hyde shuffled from his chair and moved over to the blackboard, and with one enormous sweep of his arm produced a blank space in the midst of his writing, now consigned to history and the loss of which he did not appear to lament. Picking up a well-worn piece of chalk, he drew a large circle in the middle of the board, writing within it three large capital 'Hs' evenly spread.

"You see, in my view, Project Triple H wasn't so much a project as a code, perhaps even a sum."

"What, like an algebraic calculation or something?" Lucie picked up, "Find the value of 'H'?

"Mm," Hyde nodded, "But given that we have three units of 'H', perhaps it's something more straightforward."

"Well, given that we have three men, Hurndall, Huxley and Hartnell, all together in Prague at the time this 'project' was being bandied about, it's reasonable to assume that it's got something to do with them."

"Forget Hartnell, he's the red herring in all this." Hyde snapped his assertion, taking Lucie somewhat by surprise.

"Forget Hartnell? Why?"

"Because I believe that, if you'll forgive me adding to our list of 'aitches' for a moment, his name is a coincidence, that's all, at least as far as the Project goes."

"What makes you say that?"

"Let's come back to that shall we? Now at the time the Project was mooted, however obliquely, Alexander Huxley was an agent seconded to the British Embassy in Prague, reporting to Sir Barrington Hurndall. Now, Hurndall had an extensive military career as a leader of men and had developed a not undeserved reputation for efficiency; he 'got things done', a trait with which he continued in the world of espionage. That, along with certain familial connections was enough to win him a great number of influential friends in and around Westminster at that time, including Lord Mountbatten and Cecil King…"

"Cecil who?" Lucie queried.

"Cecil King," Hyde repeated. "He was the Head of the IPC

which at the time was the biggest publishing company in the world with something like two hundred newspapers under its umbrella. Both King and Mountbatten gave interviews for my book and, at least at some stage, had a degree of respect for Hurndall, although it did seem to have dimmed with the passage of time... King was also alleged to have been behind the '68 plot against Wilson."

Lucie, intrigued, came to stand beside Professor Hyde at the board, both staring intently at the 'code' written upon it as though it would merrily reveal itself through their persistence alone. The elderly man reached up with the chalk and drew a straight arrow from the first H, writing the word 'Hurndall' beneath it.

"What was the '68 plot all about?" Lucie asked.

"Well you must understand this is all based on hearsay and anecdote, but essentially it's alleged that a meeting was arranged in May of that year at King's request, and attendees included Mountbatten and Sir Solly Zuckerman, then the government's Chief Scientific Adviser. On the agenda was the dismay of certain sections of the media and the military with the direction of the Wilson government and its inability or otherwise to counter the communist threat from the East. It was put to Mountbatten that it would be in Britain's best interests for the government to be overthrown and for him to lead what was described as an 'Interim Government of National Unity'. The suggestion was that there were up to thirty high ranking MI5 operatives who would support the move in conjunction with the military, the upper echelons of which were very much on board."

"But, obviously that didn't happen, so?"

"No, indeed. Zuckerman for one was dismayed at the suggestion and pointed out that the idea itself was treasonous and Mountbatten refused any part of it, so the plans ended there.

Heath's election in 1970 took away the urgency of any further movement but the threat of conspiracy reared its head again in '74 after Wilson returned to power, although all that eventually amounted to was a lot of arsing about at Heathrow Airport. Can you guess though the connecting feature?"

"Hurndall?"

"The very same. In '68 Hurndall was a well-connected senior figure with deep inroads into both the intelligence and military services. In '74, he was the officer who ordered the occupation of Heathrow Airport by military forces, ostensibly as a training operation in the event of an IRA attack, but in reality, at least as far as the theory goes, a show of force designed to trigger a coup that never arrived."

Lucie weighed up the information, looking at the dates and timelines Hyde had chalked onto the board as he spoke.

"So," she pondered, "Two conspiracies, neither of which came off, and one man connecting the two, perhaps driving them?"

"That's supposition," warned the professor. "You must understand, Miss Musilova, that while I may be inclined towards a theory, if I lack the evidence to support it then I consider it unproven. My business is facts."

"I understand," she nodded, "and please, call me Lucie."

"But, Lucie, while we're enjoying a hypothetical discussion, let's assume for the sake of argument that the suggestion of a conspiracy is correct, that still leaves us a couple of Hs short of a broken code. Now what was happening in Prague in 1968?"

"The Prague Spring was in full flow, a lot of tension with Russia and the invasion occurred in August."

"Precisely. Now, if we accept that the May '68 meeting with King and Mountbatten took place as described, and we also accept that Hurndall was connected to both men and was well placed in

BLOOD, WHITE AND BLUE

both the agencies they would be forced to rely upon in the event of any coup, then it's reasonable to speculate that he would have been a very unhappy man when Mountbatten refused to go along."

"So unhappy that he'd want to force the plan through however he could, using whatever means were within his power."

"Which were considerable," reminded the professor.

"I'll say… You said around thirty agents were involved, or at least sympathetic to the idea of a takeover?"

"So the theory goes."

"And Hurndall oversaw a fair few of them, sat in Prague, licking his wounds because the man they'd chosen for their coronation refused the crown. So, he decides to do something about it… but what?"

Hyde placed his chalk beneath the second H and drew a further downwards arrow, scribing in capital letters beneath it, the word 'HUXLEY'.

"But how could Huxley help with Hurndall's plans?" Lucie quizzed, "He was a Communist traitor."

"Was he?" The Professor's wide stare returned, and Lucie suddenly felt as though she were naked before her classmates.

"Well yes, everyone knows that, it's…"

"Conventional wisdom?"

Lucie looked again at the board, her eyes beginning to open.

"The cipher that Huxley supposedly sent to the Russians, warning them of imminent NATO occupation in Czechoslovakia was never released to the public," Professor Hyde elaborated, "only its alleged contents. What if he never sent it at all? What if Huxley had actually been working with Hurndall in support of the coup?"

"But something must have been sent," Lucie protested, still unwilling to abandon her long held assumptions, "it sent the embassy into panic stations and the invasion happened immediately afterwards. Huxley was in charge of the cipher coding; if he didn't send it then who did?"

"Perhaps you should ask the one who exposed Huxley in the first place?"

Lucie laughed in defiance of the awareness dawning on her.

"But that's…" her laughter ended, replaced at once by a confusing but profound shock, bordering even on sadness. "But that's Hartnell…"

"Yes, Lucie," the big eyes shared the melancholy that had so suddenly struck her. "That's the man whom the public, the press and the world expect to be Prime Minister of Great Britain and Northern Ireland within days. That would be Sir Geoffrey Hartnell."

TWENTY-NINE

The revelation had taken her by surprise and it annoyed her quite how much she seemed to be affected by it. Had Hartnell really framed Huxley? Was that the source of the death threats now, years later when he stood so close to claiming power? But if so, who was sending them was still a mystery as the body in the statesman's closet was undoubtedly that of the infamous and derided defector, the intelligence back from Prague confirmed as much. Alexander Huxley was the conspiratorial equivalent of a Norwegian Blue.

Lucie shuffled back through the front door of the Professor's flat, having taken a few moments to compose herself outside, where the grey clouds had once more gathered to collectively grieve on the people below. The elderly academic was waiting for her back at the blackboard, a cup of hot, steaming tea in his hand which he held out to her, those expressive eyes of his now displaying only sympathy at the reaction his theorising had provoked.

She accepted it gratefully despite her earlier reservations and returned to looking at the board.

"Please, do remember, Lucie, these are only theories, hypotheses and you should treat them as such; I have no evidence for their veracity."

"I know," she replied, "it's fine, go on."

The Professor looked uncertain but nonetheless returned to his chalked ponderings.

"We suppose then, that the damnation heaped upon the shoulders of Alexander Huxley is ill deserved, and that instead he was a lieutenant of Hurndall."

"And that still leaves us with a mystery 'H'," Lucie chipped in. "If not Geoff then who?"

"Well if the theory holds any weight I can only think of one."

Drawing a third straight arrow down from the final letter, he paused and turned to Lucie.

"Would you like to do the honours?"

Lucie placed down her tea on a pile of papers and took the chalk stump from Hyde's aged fingers, stepping towards the board and pressing it against it, writing in large, capital letters the word: HAROLD.

She looked back to the professor, who nodded grimly, retrieving from her the chalk and adding symbols between each of the Hs he had first drawn.

"Hurndall plus Huxley equals minus Harold," Lucie voiced as the pair examined their work. "A well-connected Hurndall, angered at the failure of the first attempt to overthrow Wilson, manufactures a plot involving Alexander Huxley's cipher expertise to provoke a second attempt. But, for some reason the attempt never happens, Huxley is condemned as a communist traitor and Hurndall's other intelligence contacts ensure the whole thing is wiped from the record."

"It would fit the circumstances," nodded Hyde.

"Which begs the question, what is it doing in your book?"

The elderly man returned his chalk to the rim of the black board and turned back towards his desk, easing himself painfully onto it, a look almost of shame on his features as the creaking wood bore his weight.

"There are two editions of my book, Lucie," he began in his deep, operatic voice, "you have been fortunate enough to read the first. Had you sourced a second edition you would have found even the minor reference I had made omitted."

The old man had become emotional and Lucie sat alongside him in concern, placing her hand over his and urging him to go on.

"I only heard mention of the Project by accident," he explained. "Interviews with Hurndall always took place in the evenings and I'd endured many an hour of tedium with him by that day. He was a master of self-aggrandisement, even for one in the Westminster bubble, and he could talk for hours without giving anything of substance away. Except for when he drank."

Hyde paused to fill his lungs, a slight wheeze evident inside them as he prepared to continue.

"His secretary had told me of his drinking problem. His family had intervened, and I understand he'd been teetotal for a period of some months by that point. I was also aware from others I had interviewed that he could be loose lipped and capable of quite unpleasant behaviour when under the influence. Being quite prone to over indulgence myself in those days I managed to sneak a bottle of eighteen-year old single malt into our next meeting."

Lucie could see from where the sense of shame grew, and she squeezed his hand tighter in an effort to show he was free from her judgement.

"You got him drunk," she stated quietly, not needing his confirmation.

"I was hungry for my story," the Professor replied, "I would have done anything to get it, even kick a man from the wagon and watch him fall under its wheels. I attempted to tell myself he deserved it because of how unpleasant a fellow he by many accounts was, but it wasn't ever my place to take such an action."

Tears were beginning to form in his eyes, just as the renewed and invigorated rain began to patter against the glass beside them.

"His grandeur grew with every sip he took, and with every glass came more and more outrageous claims of his importance. I drank my fair share but kept sufficient control to remember what he told me. The following morning, while my head pounded and my stomach churned, I wrote it all down, here, in this file."

He tapped the folder he had earlier retrieved and continued.

"Most of what he spoke about that night was pure bluster, but I was intrigued by a slip of the tongue he'd made and which he wouldn't, even with the drink inside him, be pressed on."

"Project Triple H," Lucie guessed, to the old man's nodding.

"That was the name he gave it, something way beyond Top Secret which could have, in his words, brought the government down - but raised the country from its knees. from its knees. It was in many respects the typical ultra-right wing lunacy one hears all too often from inadequate politicians, but coming from him… I pressed and pressed but he wouldn't be drawn on it. And that's when I realised it must be serious."

"So, you put a casual reference into your book and hoped that would serve as a gateway to finding out more."

Hyde nodded. "But instead, I was paid a visit here by a trio of Hurndall's associates. It transpired that the great man was less than pleased at my including details, however shallow, of our conversation in the book and I was, shall we say, 'discouraged' from investigating further."

The tears had become a cry and Hyde strained to compose himself, Lucie looking at him with concern.

BLOOD, WHITE AND BLUE

"I'm not a coward, Lucie," he said, suddenly. "I may not run from trenches into machine gun fire or leap tall buildings in a single bound, but I have never allowed myself to be intimidated out of following a story. I had no intention of doing otherwise when Hurndall's men came to call, but my daughter…"

His voice broke off and Lucie knelt in front of him, ignoring the shooting pain in her knee, and lifted his sunken head from his chest, looking into the large, soulful eyes.

"Hey, hey," she whispered softly, almost inaudibly against the ever-heavier sound of rain against glass. "It's ok, it's alright."

The professor smiled back, but only slightly, emotion still clearly welling up inside him.

"She was so tiny, Lucie, so precious. They said they could see to it her treatment was disrupted and I couldn't… I couldn't…"

The damn of his reserve cracked finally and succumbed to the flowing tears behind it, weeping openly into Lucie's sincere embrace. As had been her problem since the day she crawled out of the desert, despite her faith, despite the feelings she wished she could share to ease the old man's distress, she simply no longer had the words to do so. She vainly searched within herself for something to say, but her mouth was numb. And it struck her as he sobbed into her arms that nowhere in the room was there a picture of the daughter whom he had yearned to protect, nor were there pictures of anyone, the room decorated solely in the hallmarks of academia and journalism.

When he had wept as much as he was able, he eased himself upwards, his wild eyes tamed by the tears that had washed through them, and he took Lucie's hand, clasping it between both of his as he gave her his thanks for the concern she had shown.

"The file is yours, Lucie," he said, "but I'm afraid it will do you little good. It contains nothing more than what we have already discussed here; my thoughts and theories of what may have happened fifty years ago, all supposition and hearsay."

Lucie nodded gratefully, understanding but lamenting the lack of specifics.

"I realise that, Professor, and thank you. I just wish there was a smoking gun in there somewhere too."

"As do I Lucie, as do I," the aged face replied. "But all I can give you is the theory, now it's down to you to find the facts."

THIRTY

Hartnell had either dodged each attempted phone call, e-mail and appointment, or had his Parliamentary Secretary do likewise since they had returned from Prague, but he would not succeed in avoiding her this time.

Sitting in the dubious comfort of her chip shop flat, Lucie had pored over the file gifted by Professor Hyde. It was much as he'd warned her, crammed with hand-written observations and numerous suppositions, some of which had been crossed untidily out and others thrice underlined. Alongside the theories she had discussed with him were pen pictures of each of the key players, added to over a period of years in the case of Hurndall and Hartnell, and it was they as much as the theory that fuelled her as she flashed her Parliamentary pass to the security guard and marched towards the opulent bumptiousness of Committee Room Seven, where the statesman was chairing the afternoon's business.

The enormous double doors to the room swung open as she approached, and attendees and observers began to spill from it, as though democracy itself were spewing mistakenly consumed irritants back from whence they came. Hartnell, as was his custom, remained seated in the middle of the head table while others departed, so as to remain, Lucie suspected, the focus of peoples' attention for as long as possible. She stood like a dividing rod in the middle of the open doorway, those stragglers still remaining forced to walk either side of her while she held Sir Geoffrey in her gaze, the MP looking up to meet her eyes as though he had been expecting her and was relieved that now at least the wait was over.

The Committee Room was as grand as the man himself, the two perfectly befitting each other as though he were a proud lion majestically stalking the prey that dared to enter his lair. This was his committee, his territory; any confrontation on this turf would result in only one winner. And yet here Lucie was, present and ready to challenge the unchallengeable, to take the lion on in his own patch, and though her nerves teased her every bit as much as they would had she been called to give evidence here, her resolve never faltered.

Hartnell stood, straight, dignified and immaculately attired behind his chair in the centre of the head table, looking every bit the Statesman the world believed him to be. The pair were silent, watching each other until the final person exited the resplendent chamber and the tension between them reached its zenith.

"You know why I'm here," Lucie opened, Hartnell nodding in reply.

"I'm just surprised it took you this long."

"It's time for answers, Geoff. "

"Well there's no better place to ask questions."

Lucie walked further into the room, the doors swinging closed behind her.

"You lied to me."

"The prerogative of a politician."

BLOOD, WHITE AND BLUE

"I'm not in the mood for jokes, Geoff, not since I got off the plane from Prague."

"And what have you been in the mood for, pray?"

"Reading," came Lucie's answer. "I've read tonnes since we've been back, Geoff, all sorts of stuff from case files, to old tweets, all detailing the same thing: Project Triple H."

Hartnell's stoicism fluttered for a moment and he swallowed upon hearing the words, opening his mouth a little wider to take an almost imperceptible breath.

"I was aware of no such files," he replied, his voice uncertain.

"Oh, there are bits and pieces out there," Lucie answered, "enough for someone to put two and two together."

"And come up with five?"

"And come up with an interesting theory. Do you want to hear mine?"

Hartnell made no sound or movement other than to follow her with his eyes as she took just a step or two closer to him.

"My theory, Geoff, is that Huxley wasn't a communist defector at all. All that stuff you told me and Algers in the hotel, about your friendship, about being tortured by the StB, that might be true, it might not be, I don't know. But I think you got wind of Project Triple H; a fall-back plan to topple the Wilson government. I think you decided not to let that happen and instead of the cipher Huxley was supposed to send, you sent a replacement of your own making alleging NATO involvement and set Huxley up as a defector. Now if it was as simple as that I could live with it, but that cipher brought the tanks rolling into my Mum's country and she lived under Russian boots for years afterwards. And not just that, Geoff, but I put a knife through the heart of a man who tried to shoot you because of Project bloody Triple H; a man you told me you had no knowledge of. Well my theory is that you're a liar."

Lucie's voice had grown in strength and emotion with each word through her lips, firing them like bullets at this man who refused to lie down and play dead.

"A damn liar."

Hartnell, to her surprise dropped his eyes for a moment and adopted a definite, if brief, expression of shame, before his politician's instinct returned to the fore and he raised his proud head to justify himself; Lucie still hoping against hope that she was wrong.

"I didn't know Fostrow would be armed," Hartnell said quietly, a desperation in his eyes that she believe him. "And neither did I know where he'd heard about Project Triple H; I assumed, perhaps wrongly, that he'd picked up a vague reference from some carelessly unredacted document in a stack of papers somewhere and simply wielded it and hoped for the best like a fool playing with his father's gun."

He straightened himself fully before her, as though adopting a position of contrite apology.

"But it's true, I was expecting some kind of gesture protest from him, one that may cause me some short-term embarrassment but which I could use to my advantage later. But I didn't know he intended to fire bullets into the street, that you would be there and compelled to kill him to protect me, and that's the truth, Lucie."

He spoke the last words forcefully, insistently, punctuating his statement with a firm gesture of the hand and a steely brow.

Lucie nodded, her eyes still wet but her resoluteness as strong as ever.

"And Huxley?" she asked.

Hartnell looked away again, but not, Lucie thought, in deceit, rather because of the pain of reliving his past once more.

"Alexander was my friend," Hartnell began, "but even friendship has its boundaries. Every word of what I told you about the torture is true, but… he tried recruiting me into Hurndall's scheme, there were a handful of intelligence operatives in on it and he thought I could add to their number."

"But you didn't?"

Hartnell looked the picture of indignation and he straightened himself back up to his full height.

"I may be many things, Lucie, but I am not a traitor. Wilson wasn't exactly my cup of tea, but he was the PM and that was that. When I learned what they were planning, I couldn't allow it to happen; they were talking about tanks in the streets of London! I mean that's just not the way we do things in Britain."

Lucie couldn't help but smile at his umbrage, but the reality was that the tanks had indeed rolled through the streets of Prague, and he was apparently the man responsible for that. She pressed insistently on.

"What did he tell you?"

Hartnell sighed and continued with obvious reluctance in his voice.

"He told me he was due to compose a cipher to Moscow and allow it to be picked up by the Americans. It's the same one you'll have seen leaked in the media these past couple of days, ostensibly from the British government to the Soviet Leadership, acknowledging the USSR's right to intervene in a Warsaw Pact nation in the event of any invasion and pledging Britain's public support for the removal of the liberalising regime. There had always been rumours and allegations of Wilson's connections to the Communists and a leak like that would have seen him fall from power in a heartbeat; it was to be our generation's Zinoviev Letter and it would have destroyed the Left and their icons for a generation, leaving the way open for a Hard-Right takeover designed to secure Britain's future and offer an aggressive deterrent to Russia."

"And that was a plan you couldn't live with," Lucie surmised, nodding her head in reluctant understanding.

"Once I knew the plan it was easy enough to sabotage. I knew Alexander's access codes, and I knew when his shifts were and when he'd be out of the apartment. It was child's play to head to the cipher room and send an alternative message."

It was as Professor Hyde had suspected, and though she had come here tonight to wring such an admission from Hartnell, the reality still drove a blade into her chest and she began to feel her eyes welling up with tears for an oppression from years before she was born.

"So, it really was you," she whispered through the crack in her voice. "You were the one who sent the cipher, the coded message to Russia, telling of an imminent NATO occupation. You were the one who forced their hand, who made them spill over the border, raping, beating and killing on their way. For fifty years the world hated Huxley when really you were the man who killed the Prague Spring."

An emphatic mixture of resentment and shame fought for control of Hartnell's features as he stood listening to Lucie's condemnation, his eyes narrow and his cheeks flushed and red.

"The Russians were always going to invade!" he finally snapped, his words pointed and angry and as much designed to convince himself of their veracity, Lucie thought, as her. "They would never have allowed the regime to continue, it was impossible for them to have done so; so what if I made the tanks come a day, a week, a month earlier than they otherwise would? What matters is what would have happened to Britain had I not done so!"

His vexation had become a rage as the words spewed from him, punctuating his pacing beneath the centuries-old paintings and the figures within them who gazed reproachfully down.

"It's all very well you standing there in priestly judgement, finding fault in the impossible choices of yesteryear, but look around you today at what Britain has become, what everywhere always becomes when the Far Right take hold, and maybe then you'll see the hellish options I had: Keep a friend but aid a coup, or lose him and sacrifice one country to save another."

His pointed aggression gave way to anguished regret as he spoke, his weak arm, which he had pointed in accusation at Lucie, shaking and giving way.

"If I hadn't done what I did then the government would have fallen, and the extremists taken up shop. And now, thanks to Brexit, thanks to these leaks, they're poised to take control, just as they were fifty years ago, only this time they won't need an army to do it!"

The passion of the man succumbed to the exhaustion his body had been holding off a long time and he slid back into his grandiose chair at the head table, placing his hands on the solid, varnished oak, his head facing resignedly down.

"Only this time, they'll take it, and that will be the end of the Britain you and I call home."

A silence so profound Lucie could almost hear it descended between them, Hartnell's stare firmly on his table and Lucie still blinking back the tears that clouded her own vision.

"Not necessarily," she finally retorted, forcing the words quietly through the crack in her throat.

Hartnell looked up with puzzlement on his brow.

"But when you take your story to print, first your paper then the whole damn lot of them will take me apart. There's no doubt about it, Lucie, the Right will seize their opportunity."

"If I go to print."

"You mean…?"

The naivety on his face despite his years of experience with plots and subterfuge amused Lucie, and she was more than content to allow him to continue believing her to be an aspiring journalist after a story.

"I mean I'm half Czech," she answered. "Ever since that damn vote, I've been looked at like shit on shoes by people I thought were friends and had it made very bloody clear that I'm not welcome here. It's hard enough for us to rent a flat or get a job now as it is; do you really think I want any more of this 'hostile environment' crap? If that lot never lost any sleep screwing over the Windrush generation they wouldn't bat an eyelid about us."

Hartnell sat up in the chair, her words a fresh sustenance to him and he opened his mouth, no doubt to offer some fulsome display of gratitude, but Lucie held a hand up to stop him before he started.

"But this isn't easy for me," she continued, "because a big part of me wants to see you rot. Not just because of what you did to my country, and not just because you used your position to pressure a hand job out of me, but because I know damn well I wasn't the first."

He looked away, blushing red like a schoolboy caught with a cigarette behind the bike sheds.

"Now I want you to remember something, Sir Geoffrey bloody Hartnell," she said, the anger in her voice surprising even her. "I'm not going to ask how many other people you've conned into the bedroom in your time, but what you did to me in there was nasty, contemptible and just plain wrong. If I had my way I'd never forgive you for it, just like I'd never forgive you for treating my country like an accessory in a dick measuring contest between you and Huxley. Believe me, there's little I'd like more than to see the real you getting the full front page treatment from every part of the press and your face plastered across TV screens for all the wrong reasons for a month."

She sniffed back tears as she spoke, wanting him to understand something, anything of the pain he had been responsible for in his career, and he did indeed sit before her chastened and embarrassed; the experience of hearing his failings spoken aloud by one he had wronged as humbling as Lucie had hoped. Almost.

"But luckily for you I decided a long time ago to do my best. And the truth is if your name gets dragged through the gutter then that's it for the progressives in Parliament and the people on the street. I'm not thrilled about it and believe me I wish there was someone else carrying the banner for us, but you're the best hope we have of sorting shit out and protecting people from the violent thuggery that bloody vote legitimised. Even if I struggle to think of you with anything other than contempt."

There was nothing Hartnell could say in defence of his actions and the redness of his cheeks betrayed his guilt, at least physically, and behind his eyes there was no trace of the lecherousness that had hallmarked their encounter in the hotel room. Instead, Lucie detected a reluctant acknowledgement that his political survival now lay in her hands, and she wondered how long he would be content to let things stay that way.

"Thank you," he finally croaked, humiliated, "and may I say how much I regret…"

"Stuff your apology," Lucie interjected, "you're only sorry because the balls are in my court now, and I know how to handle them; you should remember that."

She stepped a few paces closer to him, taking full advantage of the change in dynamic between them and taking a pinch of satisfaction from his sheepish expression.

"Now, if the PM is going to be toppled, the Right must think they've got the numbers to defeat you, how many people are we talking about?"

"No more than thirty MPs, but it isn't about how many people you have," Hartnell replied, clearly relieved for the conversation to be returning to professional matters, "it's about where they're placed. The Right may be numerically imbalanced in Parliament, but they hold key positions on all the relevant Select Committees and their mouth pieces sit on grand chairs in the Cabinet while their allies in the press hold the media in their palms."

"Can they really hold that much influence with just a handful of seats?"

"You'd be surprised, Lucie, they agitated for the referendum with fewer than they have now and look at the damage that has caused. This is the culmination of the game they've been playing for years, and if we don't stop them now then who knows how many more catastrophes they can ferment."

"But they have no credible candidate, it's either the PM or you…"

"They don't need to hold the Office," Hartnell interrupted, as animated as at any point since Lucie had met him, "only the person occupying it! Your premise is flawed, they've no interest in toppling the PM; they'll embrace her as she is completely under their control. They know they won't have that with me so around the PM they'll flock, until I'm discredited or worse, then there'll be no opposition to them!"

"Geoff, you're talking about a coup! There's no sign of anything like that!"

Hartnell slammed his hands on the table, his mood tripping over the edge and plummeting into anger.

BLOOD, WHITE AND BLUE

"Of course there isn't!" he bellowed the words at Lucie, his regret at the outburst immediately apparent on his typically genteel features.

"This is the twenty first century," he continued, his composure returned, "one doesn't march on Downing Street at the head of a rabble of skin heads and football hooligans if one wants to claim the country for the Right. One is subtle, moving behind the scenes, effecting change so efficiently that no-one understands there's been a coup until the bodies fall from the first shots fired into the crowd."

Still they remained apart, like warriors searching each other for weaknesses in their austerely beautiful arena, ready to slash and scourge with words for blades, the killing blow tempered only, Lucie thought, because of the inconvenient truth of their mutual opponent.

She had been a chaplain because she had wanted to be; she had chosen the role every bit as much as she had felt chosen for it, and she took what she had preached seriously. She could forgive Hartnell, but she would not forget, and neither would she trust him again, just as she was sure he did not trust her. They may be bound together by convenience, perhaps too necessity, but she was going to make damn sure he knew what he was doing and how to keep his grandeur and arrogance in check.

"Can influence alone really bring about the end of the country as we knew it?" Lucie quizzed softly but insistently, not necessarily through disbelief, but from a desire to understand his fears and motivations. He simply smiled back at her in that patronising manner she had come to recognise.

"Lucie, at a recent general election, the manifesto of the UK's governing party was substantially identical to that of the leading far right party ten years earlier. Opposition to the government is now so fractured that support is still neck and neck against one of the most unpopular governments since records began. The Brexit referendum changed everything, and believe me, influence is everything."

At last Hartnell moved from behind the desk and came to stand in front of Lucie, his features held sincerely and not in the plastic manner of so many politicians. He moved to take her hands in his, but she pulled them away and stared defiantly into his eyes, embarrassment returning to his face.

"Lucie," he began, "I have mistreated you and many before you, and whether you believe me or not, I am sorry. Yes, I may have done wrong by Huxley, but my choice was to betray him or the country and I chose him. And like it or not you said it yourself, I'm the only hope politically for you and people like you in the UK."

Lucie drew in the deepest of breaths as she acknowledged the truth of his words and shook her head at the situation she found herself in.

"You'd better be, Geoff," she exhaled quietly. "Because God help you if you're not."

THIRTY-ONE

It was the sight of the protestors, peacefully congregating by the Wilson statue in Parliament Square that exacerbated the guilt in Lucie's stomach that had clawed at her since she had left the Committee Room moments earlier.

Even as she had given Hartnell her word not to expose his deceits, choosing to accept for now that they had at least been well-intentioned, she had felt herself complicit in the activity, and the peculiar feeling within her gut that accompanied guilt by association was not one she could imagine ever sitting comfortably within her. Watching the peaceful protestors, now huddled together for the night with clearly no intention of moving on, and joined by stalwart representatives of the 48%, their EU and British flags waving proudly, did at least though begin to dilute the indirect iniquity she reproached herself for.

She was doing this for them, and all those like them up and down the country. The regular, ordinary people whose lives had been flipped around and spat on thanks to a marginal victory in a gerrymandered and deceitful referendum and branded as traitorous saboteurs when pointing out the dangers and woes the folly continued to be responsible for. Hardworking British people of all classes, origins and persuasions were and would continue to pay the price alongside their immigrant neighbours in the poisonous atmosphere that had fermented in Britain since the vote was called, and Hartnell was key to stopping that. If the PM was in hock to the hard right, or was even toppled, then the hatred would only intensify. Hartnell, for all his faults, was that rarity in the modern world: a competent politician, and one inclined to prevent, or at least dilute the travesties that were daily occurring in Brexit's name, and that, Lucie told herself, was reason enough to do what she was doing.

Hartnell's wandering hands though were a different matter, and one not so easy to ignore. While it was within Lucie's gift to forgive his treatment of her, she was not so empowered to speak for any others. Professor Hyde's file had contained scribbled references to occasional 'incidents' in the politician's career and away from the comforting reassurance of the bands of protestors and their camaraderie, she was not altogether sure this was a wrong she could overlook, no matter the urgency of doing so. She was a woman, a survivor of the most horrific of abuses and the thought that her inaction could one day lead to his taking advantage of another…

Nausea undulated through her body as her thoughts reached their logical conclusion and as she reached an unusually quiet Victoria Street, she stopped and leant into the gutter to retch her nausea, and her guilt away. Nothing would come, and Lucie leaned back against the tall, black railings, sucking deep breathes of cold, polluted night air into her lungs, acknowledging that it would not be that easy to rid herself of a feeling which threatened to tear her loyalties in two.

It was as she stood in tormented introspection that she saw them; two young men, neither no more than twenty, dressed in hoodies and jogging pants and walking uncomfortably close to a young woman, clearly distressed by their presence. The woman was speaking in agitated tones, pleading with the laughing yobs to leave her in peace; a Spanish inflection to her words which the pair seized upon as a further avenue for their mockery.

The trio were across the road, some distance from Lucie and it was as the young woman passed a narrow ginnel between buildings that they pounced, dragging her into the darkness and slamming her against the coarse brickwork of the building behind her, the sneering laughter turned instantly to callous abuse. No scream came from the alleyway and Lucie knew that a filthy hand would now be stretched across the young woman's mouth and the thought of how else they were preparing to violate her saw the nausea swiftly replaced in her gut with rage, a pure anger which grew with each passing second until it became an incandescence on a par with anything she had felt since she had crawled out from the Afghan cave, even surpassing her frenzy in the ship's kitchen. It reached from her heart to her mind, claiming her senses in righteous fury, leaving her unable, or perhaps unwilling, to think clearly and rationally; which only spelled more trouble for those with whom she was about to deal.

Within seconds she was across the road, her footsteps delicate, her breathing controlled, as she edged closer to the ginnel, close enough to hear the attackers' verbal ordure and the frustrated attempt of their victim to scream behind the hand clamped over her mouth.

"Shut your fucking mouth and open your fucking legs," Lucie heard one voice demand, "and if you're lucky you'll crawl out of here alive."

"She doesn't understand you, bruv," laughed the other, "she's a fucking Euro whore; don't speak the Queen's English this one."

"Is that right, *senorita*?" the first sneered again, "No speaky Ingles? I bet you fuckin' can when you're cashing your benefits can't you, you fuckin' dirty bitch? Comes out of my fuckin' taxes that does, don't it?"

"Yeah, mine too, fuckin' skiver."

"So, this is just a transaction, yeah? Me and him, we're just getting our money's worth, right? You're like our slot machine for the night...*Yow!*"

The first of the attackers, the talker, yelped in pain as Lucie cracked the discarded milk bottle she had picked up from the alley down hard upon his skull, sending both he and the broken glass to the floor.

"Sorry," Lucie spat with contempt, "the bank's closed."

The second of the two men pushed the frightened woman towards Lucie, who caught and turned her to the alley's entrance way and screamed at her to run, before turning back to the thug who slipped a flick knife from his pockets and slashed wildly in the air, panic and rage in his eyes, and slicing a laceration through the left sleeve of Lucie's black overcoat, more through luck than design. The cut though brought out his overconfidence and as he lunged again, Lucie grabbed his wrist, holding it and the offending blade safely beneath her armpit, and sent her other hand sailing down his neck until it chopped with force against his jugular, the aggression in his eyes at once replaced with dazed confusion. As he dropped the knife and held his neck, still lumbering towards her, Lucie sent her booted foot straight to his groin, her bad knee refusing to give way as though relishing the opportunity for revenge.

He dropped screaming to the damp and filth strewn ground, writhing in pain as his comrade, blood streaming down his face from the gash in his head, heaved himself to his feet and raised his fists towards her like a drunken boxer who refused to throw in the towel.

"Really?" breathed Lucie as his blows flew towards her, a thin

BLOOD, WHITE AND BLUE

cut opening on her cheek as she only just dodged a sovereign adorned knuckle. Parrying his next punch with her forearm, she raised her own fists, jabbing two lefts straight through the gap in his defence to his chin, following with an enormous right swing against his ear, sending him sprawling against the bottom of the urine-soaked brick wall.

Neither thug was moving but Lucie's rage was far from satiated, and she picked up the fallen flick knife from the floor and stood over the first of the animals beneath her, her grip tightening on the blade's handle as she watched him squirm. She moved closer, as though in a dream, seeing only the look of agonised fear her captor had worn the day she had fought for her freedom and a growing desire within her to see such a look on this would-be rapist's face proving impossible to simply ignore.

The fallen criminal stirred, looking up to the see the blade pointing ever more resolutely towards him and he wriggled in concussed terror, shaking his bleeding head, silently.

Lucie moved closer, and closer still, raising the blade as she struggled with her body's intent. She was a woman of God; her place was to forgive. But to forgive this creature…? Still she moved towards him until…

"Hey!"

The shout came from behind her and she turned to see the young woman she had rescued, running back up the alleyway, between two uniformed and equipped police officers, the first of whom raised her voice again towards Lucie.

"Hey you! Stand still!"

Her delirium broken, Lucie needed no further invitation to run and she set off at pace into the darkness of the alley towards its exit onto the adjacent street, the nausea she had first stopped to dispel, now once more and emphatically returned.

THIRTY-TWO

She ran until she felt her lungs would burn themselves free of her body and she leaned against one of the many plinths that decorated this part of the city, looking up and giving a mental two fingers to whichever wig adorned grim faced Dickensian nightmare stared condescendingly down at her.

The night was dark, punctuated by the flickering lights of a government at work across the myriad of ancient grey buildings and the neon of a thousand eateries, bars and coffee shops. Looking around her she saw she had sought refuge across the road from a small, but seemingly very lively church, housed in what once must have been an office tucked between some of the grander structures, and she laughed aloud at the irony before surrendering to the weeping that had threatened to overcome her since the cry of the police a few moments before.

She still held the knife in her hand and she looked at it with self-loathing growing inside her, tossing it into a nearby bin and yearning to be home. The neon light of the plastic cross above the church door illuminated her against the darkness as she fought to restore normality to her breathing after the adrenaline fuelled heaves of her flight from the police. Though her lungs were erratic, her thinking was as clear as it had been since she had first become involved in this murderous game, and while her contemplation with the blade troubled her, the real object of her thinking was Hartnell.

No. She would not allow Hartnell to escape his past so completely. His political choices might well have been hellishly difficult, he may even have been faced with an impossible choice the day he learned what Huxley was planning; and perhaps even today he tormented himself for the decision he was forced to make, but however justified he may have been, that didn't change what he was.

However charming he may be, whatever movement he personified, the only difference between his actions and those of the bastards she had just stopped was the quality of his wardrobe and the choice of his battleground. When it came to rape, charming words and whispered promises spoken in a luxury suite were every bit as effective a weapon as a knife to the neck in a darkened alleyway, and just as she had moments before, Lucie had the power to make the one who wielded the weapon pay.

Elevation to the premiership was within his grasp and she would allow him to reach it; the future of those people in the square and those like them all across the country depended on it. But he would not enjoy the trappings of his power. When the 'hostile environment' was replaced, when the damage of Brexit was tamed – or better still reversed – and when a programme of measures was in place to alleviate those issues which had led the poor and the abandoned to be swayed by the lies of the nationalists, then Hartnell's reign would end. She would see to that. She had information now, and resources. She could count on Algers and Della to track down some of the names in Professor Hyde's file, perhaps persuade some of them to come forward. This wasn't America, no prime minister could withstand a string of public sexual harassment claims and remain in power.

Lucie set off back toward Westminster, reasoning that Hartnell would still be in his Commons office. She would lay it out for him, she thought to herself as she went. He could have his place in the history books, he could have the public adulation he craved, but when Lucie told him it was time to go, go he would; that power was hers now. Blackmail some may consider it to be, but this was not for financial gain or malicious intent, it was the best way Lucie could see to twist the guts of a corrupted and hostile world into providing the best possible outcome. It may not be as attractive an arrangement as the Granita Deal, Lucie accepted, but it was one that would hopefully be more beneficial for the country and every class of its people. She paused for breath as she reached Parliament Square, praying for divine support as she delivered her ultimatum.

And it was as Parliament Square, packed as it was with protestors, friends and comrades of all nationalities and backgrounds came into view, bringing a wide smile back to Lucie's face, that the explosion echoed into the London night.

THIRTY-THREE

The eruption itself was joined in a fearsome chorus by the shrill tone of car and building alarms, shattering glass and the screams of the wounded and fleeing, rising heavenward together in a cacophony of chaos; wailing sirens and the commands of emergency personnel soon taking their place for a grim second movement.

It had been the epicentre of the protest itself that had surrendered to the explosion, ripping the very ground from under the gathered crowd as the direction of their objections changed in one hellish moment from the political injustice they had gathered to defy, to impotent objection to the randomness of death to which so many now succumbed and more sought to escape.

Only weeks earlier, the statue of Wilson had been unveiled, standing proudly upon its plinth, attracting the political homage of a myriad of well-suited and media savvy admirers on their way to and from Parliament. Its honeymoon could scarcely have been shorter, the former Prime Minister's likeness providing a focal point for those for whom the revelations and leaks of the past few days were abhorrent. And now it lay twisted and broken, much of it scattered across the green; so many of the shining bronze metal shards now dulled with concrete dust and mud, or resplendent with the blood of those it had so brutally slain. The likeness had blown forward leaving the gathered protestors no chance as it tore through their ranks with disdainful contempt, an action repeated by the wretched internet warriors and faux journalists who, though initially wrong-footed by the absence of any brown or black faces to blame, swiftly decreed that it was an element of the protestors themselves who had surely planted the device.

Wiser heads defied the suggestions, pointing to the illogicality of such a premise not to mention the lack of evidence, but by then the seed had been sown and was being gratefully harvested. Many an occupant of the usual political sewer were eagerly spicing it with their own particular blend and sending it out wider still for mass consumption.

Within hours, the merchants of grief, whose livelihoods depended on the misery of others, wheezed out their 'told you sos' into their cameras and jabbered their 'now will they listens' into their columns, without needing or desiring even the scantest of evidence to demand the harshest of penalties against any and all who happened to be there, blaming the dead and dying for their own lot and condemning the liberal elite who traitorously allowed this travesty to happen, by permitting so many of those workshy foreigners who gleefully stole British jobs to bring their unjust protestations so close to the cradle of parliamentary democracy itself. Make no mistake, they warned through laptops, tablets and smart phones, Britain was under attack, and the bombing was the proof, the finger pointing squarely and unashamedly now at the 'enemy within', the EU nationals who had proven so damn ungrateful for the lives Britain had graciously permitted them to lead.

That same narrative combined with the list of the dead containing so many names that could be described as 'wholly'

BLOOD, WHITE AND BLUE

British, spilled over into the displays of grief that came over the next couple of days. The candle lit vigils were less well tolerated, the silences less well observed and interrupted by mutterings of the dead having 'done it to themselves', so readily were lies of the snake oil sellers believed. The usual platitudes were paid of course, the Prime Minister's standard 'tribute' to the efforts of the emergency services so professionally delivered that the unfortunately timed announcement of the latest cuts to those same bodies went practically unreported by the bulk of the media, although the powers that be were by no means praised. The most powerful of the media groups vomiting daily headlines onto the people, containing tales of unsettled backbenchers, indecision at the heart of government and the perennial need for a 'strong leader' to emerge to rescue Britain in its moment of crisis – one who could unite the country, and who was respected, even admired on the world stage.

When so many typically hard right papers combined to suggest Sir Geoffrey Hartnell as that man, his public reaction of surprise was matched by many who refused to accept that the Party would stand for it. The Party though, seemed to feel otherwise. With only one or two of the more eccentric members voicing sometimes elaborate and profane objections, the bulk of the papers and the mainstream news channels carried all manner of quotes from 'colleagues' of prominent figures and 'sources close to' cabinet ministers nervous about their security of their seats, mostly opining that Hartnell would prove a strong leader who understood the need to unite behind the referendum result and deliver a deal for Britain. Hartnell for his part refused to comment in detail other than to repeat the line that he wouldn't stand against the PM and in any event could never dream to carry the support of his Party's right wing.

Lucie, still some distance from the explosion as it went off had been unharmed, physically at least, though her efforts that night in dragging people to safety and tending to the wounded had sent her mind to the familiar edge of a chasm of depression. And when the young man whom she had pulled from the blast zone had realised he was dying and begged for a priest, her compulsion to offer the last rites as he slipped away in her arms had thrown her violently from the precipice. Laying him gently to the grass, she had stood in a stupor, her eyes unblinking yet sightless as her body found its way on foot to her Camden flat where she remained, sitting cross-legged on a couch as frayed and weathered as were her emotions, as the political merry-go-round clicked into gear outside.

The plethora of phone calls and messages she had missed on the first day only served to hasten the battery's demise and grant Lucie the silence she so desperately craved, trapped by the emptiness of her depression and lacking yet the desire, let alone the ability, to begin clawing her way out of it. And so she had remained until she heard the sound of her front door banging open and the panicked thump of foot upon stair as whomever it was reached the door to the living room and stood there for a moment, heaving breath back into their lungs.

"And just what the fuck do you think you've been playing at?"

The hint of a smile began to ache at the corner of Lucie's mouth as she heard the words, though she didn't straight away move her head.

"Spies, Kasper," she croaked in a voice unused for days, "I've been playing at spies. And now I've stopped."

Algers sighed, the anger in his initial question giving way to an obvious care and concern that Lucie couldn't help but be touched by. He came and sat beside her on the sofa, perching on the edge and sighing again.

BLOOD, WHITE AND BLUE

"The game's not over yet, Lucie," he gently said.

"It is for me. God knows what I thought I was playing at, what any of us are playing at. Whatever happens, some poor innocent bastard dies. Sometimes I wish it was me, only I'm no innocent…"

"Don't go getting suicidal on me," Algers snapped.

"I'm not suicidal," Lucie assured him, calmly. "I just sometimes hate this world, hate what goes on in it, so much that I just don't want to be alive anymore."

Her words were not delivered in melancholy or with self-pity, but a simple matter of fact expression of her feelings. She could feel Alger's eyes on her, though she was not yet ready to meet them, but more still she could feel his understanding; that his lack of response was not an inability to find anything to say, but a realisation that there were no words he could offer to break her from the grip of the mood currently claiming her.

"There's no point in telling you that he'll come after you," Algers began, sadly. "Lake, I mean. I don't know what it is he has on you, but I know he has something on all of us, that's how he works. If you give up before the job's finished he'll cash in your chip."

"No," Lucie answered. "There's no point in telling me."

"And what about your mum?"

This time his words were met with a tear, not even blinked back but allowed to trickle freely down her cheek.

"Knowing what happened to her won't bring her back. Just like the boy I held in my arms the other night won't come back if I finish Lake's job, and nor will any of the others. I might end up in a prison cell but at least I won't have killed anyone else. I'm sorry, Kasper, this just isn't for me."

Algers took in her words and nodded quietly. He placed one of his large, bony hands on hers and patted it with affection, then stood and headed back towards the living room door.

"What will you do now?" Lucie shouted as he went.

"I'll have to stick close to Hartnell for now, at least until he gets the top job," Algers answered, pausing at the door.

"Top job?"

"Aye, after the bomb the PM's position is even more unstable and the word is a change is brewing. The papers have all come out and proclaimed Hartnell as the Chosen One."

"What, all the papers?" Lucie quizzed, a tiny spark of curiosity awakening in her.

"Yeah, it's bizarre," Algers elaborated, "even the right wing papers have swung behind him, seeing him as a 'Strong Man' who can unite the country and lead it through its…"

"… Time of Crisis," Lucie echoed, finally turning around and looking Algers straight in the eye. "Kasper," she said, "wait here while I take a shower; there's someone I need to see."

BLOOD, WHITE AND BLUE

THIRTY-FOUR

Though he didn't move from his position in the grand, red leather armchair, Lord Hurndall painfully strained himself upright within it so as better to look down his nose at the newcomer, or at least that was Lucie's interpretation of his body language, and it was certainly one she could be forgiven for.

It had been Algers' reference to the improbable en masse manoeuvre of such great chunks of the press behind Hartnell that had given her the impetus to pull herself back to sufficient stability not only to follow the lead, but crucially, to want to. As Algers filled her in on the detail of the days she'd been out of action, that desire had only grown, leading her to the door of the ancient Lord Hurndall's Westminster apartment, her renewed vigour tempered only by the news that Della was herself still racked in a despair of her own. Lucie resolved to do what she could to help her from it, and her nervous wondering of what else that may lead to, was an additional shot in the arm. For now though, such pleasant distractions would have to wait as she finally set her eyes on the twisted figure before her.

The Peer's face was rigidly defined, his once strong jaw line framing features which though strong were devoid utterly of warmth or charisma. Instead his eyes flashed at once with the demand for respect and a resentment of anyone in sight who didn't offer it. What remained of his hair was pure white and militarily clipped, guarding the sides of his head as though at attention, while his bald pate reflected sharply the light from the lamp above his desk.

His jacket was tweed, as were his trousers and waistcoat, while his collar and tie, despite his intended solitude, were buttoned and knotted impeccably. This was clearly a man for whom pleasantries were an unnecessary distraction and audiences a rare occurrence. The demanding eyes at once scanned Lucie as she entered the room, ignoring the hand she stretched out in greeting and fixing her with a stare which bordered on contemptuous.

"You're not the usual girl," he sniffed, "they told me the usual girl wished to see me. Go out, madam, at once, you've no business here."

"Maybe there's more than one girl," Lucie responded unperturbed, standing in front of the elderly man and keeping her hand outstretched.

Her display of considered defiance seemed to intrigue him and with a perhaps over-emphasised caution, he reached up an ancient hand to accept hers, though the mistrust did not leave his face.

"Is there, by jove?"

"So it would seem."

"I see. And whom, may I ask, holds the dubious honour of being the other woman in this case?"

"Lucie," she answered, "Lucie Musilova."

The speed which had been absent in taking her hand was very much present as he released it upon hearing her name, and the eyes that had scanned her upon her entry to the room now sat beneath a brow frowning in unabashed disapproval.

"Musi-what? Musi-what?" Hurndall stuttered. "What kind of a name is that?"

"It's Czech," she replied calmly, not rising to his display of unguarded prejudice.

"But you sound English?"

"Well half of me does, I'm Czech on my mum's side."

"Czech?" the old man's voice was rising with each syllable, "Czech?"

"Yes, Czech," a mixture of sarcasm and annoyance began to invade Lucie's own voice in response. "You know? The place with all the beer, goulash and Brits feeling up strippers?"

"I know about the Czechs!" Hurndall snapped in irritation at her, "I spent enough bloody time in their company after all. Oh no, this won't do, this won't do at all…"

"Your Lordship," Lucie interrupted the beginnings of what was surely to become a rant, "with all due respect, if you can't say anything nice, then shut the fuck up."

Hurndall's mouth hung wordlessly open at the impertinence, the elderly officer cowed into silence by the steel in Lucie's voice and the ferocity of her stare. Harrumphing his voice back into his throat, he pulled himself up in his chair and spoke in an equally cold, but altogether less aggressive voice.

"What do you want here?" he asked. "What do you want of me?"

"I just want to talk," Lucie answered with measured calm. "And believe me I don't want to be here in this mausoleum a second longer than I need to be."

A mausoleum it certainly was, with the decrepit Hurndall sat at its dusty, loveless heart, like an ancient spider whose web caught only the grime of ages past. The room was large but devoid of life, the oak bookcases which clung to the wall as dirty and forgotten as the tomes they bore, while faded paintings and metallic trinkets which may once have held some emotional value, now sat hanging or lying, tarnished and uncontemplated on hooks and shelves nailed to walls designed to push the modern world far away.

"You're the one I was told to expect," Hurndall slowly discerned. "Yes… you're the mongrel."

The barb was designed to hurt, as was the casual nature of its delivery, but Lucie resolved to ignore it for now and keep control of the conversation.

"I've come to tell you a story," Lucie said, sitting herself down uninvited in the second of the red leather armchairs. "A story about a man who tried to bring down a kingdom, and then fifty years later tried again."

Hurndall's creased and wrinkled features turned downwards and his greying eyes narrowed.

"I've heard of that story," he replied. "I'd hazard that you would dislike how it ends."

His stare was unbroken. She had his attention now and she fully intended to use it, as she rested her elbows on the arms of the grand chair and clasped her hands beneath her chin.

"Oh, I don't know," she teased, a hint of malice in her voice. "You see in my story the ending is still up in the air."

"Then pray, continue."

The malice was echoed in the peer's creaking words and she smiled, drawing strength from and relishing the hostility of this particular environment.

"It seems there were three men," Lucie began, "in Prague in the sixties. One of these was a very important person, not least in his own mind, and was very unhappy with the PM in charge back in London and wanted to get rid of him, but nobody else wanted to help. And so, our very important person made a plan."

She paused to gauge Hurndall's response, but the cruel face was largely unreadable, save for the slightest of sneers curling its way onto the thin flap of skin that was his top lip.

"He asked one of the other men in Prague to send a nasty letter to some horrible men in Russia, making it seem as though the PM in London wanted to be their friend. If a letter like that got into the newspapers, then the PM would have to leave, wouldn't you say?"

Hurndall's sneer grew wider and he raised his chin to emphasise it.

"But the plan didn't work," she continued. "The third man found out about it and sent a different letter instead, meaning his friend was forced to run away and the very important man didn't get the change he wanted. And that made him bitter and twisted, and ultimately..." she paused before delivering the final word, allowing herself the momentary indulgence of cruelty, "... impotent."

A gurgling sound emanated from the husk-like man opposite her, as he drew an angered breath over tar filled lungs.

"You think you're so bloody clever, don't you?" the octogenarian barked in sudden retaliation. "All you treacherous creatures who call yourselves British when God alone knows what mixture of races you are..."

"I'm a mixture of God knows what, am I?" Lucie didn't rise to the bait as he had, but rather hoped he would continue until he filled in the blanks in her mind.

"Oh, of course you are," he sniffed, a malicious chuckle in his throat. "My girl, you are the very embodiment of the kind of mixture I despise; a soiled, if admittedly attractive, mongrel."

"My heritage amuses you?"

"No, your blindness does. You're like all the others, strutting around, flaunting your shame and calling it 'progressive'; declaring your love of all freedoms except the right of your opponents to voice their opinion. You haven't silenced anyone, all you've done is driven the voice underground. It's still there, it still speaks to people, but now it's the voice that whispers to people behind curtains, around the table in the pub or the terraces in stadia, and into the ears of the people in the voting booths. It's the voice that tells them they are hated, that their fears are justified and themselves loathed for expressing them. And the more that the other side clings to their 'safe spaces', the more they disrupt the speeches of those that promote our cause, the louder that voice becomes."

"Is that what you told yourself when you tried to topple Wilson?"

Hurndall shifted in his chair, the hate behind his eyes emphatic. If he felt any shame for his role in the aborted plots of yester-year then it failed to show on his unkind and brutish features.

"Patience is a virtue, young lady," he replied, almost cackling. "The takeover was merely delayed, not prevented; and thanks to you and your ilk's condemnation of the Right we have managed to persuade the moronic turkeys who scuttle to and from their pathetic workplaces in their squalid little lives, to vote for Christmas! Lambs literally voting for the slaughter! And they can't blame anyone but themselves for each job lost, each family broken, each family ruined, because as they keep saying, they 'knew what they voted for.'"

His cackle gave way to a full and heavy laugh, wheezing its way from his lungs; his callous disregard for the effect of his ideology on people's lives enough to tempt her down to his own level.

"Brexit won't last forever," Lucie retorted, giving in to her urge to call the bigoted old fool out on his nastiness. "People like you are a dying breed. Sooner or later the younger generation, the ones whose futures your precious Brexit has stolen away will come of age, and they'll demand their country back; the Britain

BLOOD, WHITE AND BLUE

proud to be part of a union of nations, facing the world and its problems together. The Britain comfortable enough with its own identity that it doesn't care what colour its next-door neighbour is and doesn't spend its days twitching at curtains in case the new couple down the street have more than one penis between them. And people like you can either join in, be welcomed and valued for your own individuality and how it helps the rest of us grow together, or you can sit in mausoleums like this, pining for your 'golden age' that never was while the rest of the world grows up."

She stood up, breathing the temper that had overcome her back into control and she turned her back to him, looking up at a wall mounted Union Flag, tattered and dirtied behind its glass veneer, its colours once proud, fresh and new, now weak and tired, like a faded memory. A brass plate was affixed to the bottom of the wooden frame encasing it, inscribed on which was one word: Amritsar.

"And you can gather dust," she continued quietly, "on your way to the grave…"

Lucie stopped her rant, a part of her regretting her outburst even while she was making it. Hurndall, meanwhile, merely sat in his great leather chair, his grey eyes never leaving her.

"What do you think of the flag?" The peer suddenly demanded.

Turning back to him, she looked straight at Hurndall, not disclosing her knowledge of the infamous massacre from which it had been preserved.

"It's seen better days," she finally replied.

Hurndall simply nodded in as sagely a manner as he could muster.

"It has, young woman, it most certainly has. Alas, the flag isn't today what once it was… It's the colours, you see?"

"The colours?"

"I wouldn't expect you to understand but getting the colours right in a flag is a tricky thing."

"Is it really?"

"Oh, absolutely. You see, a lot of people today, you youngsters particularly, think all you need to do to make a flag vibrant and resplendent, is to add more colour to it."

The ancient frame heaved itself from its chair and crossed to the glass case, Lucie keeping him at a cautious distance as he gazed at the torn cloth within.

"In my view we've had too many damn colours thinking they could make our flag brighter, thinking they could ride it to their own personal glories, sully it with their shameful practices… In they poured from India, Africa, all over the Empire, thinking we owed them something, thinking all they had to do was squeeze out a few babies and we'd fall over ourselves to feed them and clothe them and call them British. Well not I, Madam, not I."

Hurndall looked away from the case and straight at Lucie, who though unintimidated was certainly less comfortable than she'd felt a moment ago.

"And they never stopped coming," the elderly voice continued, "and soon the likes of you were joining them: thieving gypsies and greedy Slavs crawling out of your Communist sewers and claiming right of abode here! In my homeland!"

The ancient chin jutted outwards in indignation, the sincerity of his feelings not in doubt, even though their taste was.

"Too. Many. Colours." He punctuated the words as sternly as he was able, his eyes piercing Lucie's very flesh in accusation. "And all that happens to the flag when you add too many colours, is that it fades, it weakens, until it's just another tattered rag, fluttering about somewhere alongside twenty-seven others, without influence, without *pride*."

BLOOD, WHITE AND BLUE

Lucie swallowed the contempt she felt for the opinions of the man before her and while a thousand counter-arguments queued impatiently in her head, demanding release, she turned away, back to the door, unwilling to waste energy on a closed mind. Instead, she simply shook her head sadly and reached for the knob.

"Nothing to say, have you?"

The words came carried on a malicious cackle, Hurndall's tone expressing a desire that she acknowledge her wounded sensibilities to him.

"I've better things to do than waste breath on a lost cause," she replied over her shoulder, disdainfully. "But I will tell you one thing."

"Oh?"

"Yes. I'll tell you how the story ends; and I'm afraid it'll be you who doesn't like it. And that's because you lose."

The sneer returned to the ancient visage as he questioned her certainty.

"Do I?"

"Yes, you and everyone like you. Everyone to have spent years crippling the poorest in society and exploiting them to create the environment for your Brexit to flourish. But just as I know what you got up to in the sixties, using Huxley to try to bring down the government, I know it was Hartnell who foiled you, and now he's about to foil you again."

The sneer gave way to puzzlement and a palpable worry impossible to disguise.

"Foil me?" the aged Lord repeated. "What do you mean, foil me?"

"He's taking over, Your Lordship," Lucie smiled. "The rug's being pulled from under the PM and Hartnell is taking over Number Ten. And for all his faults, and believe me I know there are many, he'll put this nasty, cruel, fascistic little Brexit of yours back in its box, and eventually, with time and effort, it'll start to feel like the real Britain again. And with any luck, you'll live to see the day when everything you've worked for crumbles away into dust… before you join it."

Lucie turned triumphantly on her heel only to be stopped in her tracks by a reprise of the sickening, gurgling cackle drawn from the aged throat, the malevolent confidence it contained sufficient for her to turn back, her eyebrow raised quizzically.

The old man laughed maliciously at her, clearly relishing his apparent moment of advantage.

"You still haven't worked it out have you?" he cackled, "That's the trouble with all of you damn mongrels; you might be good for a fumble, but you only have half a worthwhile brain to devote to thinking."

"I can assure you, Your Lordship, I've thought through every detail…"

"Except the most obvious," he crowed. "Hasn't it occurred to you yet that your precious Sir Geoffrey is doing exactly what we want him to do?"

Lucie frowned, stepping back from the door and towards her tormentor.

"Meaning what, exactly?"

"Hartnell isn't some progressive hero of liberal Britain," Hurndall's laugh eased, giving way to a tone of cold and deliberate cruelty. "Like all politicians, he's simply a puppet. My puppet."

THIRTY-FIVE

Lucie stood frozen to the spot as the wizened figure before her continued its gloating, only too eager to articulate to the young woman before him what a bloody fool she'd been, Lucie even prompting and prodding him for detail.

"So, it was you, with your connections and your influence who swung so much of the right wing press behind Geoff. Just like you tried turning them against Wilson in '68."

"Child's play, young woman," he smugly confirmed. "With so much of the media concentrated in so few pairs of hands it's easier than it's ever been to twist opinion in the direction you want it to go."

Lucie nodded in understanding.

"And then, let me guess, once he's taken over, you stage another little accident, like the bomb in Parliament Square? Hartnell is killed, giving the Right the excuse to declare a State of Emergency and impose Martial Law, while simultaneously getting rid of their most influential opponent."

Hurndall's mirth had all gone, leaving only malice behind. He creaked back to his voluminous leather chair and settled himself into it, eyeing Lucie with undisguised contempt.

"So near and yet so far," he dispassionately intoned. "The redoubtable Sir Geoffrey will indeed fall, and as violently as possible, but not before he himself has declared the very State of Emergency you fear."

"What?" Lucie frowned in incredulity.

"You poor, pathetic mongrel," Hurndall shook his head in faux pity. "Somebody really ought to have put you down. Hartnell is one of us, he was always one of us. You and your ilk are about to place him in Number Ten, where he will continue and intensify the campaign against you and bring the Europeans to their knees. One would almost feel sorry for you if you weren't so gullible."

Lucie felt a sickness rising in her stomach and she gripped the shelf beside her for support as she battled the weakness threatening to claim her.

"Bullshit," she finally whispered.

"Language, young woman."

"Bullshit!"

She screamed the word at Hurndall with every ounce of fire and passion she could muster, unsure if even it was warranted but determined not to show this monster any sign of frailty.

"If Hartnell was one of you then why would you want to kill him?"

"Because he betrayed us," came the simple response. "In 1968 he and Huxley were my lieutenants, we planned the Wilson cipher together and the plan would have worked if Hartnell hadn't lost his stomach with the embellishments…"

"Embellishments?" Lucie frowned, "what embellishments?"

"His torture of course!" The deep scowl returned to the ancient face as though marvelling at Lucie's stupidity.

Lucie stepped forward, struggling to comprehend what she had heard.

BLOOD, WHITE AND BLUE

"His torture?" she softly asked. "You arranged it?"

"The torture was necessary," the aged Lord defensively proclaimed, "Alexander understood that; the suffering was crucial if the public were going to buy into the story. He would leak the cipher and Hartnell was to be our poster boy; a living example of the evils of Communism and an ideology our own government sought to support. He was to be the trigger! The press was prepared, the cipher was ready, the government was poised to fall…"

"But nobody had told Hartnell that his capture had been part of the plan." Lucie's voice was coated in disgust at the old man's actions; his and Huxley's, which dawned unforgettably on her as the withered jaw creaked out its potted history.

"You arranged the capture, the torture of a young man you claimed to be one of your own, and why? So you could parade him to your treacherous friends in the press and hand the blame to Wilson?"

"It was necessary!" Hurndall objected, clearly angered at the questioning of his motives by one such as she. "Alexander understood that!"

"But Alexander wasn't the one to be tortured."

"I needed to protect Alexander," the age-old memories and justifications came shuffling through the elderly lips. "He was the crucial one; the one I could hand the government over to after the coup."

"And Hartnell?"

"He was a side show, a tool to bring about the takeover. Alexander took some persuading as to that fact, but he finally understood, it was only a dalliance after all…"

Lucie laughed out loud as the pieces began to connect in her mind: Hartnell's veiled references to their closeness, the venue where he'd been captured which catered for gentlemen of 'discerning' tastes, and now the revelation of what Hurndall called a dalliance…

"A dalliance? Hartnell and Huxley were lovers, weren't they? No, more than that, they were in love!" Lucie's laugh defied the anger growing inside her and the contempt for the elderly man's unrepented actions. "They were partners and you made Huxley betray him, you evil old sod!"

"Love?" He huffed in a combination of unbelief and distaste, "Oh, dear me, no. Not on Alexander's part. An infatuation at best, that's all."

"And so, you persuaded Huxley to lead the man who loved him to torture at the hands of the Communists, just so you could have, what? Some extra window dressing for your coup?"

"It was necessary!"

Lucie pulled herself away from in front of him before the temptation to unleash her fury grew too strong. Instead, she kept her back to him, trying to block the image of his wizened, ruthless features as she assimilated all he had told her.

"And so Hartnell found out that his love had betrayed him on your orders. Maybe Huxley couldn't handle the guilt and confessed all? Maybe Hartnell just figured it all out? But whatever happened he got his revenge on you both. He set up Huxley to be damned as the man who killed the Prague Spring and condemned him to life as a Communist defector, while blowing your chance to topple the government."

The silence that greeted her words convinced her of their veracity and she turned back round to see the soulless old man, still sat in his chair, his forearm resting on its arm, only now with a metallic black, long barrelled Webley held tightly in his hand.

The weapon did not intimidate her, she had stared down worse in her time, and she chose her words intentionally to show him her lack of fear.

"It must burn to see Hartnell on the steps of glory when it was Huxley you wanted to see there…"

"It's of no importance. What matters is the project can move forward at last, that I'm still alive to see it and that the last thing Hartnell understands is who was behind his rise to power and who put it to an end."

"He doesn't know you're involved?"

"Of course not," Hurndall huffed. "He thinks he's done it all himself, as if he were ever that competent. He thinks he's fooled all of you, he boasts of it every day and night to my spy in his camp."

"Your spy?"

"Oh yes," the wicked grin returned. "But now, I'm tired of entertaining a foreigner in my home; I believe it's time for you to say whatever prayers you think will save you."

Lucie's eyes flicked around, looking for something, anything to save her from the rising gun.

"It'll take a lot of explaining if you shoot me in here," Lucie said, desperately trying to bide time.

"Not at all," the Peer grinned. "A Czech protestor forcing her way into the home of a prominent elderly Brexiteer, making threats to kill? With any luck, your death may even result in one or two others of your kind feeling the wrath of my countrymen."

His nauseating, gurgling laugh returned and Lucie gave a grim smile in return.

"Yeah?" she answered with venom in her voice. "Well they're my countrymen too."

She turned in an instant, lifting the framed and faded flag, frame and all, from the wall in one swift movement and threw it at the aged Hurndall, who in shock, shot at the object hurtling towards him and screaming in pain and rage as it shattered into a million shards around him, while Lucie was through the door, vaulting the inner steps to the building and skidding through the door. She cursed herself loudly as she ran into the early evening half-light for her gullibility and her own willingness to believe that Hartnell was the man to save the nation. And as the sun began to set over Westminster and the country, the damning sensation that by coming to Hartnell's aid in Prague, she had saved the man who would kill the Britain she knew for good.

THIRTY-SIX

Lucie pushed her way onto the Commons Bar terrace, earning the disdainful glances and impassioned tuts of several Members, before spotting Algers and rushing over to him.

"Run," she hissed, taking his arm and leading him back through the disapproving politicians and towards the street, overriding the objections he raised on behalf of his knees and filling him swiftly in on her evening chat with the cackling Lord Hurndall.

Across the Thames, dusk was settling upon the city and the first of the bright lights began to flicker on to the sound of beeping horns and revving engines from the rush hour traffic, and for a moment, Lucie allowed herself to drink in the intoxicating sight, before turning her back to it and looking instead in earnest into Algers' eyes as they settled into an erratic jog.

Hartnell was hosting an impromptu drinks reception that evening and had hired the function room at the nearby Florence Nightingale Museum on Lambeth Palace Road just for the occasion, Algers explained to her somewhat breathlessly as they jogged. And in political circles, impromptu drink receptions were as loaded a gun as could be imagined, not least because of the inclusion of select members of the press, for purely social reasons of course...

The rush of heavy traffic and the tortuous delay in the changing lights gave the pair pause to refill their burning lungs, Algers questioning whether Lucie was sure about her theory.

"Look," she answered in earnest, "the Hard Brexiteers in the Party barely reach thirty, they wouldn't even be able to trigger a challenge by themselves and their candidates would never secure sufficient support to take the top job. Instead they need a figure that the centre and left will rush to crown but who will turn on them the moment he takes office and steers the country to an extreme and absolute Brexit. Somebody like...?"

"Hartnell?"

"Hartnell!"

"But that's insane! Hartnell's about the only government figure we still have who carries any kind of respect past Dover; he's pushed for greater integration his whole career!"

"It was a long game!"

Lucie shouted the words at Algers, in exasperation, the MP shaking his head in incredulity, as she gripped his hand and set off again with him across the road, pushing their way through pedestrians in as polite a manner as they could as she continued.

"Project Triple H, remember? Hurndall might have betrayed the coup in '68, but what if he's been biding his time to take over bloodlessly, not through a military revolution but through a coronation?"

They reached the other side of the road and the older Algers raised his hand in insistence of a breather, his age not conducive to debating politics while running through traffic.

"Fifty years is more than just biding time, Lucie," he wheezed, "and you have no idea how many people have been waiting for Hartnell to throw his hat in the ring; there's talk of defections

BLOOD, WHITE AND BLUE

from other parties to support his candidacy; shit, they even had the balls to approach me!"

Lucie frowned.

"And what did you say?"

"I told them to fuck off. But there are plenty who haven't and all they're waiting for is his word; they're not going to abandon him just because we've pulled a conspiracy out of our arses and run in there waving it around."

"The word they're waiting for is what he's about to give. And the second he takes power he'll bring us crashing out of Europe without a deal, revoke the rights of EU Nationals living here and invoke martial law and suspension of elections to contain the fall out."

She spoke the words desperately, imploring him to believe her, the sad eyes beneath the firesome brows squinting at her as he processed what she'd told him, and for the longest second the fear that he would dismiss her theory teased and tormented her, until eventually he spoke.

"Then we haven't got much time," he said, a soft smile forming on his wrinkled face. "Come on, run."

THIRTY-SEVEN

The museum was housed within the concrete and glass monolith that was St. Thomas's Hospital, and the pair slowed to a walking pace as they approached it, slipping as casually as possible into the stream of lounge suit and cocktail dress wearing attendees milling around the entrance way. Feeling suddenly out of place, Lucie wrapped her trusty overcoat around her and hoped her more casual dress wouldn't attract attention.

"If we get through this, remind me to invest in a bit more evening wear for the next job."

Algers smiled down at her with a look of pleasant surprise and she realised that whether light hearted or not, her comment was the first indication she had given that she may not after all disappear straight into the sunset after the mission.

"I should think so too," her comrade replied, "I'm not paying for the next lot."

Finally making their way inside and collecting the obligatory glass of champagne, Lucie looked around the theatre Hartnell had chosen in which to give his performance. The walls of the function room were clinically white, almost all indications of its devotion to the heroine of Crimea removed, save for a portrait hanging reverentially alongside pictures of Disraeli, Butler and other of Hartnell's publicly professed political heroes specifically chosen for the evening. There was no lectern upon which to lean and nothing in the room to demonstrate an announcement was due, just a plethora of tables laden with expensive canapés and a team of white aproned, waiting staff gliding between guests, silently encouraging the consumption of the champagne which they so gracefully bore. This, after all, was play, not work.

"So how do we do this? Lucie asked of Algers, the room's ambient buzz sufficient to mask their conversation. "If I can get him alone I can talk to him and try to…"

"There's no talking anymore, Lucie," Algers interrupted her, his voice suddenly cold and ruthlessly professional, the change in his demeanour unsettling her and she looked around to see his face as solemn as the grave.

"If what you say is true then Hartnell's spent fifty years planning the perfect takeover; he's not going to be dissuaded by a friendly chat over a Scotch egg and a glass of bubbly."

"Then how are we going to…?"

"You know."

Lucie went cold. She did know. She had known Hartnell just a few days and in that time her feelings towards him had roared from admiration, to mild attraction, to resentment, and even hatred, but through them all had been an undercurrent of sympathy. Whatever this man may represent and however deeply she wished she didn't, she felt for him, and now Algers was telling her that there was only now one way left to prevent the rise to power he had planned for so long.

"Do you want me to do it?" Algers quizzed, sympathetic understanding in his voice.

"No."

"Are you sure? I can…"

"I said no. I'll do it; it should be me."

Algers inhaled and looked around, the eyes beneath the grand brow scanning the room for possibilities.

"Ok; the room's probably as full as it's going to get. When Hartnell starts talking, as surreptitiously as I can I'll set the fire alarm off. Everyone will head to the fire exit over there. Make sure you're close to Hartnell when it goes off and when you're in the scrum, give him two shots to the abdomen then dump it and blend in as best you can. Try to scream."

"Two shots from what?" she asked, in as cold a manner as he.

"My gun," he hissed in response. "I'll leave it under the basin in the first cubicle of the gents', it's silenced already. You go in after me and retrieve it then spot Hartnell and stay close to him."

"And how do I explain what I'm doing in the gents'?"

"Just say there's a queue for the ladies."

"There usually is."

"Yeah but that's made up for with the flowers and the scented handwash. Now stay alert, I'll be back in…"

The sharp clink of metal on crystal interrupted them as the self-important conversations and intoxicated chatter died down and all eyes turned towards the far end of the room where the Man Who Would be King emerged from the clutches of a group of admirers to accept the wider adulation of the gathered crowd.

All eyes turned to him and he was if anything, Lucie thought, even more imposing than usual, as though provoking awe were the simplest of pastimes for him. His silver hair was impeccably swept back, his pink shirt and dark blue suit and tie presenting a knowingly Prime Ministerial image of authoritative modernity.

"Thank you all for coming," he smiled in gratitude for the quiet, his eyes expertly scanning the crowd. If he had seen Lucie, his features betrayed no moment of recognition, "and I'm sorry to distract you from enjoying your evening."

The doors behind them were closed, cutting off Algers' route and he cursed to himself, Lucie sharing his frustration as Hartnell began his oratory.

"This evening," he began from his vantage point at the end of the room, his frame emphasised by the brilliant white of the tall and wide wall behind him, "was intended to simply be a gathering of friends; a meeting place for those of us across several Parties, dismayed at the direction the country we all love is taking. But I fear, I must provide a deeper significance now."

Murmurs of approval played over the grumbling of wing filled bellies while Lucie could see Algers' fingers twitching, his hand reaching for his inner pocket and dropping back again and her own trepidation brewing.

"We stand here this evening in a museum to the memory of Florence Nightingale, who in 1854, despairing for the plight of the wounded, travelled to Crimea to do what she could to help." He scanned the room, meeting the eyes of each person in turn to be sure they understood his comparison.

"My friends, our people are as wounded today as they were then. Not by war and weaponry in some far away land, but here. Our countrymen and women have turned on each other, while people, as evidenced by events this week only yards from here, are under a very real attack. From the Prime Minister and the Cabinet however, there is nothing, no trace of leadership, no answers and no plan to unite this country and see it move forward with pride once again. And that is why, tonight…"

The sentence hung unfinished in the air as its speaker was distracted by the instant sound of nauseated shock and sickened profanities and the sudden cutting off of all lights in the room.

Hartnell squinted at his audience and realised at once that none were looking at him, rather the horrified expressions he could make out were worn in response to something directly behind him. Both frustrated by the robbing of his moment and curious as to what was responsible, Hartnell turned to face the wall, his stomach yearning to retch and his mind turning to jelly in less than an instant.

There before him, projected from the tiny camera projection box in the centre of the ceiling, was the horrifying image of Alexander Huxley's fetid corpse.

Hartnell's mouth hung open in mute objection as further images were spliced and overlaid atop that of the grim cadaver; the first a copy of the now infamous death threat allegedly penned by the skeletal remains – a prospect now proven to the room to be ridiculous. The pictures and patters appeared and disappeared faster and faster to the palpable disquiet of the other guests and the utter horror of Hartnell, who simply stared, wide-eyed at the spinning display of Huxley's proxy revenge.

The room was beginning to panic, realisation now inescapable that this was not some kind of joke. Hartnell was deeply troubled by the images which continued to spin, accompanied by the deafening screech of a poorly played violin, the volume high and uncomfortable. One word was super-imposed across the picture: Murderer.

As cries rang out for the doors to be opened, the mortified Hartnell, sweat broken out on his forehead and the flesh of his cheeks as pink as the collar beneath them, turned back to attempt reassurance, only to freeze again as though trapped in a hellish nightmare. Standing in horrified confusion, his weak arm pointed unsteadily towards the door. Lucie followed the arm to see a figure, almost heroic in appearance, standing in the entranceway as if making some grand entrance in a low budget feature, pausing just long enough to catch the stuttering old man's attention before turning on its tail and fleeing.

People had begun to funnel through the doors, but Hartnell, looking to all the world as though his own were crashing down, roughly pushed past those headed outside, squeezing through and heading off in pursuit of the terror from his past.

Lucie too made an inroad for the door, Algers shouting her back to himself. The confusion had everybody's attention focussed on either the still rolling video or the manner of Hartnell's exit.

"Lucie!"

She paused at Algers' exclamation and he reached out, pulling her close to him by her arm as he slipped his hand inside his inner pocket.

"Take this and for God's sake, be careful."

He pressed the gun into her palm, the view shielded by the jostling people and the horrors of the screen.

"Thank you," she whispered, before forcing herself through the door and scanning the streets for any sign of Hartnell, finally spotting his silver mane flowing as he crossed, several meters ahead of her and heading back towards Parliament. Heaving herself a full chest of air, she looked down at the weapon in her hand and slipped it into her pocket, setting off at pace in pursuit, knowing that she wasn't simply chasing Hartnell to apprehend him, but to be his executioner.

THIRTY-EIGHT

"Majestic, isn't it?"

And it was. Lucie gasped for breath as she bounded the last few stone steps and through the tall, narrow entrance to the Public Gallery in exhausting pursuit of her quarry. And there he stood, barely a few feet away from her, leaning on the banister above the Speaker's Chair. Beneath them the Commons was dark, save for sparse lighting which afforded miserly glimpses of the smooth, green leather benches either side of the long table upon which rested the Statute Books; an imposing altar to Parliamentary Democracy.

"That shouldn't be the word of course," Hartnell continued. "Everything about the place should symbolise the People's Mastery of their own futures, but sometimes there are few words which suffice, and fewer people deserving of the freedom to rule their own affairs."

Lucie stepped closer, half expecting him to run again, but he stood still and resolute, gazing down at the seat he had come so close to occupying.

"Have you ever thought how easily someone could do just that? Master the future?" He voiced the question without turning to look at her, then continued as though working through a conundrum in his mind.

"Any disenfranchised nobody could walk into public gallery with a bag of something, anthrax or whatever, dump it over the side and change the world… a shake to the right to take out the Cabinet, a shake to the left and their shadows are gone. All it really takes to bring about a constitutional crisis in Britain is a willingness to kill and be killed in the act."

Hartnell turned around finally. The sweat from his exertion glistened in the low light and his eyes stared at Lucie without malice or aggression but with the unsettling intensity of a mad man.

"We over complicate things, you know?" He opined. "Most of my life I've spent plotting and planning and inching oh, so cautiously towards the Despatch Box, and for what? Nought, it seems."

"You could have gone there without the plots," Lucie offered, giving in for a moment to the part of her soul which still held sympathy. "I know you betrayed Hurndall's coup in '68 when you found out he and Huxley were behind your torture. Why didn't you take that as your fresh start?"

He looked at her with the eyes of a broken mind.

"Just because one dislikes the chef doesn't mean one doesn't enjoy the recipe. Hurndall may have been a bastard, his methods sloppy and unnecessarily militaristic, but the principles were right."

"And Huxley?"

The mad eyes dropped for a moment, a tear of regret beginning to form.

"I only told you half the truth," he said, Lucie looking back at him sadly. "Huxley was there, by the riverbank, squirming pathetically in the mud, all his arrogance, his smug over-confidence stripped from him. The life of a defector is never more than barely tolerable and after thirty years he wore it particularly badly."

"He wanted to come home, didn't he?"

"Of course! He had nothing there and was about to have less. Even after a show trial and prison sentence he could be sure of some form of compassionate release in a few years and then he could retire into the life of a minor celebrity, touring the chat shows and writing his memoirs. I wasn't a jailer to him, I was his ticket home! His and that nasty little handler that shadowed his every move."

"The handler wanted to be snatched too?"

"He attempted to bargain with me," Hartnell explained. "He was a desperate, pathetic little man, terrified of what the revolution would do to him. But all he had to offer were low-level secrets of a dying regime, shortly to be worth less than the shit he stood in. I killed him before I even spoke to Alex."

Lucie empathetically felt the torment of the man as the undiluted truth began to pour from him.

"I had to kill him you know? I had to. He would have exposed me if I'd taken him back."

"I understand why you wanted to," Lucie nodded, "but I don't know how you could go through with it, killing a friend like that, murdering a lover..."

The Statesman's eyes glazed once more at her use of the word and his shoulders began to heave as his body succumbed to the force of its own weeping.

Lucie took no pleasure from the sight, but she needed more, she needed every inch of the mystery solved before she could do what she had to do.

"And so, fifty years after you destroyed one coup, and nineteen after you killed the man who said he loved you, you engineered your own elevation. But who helped you, Geoff, who did the dirty work for you?"

"Haven't you got enough for your damn story yet?" Hartnell sobbed as he leant against the wood.

"For God's sake, Geoff, I'm not a journalist, I'm a British agent! Haven't you worked that out yet?"

Hartnell frowned, pulled from his haze of disorientation by the even stronger power of incredulity.

"You?" he smirked as he spoke, his face a tapestry of amused puzzlement.

"What, a woman can't be an agent?" Lucie retorted in annoyance at the re-emergence of the politician's misogyny.

Hartnell laughed, as though in some pleasantly distracting daydream.

"Well, an agent perhaps, but come on!"

"Come on, what?"

"Well, you're hardly British, are you?"

Lucie's face dropped as hard and as fast as her heart at this new and ultimate betrayal, this final shedding of the last remaining cloth covering the Hartnell she had thought she knew; his progressive advocacy joining the discarded robes of honesty, integrity and gentlemanly conduct.

"At least that's one thing we can agree on, boy."

Lucie and Hartnell turned at once to the voice which came from across the partition in the senate gallery, in which stood Lord Hurndall, as withered and vexatious as ever, his Webley still lodged tightly into his hand, where Lucie had last seen it before he had fired at her.

"You!"

Hartnell leaned forward, his delirium returning at the sight of the elderly man and his gun, but no word of sympathy or affection, even a broken affection resentful of historical betrayal came back in response. Instead, the elderly peer curled a snarling lip around gritted teeth as he spat his condemnation.

"All you had to do was keep your bloody nose clean and you'd have made it!" Hurndall spat, "we engineer this support for you, this chance for you to do what should have been done years ago, but you couldn't even get that right!"

The rage rattled the very bones of the wraithlike old man and Lucie thought she actually saw Hartnell cower from him in his delirium.

"You betrayed me," Hartnell weakly retorted, earning even greater ire from the monster nearby.

"You considered yourself of greater importance than the Project! And because of your weakness, you betrayed it, you betrayed Alexander, me, the country! Good god man, look at what they've done to the country! A thousand languages on every street and precious few of them English! We could have stopped all that, but for your cowardice!"

The ancient, blimpish frame shuffled closer to the edge, his eyes displaying nothing but angered resentment.

"It's because of your betrayal that Alexander spent the best years of his life drinking his mind away on cheap spirits when he should have been at my side in power! He met his death, drunk and incontinent at the end of your gun…"

His overcoat was pushed aside, the gun from the cabinet in the old man's apartment clasped within the skeletal hand; a bony finger squeezing on the archaic trigger.

"Well, I'll be buggered if I'm going to let you take the mantle he should have held for years. To your grave you go, coward."

The aged finger squeezed tighter and the shot echoed around the chamber like a judgemental bolt of divine thunder. Hartnell had made no effort to move, and simply stood there in melancholy catatonia, as though welcoming the escape route the bullet would provide.

Lucie though was restrained by no stupor, and she gripped Hartnell powerfully by his shoulders, forcing him down across the rail and herself atop him, protecting him from his own inaction as much as Hurndall's murderous intent. Within a second of the shot firing, she had rolled from the politician's back and slipped her own despised weapon from her pocket, standing poised and ready to use it.

She shouted her warning as the almost emaciated arm began to rise again and Hartnell, still in the grip of delirium, staggered back to his feet, directly in the line of fire.

"Get your arse down," she hissed at the blundering Hartnell, drawing Hurndall's mockery.

"Hiding behind a priest with a gun? Do you intend to shoot me, young lady? Did the Ten Commandments elude you wherever you trained?"

"No," she hollered back, clearly. "Thou shalt not commit murder, is the one you're thinking of. It's not murder if it's self-defence."

Hurndall's vicious cackle returned, as though he relished the reality that she would not back down.

"Then die with the traitor, foreign whore!" Hurndall bellowed across the divide, "It's one less for us to deport!"

He fired again, but weakness and age threw his shot off course, the bullet wedging home in the oak beneath them. Lucie, her instinct overruling both every rational thought and spiritual intention inside her, raised her own weapon and fired.

"Sorry," she whispered as the shot met the bigoted Peer's skull and he fell back against the seats, dead, "that ship's been cancelled."

It was only seconds later that the sensation of the weapon's ridged grip against her palm cut through her instinct, pushing it back into the recesses and allowing her rational self to come to the fore once more. Hartnell too it seemed was beginning to return to some semblance of normality, the shots enough to wrench him from entrapment within his own mind.

He was pale, devoid utterly of any of the usual quirks and mannerisms that Lucie had come to know; his eyes fixed on the gun she still held by her side, his fear that she may be tempted to use it again apparent in his cold stare.

Though disgust was making her nauseous, Lucie realised that it was disgust aimed as much at herself as the man standing before her, his every lie exposed, his every piece of armour pierced, but nonetheless she felt the pull and the power of the weapon in her hand, cold, simple and undoubtedly deadly. She stared back at the man she had once believed would restore Britain to the country she had thought she had known, but who had betrayed her and everyone so completely and for so long, the temptation to simply fire and forget gnawing at her, each bite a thousand times sharper than the last.

He began to recoil, his cold expression twisting into one of fear and for a moment she wondered why, until she saw her own arm rising, pointing the gun directly at him. She held his life in her hands for seconds that felt like eternities, two separate and powerful urges within her fighting for supremacy while her trigger finger awaited a victor. The hatred he embodied, the pain he and those like him yearned to bring to the world; all was encapsulated within him and with one moment Lucie could rid the world of that evil. It would be no less than he deserved after everything he had done, surely no-one could condemn her for such an act, and how many people ever found themselves with the chance to

BLOOD, WHITE AND BLUE

take revenge on their enemy? The one who could do them wrong? Their own Judas…?

Hartnell stood shakily before her, as humble and as wordless as any politician ever had been, a pre-emptive wince forming on his face in what must surely be his final expression, waiting for the shot that must certainly come.

It did not.

Instead, Lucie relaxed her finger, clenching the grip tightly and hurling the weapon past Hartnell and far over the rail where it landed with a metallic clatter on the floor between the two sides of benches. Gasping for breath, Hartnell began to mumble incoherent words before Lucie gripped his lapels and pulled him to his full height.

"Love your enemies," she voiced into his face, her eyes boring into his. "Pray for those who persecute you, that you may be children of your Father in Heaven."

Her anger spent, she pushed him back against the rail where he squirmed in humiliated discomfort.

"Matthew, Chapter five, verses forty-four and forty-five," she clarified as she reached into her pocket for her mobile phone. "No, I didn't 'lose my faith.'"

"What are you going to do with me?" Hartnell nervously queried.

"Give you to the police," she answered with disdain, "you and your hard right chums are going down for a long time. Let's see what headline the Mail can come up with when there are genuine traitors in the dock, and from their own side."

"Sorry, not good enough."

Both Lucie and Hartnell followed the new voice to the chamber below, in which stood a lone figure, the same figure that had haunted Hartnell in Prague and in London, dressed in a brown trench coat, a dark, narrow brimmed trilby pulled down over its face.

The sight of it seemed to push the unstable Hartnell back towards his delirium and he leaned over the rail, squinting in frightened disbelief.

"Alex?" He asked, all traces of dignity gone from his trembling voice, his sanity not far behind. "You've come for me?"

"I'm not Alex," the figure said as it removed the trilby and shook its long hair down against its shoulders. From its pocket, the figure produced a gun of its own and pointed it at the bewildered Hartnell who looked on in confusion. "But I've definitely come for you."

Before Lucie could react, the gun had fired and Hartnell, clutching his shoulder, staggered for a moment and toppled over the rail, his falling body tearing through the patterned canvas above the Speaker's Chair, into which he crumbled, bloodied and broken.

The figure, watching him fall, carefully unhooked the ancient ceremonial mace, the heavy silver and gilt club that dated back to Charles the Second; the very symbol of royal authority and the ability of Parliament to make law. As the figure approached the stricken Hartnell, Lucie realised with horror its intent and screamed her defiance.

Oblivious to her protest, the figure raised the shining bludgeon high above its head, Hartnell giving one final look of terror as it came thudding down onto his sweat drenched skull, landing with a stomach-churning crack.

"Della!"

Lucie screamed her friend's name, almost sobbing at what she had witnessed her do and the figure finally looked up in answer, Lucie's damp eyes mirrored by its own.

"I had to," Della answered with earnest but horrifying sincerity, "believe me, Lucie, I had to."

BLOOD, WHITE AND BLUE

THIRTY-NINE

The heavy tap of Lucie's shoes echoed around the ancient stone palace as she ran, her coat flailing behind her and the portraits and busts of a hundred statesmen watching her go with patriarchal disapproval. Ahead of her Della rushed towards the entranceway, pushing the guard who stepped out to confront her against the wall. Another guard, stocky and with a face that looked as though it relished conflict, appeared beneath the archway that led to freedom, and Lucie watched as Della increased her speed and threw herself feet first towards the man, striking him with both boots in the centre of his chest, whence upon he staggered backwards unbalanced and fell against the hard, concrete floor, a sickening thud echoing as his head banged against it. Lucie couldn't stop to tend him, Della was fast disappearing and her capture had to be the priority.

Blue lights and howling sirens signalled the arrival of the emergency services, their airwaves no doubt overflowing with chatter of gun shots at Westminster, a pair of motorbike cops the first on the scene, screeching towards the entranceway with elaborate skids and the stench of burning rubber.

Stopping at the side of the first officer, Della gasped for breath and Lucie could hear her screaming for help, adopting the role of terrified bystander as easily as she had that of the haunted figure of Hartnell's nightmares. As the officer dismounted, Lucie could only holler in warning as Della slipped the gun from her pocket and discharged it point blank into the man's side.

He crumpled in an instant, his eyes wide in shock as Della dragged him callously from the bike, casting the briefest of glances back towards Lucie as she set off at speed past the ambulance pulling into the scene. The second bike cop had left his own vehicle and leapt to the aid of his fallen colleague, clamping down on the wound and calling for the newly arrived paramedics, and as he knelt there, Lucie jumped onto his discarded bike, revving the accelerator and screeching out in pursuit of the woman she had thought she knew.

Della had a head start and began to move faster still onto Westminster Bridge, until a cavalcade of late-night buses blocking the lanes began to hamper her progress. Knowing the older woman would try to accelerate between them, Lucie wrestled her bike onto the pavement, free completely of pedestrians and throttled down hard to pull ahead of her, skidding the machine into a stop further down the bridge. When Della came through the buses, Lucie was ready. She stood astride the bike, her gun in her hand and pointed towards her murderous friend. Della in response gave only her customary mischievous grin and thrust down on the accelerator towards Lucie.

She fired once.

Della's front wheel twisted into a treacherous spin, sending the heavy bike and its rider careering towards the stonework of the bridge, smacking it headlong and sending Della over the handlebars and off the top of the bridge, her hands grasping frantically for support as she went.

Lucie reached her before she could fall, grabbing her arm and taking the weight as Della's momentum propelled her into a swing on the wrong side of the bridge.

"It was you," Lucie shouted accusatorily, her eyes misty with anger and tears. "You were Hurndall's spy in Geoff's camp, the one who sent the letter and leaked all that stuff to the trolls."

"I saved your life too, in Prague," she hissed back.

"You? You were the shooter on the rooftop? Della, why?"

"You're not the only half British girl in the world you know," the woman laughed. "In Prague, in the sixties, all three of those murdering Nazi bastards used to go whoring at that goddam brothel; treating the women like animals. Well some animals never forget… and neither do their daughters."

Lucie reeled at the revelation, Della sliding just a couple of inches down before she readjusted her grip painfully, her tears beginning to break down her resolve and leak through.

"You double crossed them," she mulled, "you had your foot in both camps to bring them both down."

"They deserved it!"

"Maybe they did, but Della, you didn't stop there! What about the guard you just took out, what about the cop?"

"Collateral damage, Lucie."

Della spat the words without a shred of compassion in her voice, not the slightest twinge of regret.

"This country has voted for its own destruction and wants to take me, you and everyone like us down with it. That makes them all fair targets to me."

"You can't execute someone because of how they voted!" Lucie screamed at her friend's murderous illogicality. "And what about those who didn't vote that way? Are you going to ask everyone for their ballot paper before you pull the trigger?!"

"It doesn't matter now, you have to let me drop."

"Like hell I do! Get a foothold!" Lucie demanded, but Della refused, simply letting herself hang from her friend's grip, her unstable smile and her now tearful face hovering somewhere between hilarity and despair.

"You bitch," she laughed through her tears, "you fucking bitch."

"I learned from the best," Lucie answered sadly, struggling to keep hold of the dead weight she clung to.

"So that's your choice is it? Take me in and stand me in front of the apes, ready for them to throw their shit at me, while you fall in line and risk your life for a country that despises you and everything about you? Brexit Britain's new champion, out for revenge against anyone who betrays it?"

"Fuck Brexit Britain," Lucie hissed. "You betrayed me."

Della narrowed her eyes in understanding, nodding slightly at Lucie's words.

"Good girl… let me go," she said softly, almost in a whisper.

"Don't be stupid, get a foothold and push up."

"It's pointless."

Lucie began to panic. She didn't mean it did she? She wasn't really going to let her die? Not Della, not this fiery, brilliant woman who had done her best to awaken Lucie's joy, to help her heal… Lucie's tears were now dampening her cheeks, and the crack in Della's voice mirrored in her own.

"No, it isn't!" Lucie insisted, "Please… I can save you."

Della smiled up at her, all anger and bitterness gone from her features, replaced instead with a serene acceptance.

"Save yourself."

Lucie's arms were aching under the strain of holding her and she felt herself leaning further and further over the edge. Before she could make another plea, Della reached her free arm up and knocked Lucie's hands away from her wrist. She dropped into the depths, her face remaining fixed on Lucie's own until the moment the broken waters rushed back in to envelope her in blackness.

FORTY

Lucie had reached the bench in Hyde Park over an hour earlier and her eyes had not moved from the monument to Prince Albert in all that time, not through any devotion to the structure itself but simply to avoid making eye contact with a real person and risk them replacing the sight of Della's face as she fell beneath the waters in her mind.

She retained her posture even when Lake sat beside her, joining her in silent admiration of a queen's fallen love.

"Hurndall and Hartnell died at the scene," Lake eventually confirmed, a degree more uncertainty in his voice than Lucie had become accustomed to. "It's been fed to the press that they died preventing a terrorist attack on Parliament."

Lucie laughed in contempt.

"Heroes' deaths?"

"I'm afraid so, one from each side of the divide, a hard core Brexiteer and a die-hard Remainer, at least as far as most are aware."

"And that's that is it? What about the people behind Hartnell in Parliament? What about the figures in the press Hurndall could so easily manipulate?"

"Returned to the undergrowth from whence they came," he replied with frustration. "No-one ever came forward publicly and as far as we know there's no smoking gun list anywhere, but Algers is making what enquiries he can."

"What about the bomb?"

"The same; we've one or two leads."

Lucie stayed quiet for a moment, not wanting to ask but compelled to.

"And Della?"

Lake's sigh was both heavy and profoundly sad. "She was behind the leaks, she set our friend Fostrow up to be killed by you – he'd apparently proven too erratic for her to control – and she managed to persuade that young boy, Underfoot, to send the original threat in the diplomatic bag."

"And was it true? Her mother had been one of the whores Hartnell and his friends used to abuse?"

Lake squinted a moment.

"It could be," he answered, "we're still looking into that. She left you a note, she must have realised that one way or another she wouldn't be seeing you again. Would you like it?"

He reached into the pocket of his overcoat and handed out a white envelope.

"No," came Lucie's quick response, Lake pocketing the note once more.

"You should let him go you know? Kasper. Whatever hold you have on him just stop it. He's a decent guy, he doesn't need to be mixed up in all this anymore."

"My arrangements with Mr Algers are precisely that," Lake replied sternly, "mine."

"And his, and it strikes me you delight in rubbing his nose in it."

"Well that may be," Lake conceded. "But for now at least I need

Algers where he is; the by-election will be interesting, might even shake things up a bit and get the country thinking straight again. Who knows? It might even provoke a General Election."

"So, what if it does?" Lucie answered despondently. "Even if it did, even if all this Brexit stuff got reversed and they tore up the Article 50 letter tomorrow morning, it's not going to stop the hate, it'll just make it worse. The only thing Brexit achieved was the normalisation of racial violence, and I don't know how many social trends you've tried reversing but it'll take years to recover from that damage, who knows if we even can? But until we do we'll be the ones to pay the price for the prize being plucked from the xenophobes' grasp."

"You don't know that."

"Don't I? They don't listen to reason, they don't listen to argument. All they know how to do is hate... And I don't think I can change anyone's mind in a job like this..."

"Ms. Musilova," Lake began, his eyes still over the park. "Lucie... Immorality is rife in this business and I can't claim any special immunity. You think I'm a callous bastard, and you're right; I am. But when I do wrong, I like to think at least I do it for the right reasons. There are real bastards out there, Lucie, real people who not only do wrong to people but desire every day to do so to more, and for no other reason than their discredited ideologies or their personal glories. If we're to stop them, we need to show we're not scared of stooping to their level. I'm a bastard, Lucie, yes, but I'm trying to be the right kind of bastard. The question for you now is, can you be the right kind of bitch?"

Lucie frowned. To her surprise she felt the now familiar lump return to her throat and the nag of un-resolved emotion tugging at her mind.

"I'm not sure I can," she finally answered. "I'm not sure I want to be. The one person in a million I thought I could do this for is gone, and I just can't do it for Brexit Britain; I hate the place. A friend of mine, she's Slovak, was abused in the street with her four-year-old son, for daring to speak to him in her own language. Just now, here in the park, I saw a jogger push a young couple stood chatting out of her way, calling them 'Polish cunts'.

I was raised here, my Dad was British, but this isn't my home anymore. Britain has turned its back on me and my kind, the 'half and halves'; why the hell should I fight for broken dreams on behalf of people who hate me?"

She turned finally to face the man whose actions had brought her to this bench, her face offering a vague but sincere apology.

"The Britain I know is dead. It was killed by its own people and they didn't even have the decency to bury it properly; they just chucked a Union Jack over the coffin and pissed all over everything it used to stand for; all the rest of us can do is mourn it."

Lake met her eyes for a moment as she said the words and turned back to his constant surveillance of the park's visitors, taking a moment to collect and organise his thoughts.

"You know, a lot of people presume that I live for 'patriotism', for an utter devotion to the flag," he started his reply with more than a hint of lament clinging to his words. "But the truth is, I'm every bit as sick of this bloody country and the idiots within it as you."

The bitterness startled Lucie, who could have sworn she saw dampness in the older man's eye as he continued.

"The only thing my wife ever asked of me was fidelity. She worked in the labs at 'Six', so she understood the nature of my job. She accepted the risks of my work, she accepted the secrecy, but she simply asked me to remain faithful to her in the course of my duty, and I of course was. All except one occasion…"

The bitterness turned to lament as Lake continued, blinking back the tears which stubbornly refused to retreat.

"When she found out, it didn't matter to her why I'd done it, how many lives were saved because of the information I gathered through my betrayal; all that mattered was the betrayal itself. When I found her, she was standing on the bridge at Sandbach services… one look at me and she threw herself off, right into the middle of the rush hour stream."

Silence refused to release Lucie to voice any noise of either sympathy or disbelief, and in any case, she wouldn't have known which the appropriate emotion was to express, but what was undeniable was the shake in Lake's words as he continued.

"And that's when they came; the Great British Public, crawling and squirming from their cars towards her broken body. Not to offer help or comfort to a dying woman, but to film her on smart phones and use her last breath to score likes on Facebook. And I realised, as the woman I loved died, that so had my country, the Britain I had known."

Drawing in a cathartic breath, Lake turned to face Lucie, offering her the first smile she could remember in their brief acquaintance.

"Don't do it for Brexit Britain, Lucie," he said, "do it for the Britain that used to be, and the hope that one day we can bring it back to life, even if we can't bring back the people we've lost."

Lake stood to leave, lifting the collar of his overcoat around his neck and thrusting his hands deep into his pockets.

"Your mother," he said softly, looking down at her. "She was killed, murdered by a man called Tristan Dagonet. He was one of us, did some damn good work before it got to his mind and he started seeing conspiracies everywhere. Your mother wasn't the only innocent he killed, you can believe that if nothing else."

"What happened to him?"

Lucie's voice was measured, calm, displaying no evidence of any resentment towards Lake for having kept this from her until now, and in truth, she felt none, only an understanding that this was a human being with sometimes impossible choices to make, many of which he was bound to get wrong.

"We don't know. He fled before he could be captured, possibly into Poland where he had some contacts who would have sheltered him, at least for a time. But the truth is he could be dead, alive or sitting next to you in the cinema."

Lucie kept her stare straight ahead, not wishing him to see the dampness in her own eye and struggling to vocalise a response for the lump in her throat.

"If you wished," Lake continued, "you could use the department's resources to find him. When your duties permitted, of course."

"And do what, kill him?" Lucie snapped, intoxicated on a new emotional cocktail. "I'm supposed to sit in the forgiveness corner, remember?"

"Yes, well that of course is up to you."

Lake straightened himself up and coughed, evidently having demonstrated a sufficient portion of his softer side for one day.

"Take the rest of the week," he barked, his typical tone restored, "get your head together, wail about the unfairness of it all, whatever makes you feel better, then I want you back in Algers' office at eight o'clock on Monday morning, without fail."

Lucie watched him begin to walk away, her heart resentful at the decision her mind was making.

"You really think I'll be there, don't you?" Lucie shouted after him.

"Of course," confirmed the Spy Master over his shoulder as he stomped away towards the Albert Hall. "After all, there are plenty more of the bastards out there."

ACKNOWLEDGEMENTS

My thanks to my family, friends and the Good Lord, who continue to tolerate the grumpy, short tempered old fart I become when deadlines approach and pages remain unwritten and understand my reclusive tendencies in the same periods; your love and support really does mean the world to me. Thanks in particular to Mirka, Alan and Laura Smith, Martin and Della Hyde, Mike Harrowell and Jon Healey – sorry that writing these things prohibits me from coming to sing with you Jon.

This book is inspired by so many who have stood up to be counted in these dark times, both here and throughout the world, often putting themselves at risk to do so. In particular, Lucie Musilova owes much to those citizens of other countries who work in our emergency services, putting themselves at daily risk for a country which has turned its back on them through its pursuit of the poisonous Brexit so desired by the Hard Right. My admiration and my thanks go to them for their dedication and resilience, and my regrets for the loathsome manner in which so many in this country have treated them on our imperious march to the cliff edge. This book is for you.

I am blessed in belonging to a network of mutually supportive writers, all of whom I thank for their support and time as I blunder my way along. You each know who you are, and I am grateful to all of you. Thanks especially to Simon Michael, for taking time out from writing his brilliant legal thriller series for the occasional

pint and supportive chat, and to the wonderful Deirdre Query, for offering encouragement during the increasing dark moments of self-doubt. I must also thank those splendid gents (and exceptional authors) Robert Daws and Hugh Fraser, for offering support and encouragement beyond any expectation I could have had. Their kindness is sincerely appreciated, and I hope both enjoy reading the characters I have shamelessly borrowed their likenesses for.
All those mentioned are supremely talented writers and I encourage you to seek out their work.

This book was written during a difficult personal spell, in which my mental health took something of a battering and after a prolonged period of ill health, I lost my dad, my first hero. Though he and I held different politics and different views on so many things, I could not have asked for a better father, and I hope this book makes him proud.

Finally, a sincere thank you to Matthew Smith of Urbane Publications for his flexibility and support as deadlines slipped and dark clouds gathered. I hope the final product reflects his continuing faith in me.

Lucie Musilova will be back soon in her new adventure, Sealed With A Death, summer 2019.

Finally, thanks to you for taking a chance on this book. I hope you enjoy it and that you come back another day to see what else lies in store for Lucie Musilova, as she fights for a country that hates her.

James Silvester's debut novel and sequel, *Escape to Perdition* and *The Prague Ultimatum*, reflected his love both of central Europe and the espionage genre and was met with widespread acclaim.

James has also written for *The Prague Times* and his work has been featured by *Doctor Who Worldwide* and travel site *An Englishman in Slovakia*.

James lives in Manchester.

Have you read James Silvester's earlier thrillers? Both available now from Amazon and all good bookshops.

Prague 2015. Herbert Biely, aged hero of the Prague Spring, stands on the brink of an historic victory, poised to reunite the Czech and Slovak Republics twenty-six years after the Velvet Revolution. The imminent Czech elections are the final stage in realising his dream of reunification, but other parties have their own agendas and plans for the fate of the region.

A shadowy collective, masked as an innocuous European Union Institute, will do anything to preserve the status quo. The mission of Institute operative Peter Lowes is to prevent reunification by the most drastic of measures. Yet Peter is not all that he seems. A deeply troubled man, desperate to escape the past, his resentment towards himself, his assignment and his superiors deepens as he questions not just the cause, but his growing feelings for the beautiful and captivating mission target. As alliances shift and the election countdown begins, Prague becomes the focal point for intrigue on an international scale. The body count rises, options fade, and Peter's path to redemption is clouded in a maelstrom of love, deception and murder. Can he confront his past to save the future? This is a high-quality page turning thriller and perfect for fans of John le Carré.

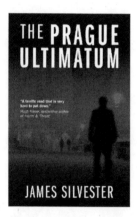

THE **PRAGUE**
ULTIMATUM

"A terrific read that is very
hard to put down."
Hugh Fraser, bestselling author
of 'Harm' & 'Threat'

JAMES SILVESTER

Fear stalks the newly reunified Czechoslovakia, the terror wrought
by international terrorism and violent extremists overshadowing
the forthcoming fiftieth anniversary of the Prague Spring, and
threatening to burn the country in its wake. Into this arena steps
Captain Lincoln Stone, a disgraced British officer, humiliatingly
scapegoated by his government for his role in the disastrous on-
going Syrian Conflict.

Plucked from his purgatory, Stone is teased with exoneration
by British Foreign Secretary Jonathan Greyson, in return for his
'off the books' aid of Czechoslovak Prime Minister, Miroslava
Svobodova. Stone, resentful of his treatment and determined
to prove himself, is driven by deeper motives than the casual
platitudes of his superiors and finds himself at the epicentre as
the country descends into chaos. Cut off from the international
community and isolated in the face of an expansionist Russia, and
with the sinister Institute for European Harmony ever present
behind the scenes, Czechoslovakia's fate, and that of the world,
hangs on the outcome to the Prague Ultimatum.

URBANE

Urbane Publications is dedicated to
developing new author voices, and publishing
fiction, non-fiction and business books that
thrill, challenge and fascinate.

From page-turning novels to innovative
reference books, our goal is to publish what
YOU want to read.

Find out more at
urbanepublications.com